HARDCASTLE'S SOLDIERS

Graham Ison

This first world edition published 2010
in Great Britain and in the USA by
SEVERN HOUSE PUBLISHERS LTD of
9–15 High Street, Sutton, Surrey, England, SM1 1DF.
Trade paperback edition published
in Great Britain and the USA 2010 by
SEVERN HOUSE PUBLISHERS LTD

British Library Cataloguing in Publication Data

Ison, Graham.
    Hardcastle's Soldiers. – (A Hardcastle and Marriott
    historical mystery)
    1. Hardcastle, Ernest (Fictitious character)–Fiction.
    2. Marriott, Charles (Fictitious character)–Fiction.
    3. Great Britain. Metropolitan Police Office–Fiction.
    4. Murder–Investigation–Fiction. 5. World War,
    1914-1918–Social aspects–England–London–Fiction.
    6. Great Britain–History–George V, 1910-1936–Fiction.
    7. Detective and mystery stories.
    I. Title II. Series
    823.9'14-dc22

ISBN-13: 978-0-7278-6860-2   (cased)
ISBN-13: 978-1-84751-213-0   (trade paper)

All Severn House titles are printed on acid-free paper.

 Mixed Sources
Product group from well-managed
forests and other controlled sources
www.fsc.org Cert no. SA-COC-1565
FSC © 1996 Forest Stewardship Council

Typeset by Palimpsest Book Production Ltd.,
Grangemouth, Stirlingshire, Scotland.
Printed and bound in Great Britain by
MPG Books Ltd., Bodmin, Cornwall.

ONE

The news on that July morning in 1917 was bleak, even to a nation inured to nearly three years of war. On Monday the ninth, two days previously, the battleship HMS *Vanguard* had been destroyed by an explosion at Scapa Flow. Only three men had survived out of a complement of 807. The official communiqué gave no reason for the tragedy, other than to say that it was an accident. But that did not stop a *Daily Mail* reporter from hazarding a guess that a German submarine had got close enough to fire a torpedo into the vessel's magazine.

'Bloody war!' muttered Ernest Hardcastle. Taking off his spectacles, he folded the newspaper and threw it into the waste-paper basket. He crossed to the open window and stared down momentarily at Westminster underground station below, just as a train pulled out, rattling the windows of his office. However, as the divisional detective inspector of the A or Whitehall Division of the Metropolitan Police, he was about to be occupied with matters closer to home than the tragic loss of HMS *Vanguard*.

'Excuse me, sir.' Detective Sergeant Charles Marriott – a first-class sergeant and Hardcastle's assistant – appeared in the doorway of the DDI's office on the first floor of Cannon Row Police Station. The station, and New Scotland Yard opposite, had been built in 1888 of granite hewn, fittingly by convicts from Dartmoor prison.

'What is it, Marriott? Not more bad news, I hope.'

'Matter of opinion, sir,' ventured Marriott. 'At about twenty past ten a railway copper called the PC on the Victoria Street and Vauxhall Bridge Road traffic point. One of the cashiers on Victoria railway station was found dead in his booth.'

'What was a cashier doing in a booth on Victoria Station, Marriott?' Hardcastle took out his pouch and carefully filled his pipe with St Bruno tobacco.

'It's an arrangement the army has with a bank, sir. The cashier in question exchanges French money into sterling for troops arriving home from the Front. Looks as though he was attacked in the course of a robbery.'

'Where on Victoria Station is this booth, Marriott?'

'On the concourse, sir.' Marriott spoke hesitantly; he knew what was coming next.

'Dammit!' exclaimed Hardcastle.

It was one of the perversities of the Metropolitan Police that responsibility for the platforms and track at the railway station rested with the B or Chelsea Division, whereas the concourse came under the aegis of A Division. Even before Hardcastle had been posted to Cannon Row Police Station, discussions had been going on among the hierarchy at Scotland Yard about transferring the responsibility for crimes committed on the entirety of the railway station to B Division.

After all, A Division – known informally as 'the Royal A' – had more than its fair share of responsibility, with Buckingham Palace, St James's Palace, Parliament, Westminster Abbey and the government offices in Whitehall within its purview, added to which was the onus of policing the royal palaces at Windsor Castle and Holyrood House in Edinburgh.

Hardcastle's view was that it was typical of the muddled thinking of the senior officers at Scotland Yard, that they had shilly-shallied over making what to him was a simple decision. Not that he would give voice to that criticism in the presence of a subordinate.

He took out his chromium hunter watch, glanced at it, briefly wound it, and dropped it back into his waistcoat pocket. 'Better go and take a look, I suppose, Marriott.' He took a box of Swan Vestas matches from his pocket and lit his pipe. 'Sent anyone up there?' he asked, emitting a plume of smoke towards the nicotine-stained ceiling.

It was Marriott's job to know the present whereabouts of every detective at Cannon Row, and he knew that Hardcastle meant an A Division CID officer. 'I've already sent Catto and Lipton up there to secure the scene, sir,' he said, naming two detective constables.

'Fat lot of good they'll be,' growled Hardcastle, seizing his bowler hat and umbrella, and making his way downstairs.

'And I took the liberty of calling Dr Spilsbury, sir,' continued Marriott, as he hurried after the DDI.

'I should hope so, Marriott,' muttered Hardcastle, who

always wanted the country's leading forensic pathologist to examine the victim of any murder that he was investigating.

Spilsbury was renowned in courts throughout the country, and defence counsel always took special care in preparing their case when they knew he was to appear for the prosecution. In particular, his evidence in the infamous Brides in the Bath case in 1915 had resulted in George Joseph Smith being hanged for his crimes. During the course of that trial, a bath had been brought into the Old Bailey courtroom and filled with water. A nurse, attired in a bathing costume, stepped into the bath. Pulling the nurse's ankles upwards and submerging her head, Detective Inspector Neil demonstrated how Smith had murdered his victims. By so doing he almost succeeded in killing the unfortunate nurse, but newspaper reports attributed the demonstration to Spilsbury. He never denied it.

Turning out of the police station into Derby Gate, and thence to Whitehall, with his sergeant chasing behind him, Hardcastle peered in vain for a taxi.

'Might be quicker to take a bus, sir,' suggested Marriott warily. 'I heard the other day that a lot of cabbies have joined the army.'

'Divisional detective inspectors do not travel to the scene of a crime on a bus, Marriott,' said Hardcastle sternly. At last, sighting a cab, he waved his umbrella at it imperiously. 'Victoria Station, driver.'

The cab driver yanked down the flag on his taximeter. 'Having a day at the seaside, guv'nor?' he asked. 'Five-and-nine on the Brighton line,' he added jocularly, quoting army housey-housey callers' slang for the number fifty-nine.

'Just get on with your bloody driving,' snapped Hardcastle. 'I've got a murder to deal with.'

The chastened cab driver remained silent for the remainder of the short journey down Victoria Street.

It was drizzling with rain when Hardcastle and Marriott arrived at Victoria Station. A troop train had just disgorged a thousand or more soldiers returning from the Front. They were borne down with packs and rifles, while others, taking a brief respite, had dumped their kit around their feet. These men had arrived on leave, although few people would have guessed it. Each had a muddied, drawn and haggard appearance, as though he had been to hell. And back.

Many of the soldiers were clustered around the three money-exchange booths, one of which was to become the focus of Hardcastle's latest murder enquiry.

In an attempt to marshal those unfortunates who were bound for the Front, Movement Control sergeants dashed around shouting orders and scribbling on papers.

Clouds of steam swirled across the crowded station and the odour of burning coal filled the air. Occasionally the hubbub of noise was punctuated by the doom-laden whistles of hissing locomotives hauling their reluctant passengers on the first stage of their journey to France or Belgium.

Little knots of people were saying goodbye to loved ones returning to the fighting. Some women clutched handkerchiefs and were crying, while others did their best to put on a brave face.

One young girl, her long black coat failing to disguise her pregnancy, was clinging to a lance-bombardier who only yesterday had done 'the right thing' by her. Her face was buried in the rough material of his tunic, and she gripped the webbing of his equipment as though trying to prevent his going, doubtless wondering if she would ever see him again.

A line of ambulances stretched down one side of the concourse, the women drivers talking to a group of red-caped nurses of Queen Alexandra's Imperial Military Nursing Service as they waited for the next hospital train.

Suddenly, as if in response to some secret signal, the group broke up, clambered into their vehicles, and drove on to one of the platforms. They stopped and swung open ambulance doors as the first of a depressing number of wounded soldiers was carried off the train on stretchers.

Once again, reminding him of his visit to the little Belgian town of Poperinghe only last year, Hardcastle witnessed the human detritus of war being loaded for the last part of its long journey to Charing Cross Hospital, some of them to recover fully, some partly, some to remain in an awful limbo between life and death. And some to die. These pathetic human wrecks were the result of jingoism, political bungling, military incompetence and ignorance. And patriotism and gallantry of the very highest order.

Few of the civilians on the station afforded a second glance for those wounded men who, in 1914 and 1915 and even in the earlier months of 1916, they had hailed as 'our brave boys', and had cheered and encouraged with cigarettes and chocolates. But now, especially since the Battle of the Somme, the human mind had become numbed to the carnage. And there were no longer military bands to greet them.

Although the victims of frequent air raids, the civilian population had not experienced the horrors of front-line trench warfare, nor had they learned much of them. A soldier returning to his family wanted to forget the mud and the shells and the screams of the wounded, and the sight of a friend blown to smithereens when seconds before he had been talking to him. Kith and kin did not want to hear how he had wiped the man's brains from his tunic before getting on with the war.

People rarely spoke of the conflict now, but were only too conscious of the mounting losses, and were beginning to wonder what had gone wrong, and to ask if the slaughter would continue until there was not a man under forty left alive in Britain.

Hardcastle and Marriott forced their way through this throng, and eventually reached the kiosk that was about to become the centre of Hardcastle's latest investigation.

A railway policeman stood in front of the booth, one of three small huts constructed of wood with corrugated iron roofs, above which was a large sign that read: FRENCH MONEY EXCHANGED HERE FOR OFFICERS & SOLDIERS IN UNIFORM.

'This kiosk's closed,' said the constable importantly, as Hardcastle and Marriott approached. He nodded at the closed hatch as if to emphasize his point.

'I'm DDI Hardcastle, Metropolitan, come to clear up a crime for you.' Hardcastle stared pointedly at the PC whose thumbs were tucked under the buttons of his tunic breast pockets.

'Yes, sir. Very good, sir.' The railway policeman hurriedly assumed a position of attention and sketched a salute. 'Your two officers are inside the hut, sir, and this here officer saw a man running away, sir,' he said, suddenly affecting an air of obsequiousness as he indicated a young army officer standing next to him.

'I'll be with you in a moment, Lieutenant,' said Hardcastle, recognizing the officer's rank from the two stars on each of his shoulder straps. That insignia had long since been transferred, unofficially, from the cuffs, in an attempt to make it more difficult for enemy snipers to identify officers in the trenches. But, in the face of that widespread practice, it had, this year, been officially sanctioned.

'While you're hanging about,' said Hardcastle to the railway PC, 'ask if any of these soldiers saw anyone running off. Meanwhile, I'll get on with finding out what's what.'

The DDI pushed open the door of the kiosk. Face down on the floor lay the body of a man. The back of his head was a mess of blood and hair, and Hardcastle did not need the services of a doctor to tell him that the man was dead, and that he had been the victim of a savage blow. Scattered across the floor, near to the man, were abandoned bank notes, both British and French.

'Learned anything, Catto?' demanded Hardcastle of the detective constable who was standing near the body.

'No, sir,' said Henry Catto.

'That don't surprise me,' commented Hardcastle, who, unreasonably, had no great faith in the young detective's abilities.

'But the army officer outside apparently saw someone legging it, sir,' said Catto, and then pointed at a revolver lying on the floor. 'That firearm was at the scene when we arrived, sir,' he added.

'I hope you haven't touched it.' Hardcastle shot a censorious glance at Catto.

'Certainly not, sir.'

'It's interesting though,' mused Hardcastle, 'I wonder what it's doing there.' He knelt to make a closer examination of the body. 'It don't look as if he was shot, and there's blood on the butt of the revolver.' He stood up again. 'Well, there's not a lot we can do until Dr Spilsbury gets here. In the meantime, I'll have a word with this army officer.' The DDI paused at the door. 'And arrange for a van to remove the body, Catto, once Dr Spilsbury's conducted his examination. I daresay the railway police have got one of them telephone instruments in their office, and we don't want the deceased taken through the streets on a hand ambulance. It don't look good.' The DDI despised the introduction of the telephone, believing, in common with other senior officers, that it was a flash in the pan that would not last.

'Yes, sir,' said Catto, and hastened to do Hardcastle's bidding.

The DDI turned to DC Lipton. 'Put that revolver in a bag once the pathologist has finished, lad, and take it to Detective Inspector Collins in the Fingerprint Department at the Yard, *tout de suite*. And make a note of the serial number, and let me have it before I leave.'

'Yes, sir,' said Lipton.

Hardcastle, in common with older CID officers, was only just coming to realize the value of fingerprints, introduced into English policing from India by Sir Edward Henry, now Commissioner of the Metropolitan Police. It had been as recently as 1905 that this newfangled science had been accepted by the courts for the first time. When Albert and Alfred Stratton, the two murderers of Mr and Mrs Farrow, a Deptford oil shop proprietor and his wife, had been convicted on such evidence, it was regarded as a significant advance in criminal investigation.

Emerging from the booth, Hardcastle turned his attention on the young army officer. Although he was wearing a cap, the officer was holding another, the reason for which was shortly to be made clear.

'Perhaps we could start with your name, Lieutenant,' said Hardcastle.

'Geoffrey Mansfield, the North Staffordshire Regiment.'

'What can you tell me, Mr Mansfield?'

'It's the most extraordinary thing, Inspector. I've been waiting here to meet my fiancée. The ticket collector wouldn't allow me go on to the platform without a platform ticket, and I was about to—'

'You weren't on the troop train that just came in, then?'

'No, not at all.' Mansfield glanced at his watch. 'I think her train must be running late. However, I was standing quite close to here when I saw a soldier come out of the bureau de change there.' He pointed at the booth wherein the cashier now lay dead. 'He saw me but didn't salute, so I challenged him. Discipline seems to have gone all to Hades since this damned war started.'

'What happened next, sir?' asked Marriott, fearful that Hardcastle might lose his temper with the young army officer's vacillation.

'I thought the fellow must've been up to no good. After all, he came out of the door at the side of the booth. If he'd been exchanging his francs for pounds, he'd've done what we all do and queue up at the hatch there.' Mansfield pointed, and gave a brief, nervous laugh. 'Well, not the officers, of course. We go straight to the front of the queue.'

'Would you get to the point, Mr Mansfield,' said Hardcastle, his mood rapidly turning to one of impatience.

'I chased after him, and shouted to a couple of military policemen to stop him, but I doubt they heard me. As he was escaping, he dropped his headgear.' Mansfield handed Hardcastle the army cap he was carrying. 'I picked it up and was about to give chase again, when this troop train unloaded. Well, Inspector, you can see how many men are milling about. Quite frankly, I lost sight of him. One moment I had the chap in my sights, the next minute the place was flooded with the common soldiery, eh what?'

'Did you hear a shot, by any chance?' Hardcastle was satisfied that the cashier had been murdered with the butt-end of the revolver that had been found, but he wondered if it had been discharged prior to the murder, perhaps by accident, or with the intention of frightening the man who now lay dead in the booth.

'A shot? Definitely not, Inspector, and believe me, I know what a shot sounds like. There's a lot of it going on in Arras.'

'I suppose you would,' said Hardcastle, glancing at the ribbon of the Military Cross on Mansfield's tunic. 'What time was this?'

The officer glanced again at his watch. 'Ten twelve ack emma, Inspector. Forty-five minutes ago.'

Grunting a response, Hardcastle turned his attention to the cap. Inside, in heavy black ink, were written the name Stacey and a regimental number. 'What regiment is this, Lieutenant?' he asked, pointing at the brass badge.

'The Army Service Corps, Inspector,' replied Mansfield promptly.

'Well, as we've got his name and number here, he shouldn't be too difficult to trace.' Hardcastle turned to his sergeant. 'Marriott, find somewhere quiet and take a statement from this officer. Then he can go.' As Marriott drew Lieutenant Mansfield away from the crush, the DDI next addressed

himself to the railway policeman. 'How did you get to hear
of this, lad?' The policeman was not much younger than
Hardcastle, but the DDI always called constables 'lad'.

'There was a bit of a to-do at the kiosk, sir. The swaddies
waiting there was complaining something cruel that they
wasn't getting served. And the hatch was shut. Most unusual,
that.' The railway constable paused thoughtfully. 'I suppose
the murderer must have shut it,' he suggested. 'Anyhow, these
swaddies was in a nasty mood, sir, and I apprehended there
might be a breach of the peace. So, I pushed open the door
to see what the hold-up was, and found the cashier lying on
the floor. Then this officer come up to me and told me about
some swaddy he'd seen running away. That's when I sent
another officer to call the Metropolitan copper off the traffic
point outside.'

'Wasn't the door locked?'

'No, sir. I always thought it was s'posed to be, but perhaps
the murderer busted it open. There was one other thing, sir . . .'

'Yes?'

'That army officer, sir. It wasn't quite right what he told
you. I was walking towards the booth when I almost bumped
into him.'

'Are you suggesting that he wasn't running after anyone?'
Hardcastle was aware that witnesses' statements often
conflicted, and attached no great importance to what the
policeman had said.

'Didn't seem to be, sir, but I might've got it wrong.'

Having gauged the efficiency of the railway policeman,
Hardcastle thought that that was quite likely. 'My sergeant
here will take a statement from you later on,' he said, not at
all happy with the constable's knowledge of what had occurred.
There was, however, some truth in what the PC had said earlier
about the entrance to the booth. The DDI's brief examination
of the door to the kiosk indicated that the flimsy lock had
been forced, and the jamb splintered, probably by bodily pressure. He turned away, and then paused. 'And did you ask if
any of the soldiers saw anyone running away?'

'Yes, sir. I enquired, but they never saw nothing.'

'There's a surprise,' grunted Hardcastle.

Two military policemen arrived at the kiosk and approached
Hardcastle.

'Everything all right, sir?' asked the senior of the two, a corporal, having been told who Hardcastle was by the railway policeman.

'Apart from the cashier having been murdered, yes,' said Hardcastle sarcastically. 'But now you're here, you can stand guard on this place until someone arrives to take possession of the cash. Is it an army arrangement?'

'I'm afraid I don't know, sir,' said the corporal. 'But it does turn up here every morning with a military escort.'

'That officer over there,' began Hardcastle, indicating Lieutenant Mansfield who was sitting on a bench next to Marriott, 'says that he shouted to you to apprehend a running soldier. Is that correct?'

'Didn't hear nothing, sir,' said the corporal.

'Don't surprise me,' muttered Hardcastle, turning away. But any further criticism of the military was curtailed by the arrival of Dr Bernard Spilsbury. A tall, impressive, tail-coated figure, he wore a top hat and carried a silver-topped cane with which he was tapping soldiers aside as he made his way purposefully towards the little knot of police officers.

'Good morning, Hardcastle.'

'Good morning, Dr Spilsbury,' responded Hardcastle, and raised his bowler hat.

'Where's the cadaver?' Spilsbury always referred to a dead body as a cadaver.

'In the hut here, doctor.' Hardcastle led the pathologist into the small kiosk.

Spilsbury put down the small Gladstone bag he was carrying and rubbed his hands together as if in anticipation of something interesting. Kneeling down, he examined the wound on the back of the dead man's head, and then glanced at the revolver, still lying on the floor a few inches away.

'I'm in little doubt that it was the revolver that did the deed, Hardcastle, but not used conventionally.' Spilsbury gave a brief laugh. 'Bludgeoned on the back of the skull with the butt of the thing, powerfully enough to fracture it severely.' The doctor stood up. 'No point in taking temperatures. I gather that you know the time of death, give or take a few minutes.'

'Indeed, doctor. About an hour ago.'

'Splendid. Be so good as to have the cadaver taken to St Mary's Hospital at Paddington, Hardcastle, there's a good chap. I'll conduct the post-mortem this evening at six o'clock sharp, but I'm sure that my original diagnosis of the cause of death will stand.' And with that, Spilsbury picked up his Gladstone bag, waved a cheery goodbye and departed.

'This cashier, lad,' said Hardcastle to the railway policeman who had returned after making his statement. 'Is he a military fellow, d'you know? Those army policemen don't seem to know.'

'No, sir. He's a teller from Cox and Company's bank in Albemarle Street. The cash comes here every day in a van with an army escort, and he meets them here. Then, every night, he checks the money and sends it back to the bank, again under escort.'

'I'm glad to see someone knows what's going on,' said Hardcastle, offering a rare word of praise.

'Not much goes on here that we don't know about, sir,' said the railway policeman, preening himself.

'Except escaping murderers it seems,' said Hardcastle, crushingly redressing the balance.

'The van's here to remove the body, sir,' said Marriott. 'And I've taken a statement from Lieutenant Mansfield.'

'Yes, all right, Marriott.' Hardcastle pulled out his watch and glanced at it. 'We'll take a stroll up to Horse Guards, and have a word with Colonel Frobisher. He should be able to tell us where this man Stacey is. Then it'll simply be a case of arresting him.' He rubbed his hands together. 'Should have it all done and dusted by tonight, Marriott.'

TWO

The taxi set down the two detectives in Horse Guards Road, and they swiftly crossed the parade ground to Horse Guards Arch.

'Funny to think of General Wellington sitting in that office up there, sir,' said Marriott, pointing at the window beneath the clock.

'Funnier still to think of a general becoming prime minister,' commented Hardcastle, displaying, yet again, his knowledge of history. 'I'd have thought he'd have had more sense.'

The dismounted sentry in the archway raised his sword in salute at the sight of the bowler-hatted Hardcastle. It was not the first time that the DDI had been mistaken for an army officer; nevertheless he solemnly doffed his hat in acknowledgment of the compliment.

Lieutenant Colonel Ralph Frobisher of the Sherwood Foresters was the assistant provost marshal of London District, and was Hardcastle's point of contact in all matters military. Attired in khaki service dress, he wore a red armlet with the letters APM in black.

The APM looked up warily as Hardcastle and Marriott were shown into his office. 'I take it this is not a social call, Inspector,' he said, smiling. The arrival of the DDI usually succeeded in presenting Frobisher with a problem.

'Indeed not, Colonel. It's a case of murder that took place some two hours ago at Victoria Station, but with your assistance I reckon I can clear it up before nightfall.'

'Take a seat and tell me how I can help you,' said Frobisher, moving a writing pad into the centre of his desk.

As briefly as possible, Hardcastle outlined the circumstances surrounding the death of the cashier who had now been identified as Herbert Somers.

'The army officer I mentioned – a Lieutenant Geoffrey Mansfield of the North Staffordshire Regiment – seized this cap.' Hardcastle handed over the runaway soldier's headgear.

Frobisher examined the cap, and wrote down the name and number that were inscribed inside it. 'You'll be wanting me to tell you where this man is stationed, I suppose, Inspector.' He looked up with a twinkle in his eye.

'That'd be a start, Colonel.'

'It might take some time,' said Frobisher. 'The Army Service Corps is one of the largest corps in the British Army, and to make matters worse this man could be from a unit anywhere in the world. France, Belgium, India, Malta, Gibraltar and Egypt to name but a few. I don't suppose this Lieutenant Mansfield happened to notice whether this soldier had any campaign ribbons on his tunic.'

'I didn't think to ask, Colonel. Although I doubt it. The man was running away at the time. Is it significant, though?'

'It might tell us whether he'd just returned from the Front. On the other hand if he had no medals, he might be in training.

Leave it with me, Inspector, and I'll get back to you as quickly as I can.'

'There was a service revolver lying near the body, Colonel.' Hardcastle produced the slip of paper on which DC Lipton had recorded the serial number.

'D'you know for certain that it's a service revolver, Inspector?'

'It's a Webley Mark Six and is engraved with the broad arrow along with the letters WD. DS Marriott here tells me that stands for War Department,' said Hardcastle, indicating his sergeant with a wave of his hand.

Frobisher nodded. 'Yes, a good weapon, introduced in 1915, Inspector, but you say the cashier wasn't shot.'

'No, Colonel, he was bludgeoned to death with the butt. I was wondering if it was possible to trace where it came from.'

'Virtually impossible, Mr Hardcastle. That particular weapon has been issued in its thousands. All I can tell you is that they are normally only issued to officers, NCOs and trumpeters of cavalry regiments, and some artillery drivers. I think I can say, without fear of contradiction, that your man Stacey of the ASC would not have been issued with one. Not unless he's a horse transport driver. However, I'll do what I can. But I must warn you that I'm unlikely to be able to help. Weapons are abandoned on the battlefield, and rarely traced. In fact, most are lost or buried.'

Once their business with Colonel Frobisher had been completed, Hardcastle and Marriott took a taxi to Cox and Company's bank in Albemarle Street, a turning off Piccadilly.

The manager, a white-haired man of about sixty, who introduced himself as Leonard Richards, had already been advised by the Vine Street police – at Hardcastle's behest – of the death of Herbert Somers.

'A terrible tragedy, Inspector,' said Richards, once Hardcastle and Marriott were ensconced in the manager's office. 'Is there any indication as to who was responsible?' He sat down at his desk, adjusted his spectacles and smoothed his hand over his hair.

'These are early days, Mr Richards,' said Hardcastle, unwilling to divulge what the police knew about the escaping soldier seen by Lieutenant Mansfield. After all, the man Stacey might have had nothing to do with the murder of Herbert Somers, but Hardcastle thought that extremely unlikely. 'But we'll bring him to book, never fear.'

'That's very comforting, Inspector.'

'What interests me at the moment, Mr Richards, is whether there is any money missing? I'm working on the basis that your teller was murdered in the course of a robbery. There were a few bank notes of different denominations left scattered about on the floor of the kiosk.'

'I've already had the bank's accountant conduct an audit of Mr Somers' books, Inspector, and the monies that were returned. It seems that some three hundred pounds are missing.'

'I take it that the missing money was sterling, sir,' said Marriott, looking up from his pocketbook.

'Yes, it was. Mostly five-pound notes, and possibly one or two one-pound and ten-shilling notes, I should think. The French francs appear all to be accounted for.'

'I see.' Marriott made a note and glanced up again. 'I don't suppose you have the serial numbers of those notes, sir, do you?'

Richards smiled at the question. 'I'm afraid we don't have the time for that, Sergeant Marriott. We're already short-staffed, thanks to the war, and more men are going off to join up almost every day.'

'I thought that might be the case, sir,' said Marriott. 'Might we have Mr Somers' address? We'll need to have a word with his family.'

'Yes, certainly,' said Richards, and he scribbled the details on a slip of paper. 'The tragedy is made worse by the fact that Somers shouldn't have been there at all.'

'Oh?' Hardcastle, who always gathered snippets like that, looked up sharply. His suspicious mind immediately wondered why.

'No, Somers doesn't usually do the services' bureau de change. It's normally a teller called Utting, Jack Utting, but he called in sick yesterday evening. Apparently he was knocked over by a lad on a bicycle that afternoon. Not badly hurt, just a bit bruised it seems, but he didn't feel up to coming in to work today.'

'How very interesting.' Hardcastle made a mental note of that piece of information, his active detective's mind immediately wondering whether there had been an accomplice to the robbery and whether his name was Jack Utting. And if so, had he played any direct part in the unfortunate death of Herbert Somers? 'D'you happen to have this Mr Utting's address?'

'Yes, I do.' Richards scribbled a Pimlico address on the slip of paper bearing Somers' address and handed it to Hardcastle. 'Having a house in Pimlico makes it much more convenient for Utting to get to Victoria than it did for poor Somers who lived in Lewisham.'

'Would the cashier usually report here first, Mr Richards? Before setting off for Victoria Station, I mean.' Hardcastle knew what the railway policeman had told him, but he always checked.

'No, he would normally go straight to Victoria Station. Then he'd wait until the military escort arrived with the cash. The army comes here every day to collect the money, you see. Except for those days when we're advised that no troop trains were expected. And the hours of work tend to change too, dependent on what the army tells us. Some troop trains arrive early in the morning; others late at night.'

'I see,' said Hardcastle thoughtfully. 'Thank you very much, Mr Richards.'

It was nearing four o'clock the same afternoon by the time that Hardcastle and Marriott arrived at Honor Oak Park railway station in south-east London. It was but a short walk from there to the Somers' terraced house in Tatnell Road, Lewisham.

'Yes, what is it?' The woman who answered the door was probably about forty years old. She looked harassed, and flicked a lock of greying hair away from her face.

'We're police officers, madam,' said Hardcastle, raising his hat. 'Mrs Somers, is it?'

'No, I'm Mrs Perkins, Mrs Somers' neighbour,' said the woman, opening the door wide to admit the two detectives. 'Mrs Somers has had terrible news, and I came in to do what I could. She's got two small children, you know. They're next door, playing with my three. I don't know how we're going to break it to them.'

'We know about the murder of Mrs Somers' husband,

madam, that's why we're here,' said Hardcastle, as he and
Marriott stepped over the threshold.

There was no pressing reason why Hardcastle should have
visited Herbert Somers' widow; the local police had called
earlier to advise her of her husband's brutal murder. But
Hardcastle was a tenacious detective and would explore every
avenue in his hunt for a killer, even though he realized that
he was unlikely to find the answer to the cashier's death in
this well-kept house.

'I'll make some tea,' said Mrs Perkins, after she had shown
the two CID officers into the parlour. A careworn woman of
about thirty-five was sitting in an armchair, her red-rimmed
eyes testifying to the grief she was suffering at the loss of her
husband. She clutched a wet handkerchief between her hands.

'I'm Divisional Detective Inspector Hardcastle, ma'am, and
this is Detective Sergeant Marriott. We're investigating the
death of your husband.' The DDI glanced around at the jumble
of bric-a-brac, at the depressingly brown decor, and the brown
velour curtains. The fire grate was filled with a newspaper
folded into a fan. But there was not a trace of dust anywhere
and the windows were sparkling clean.

Doris Somers looked up listlessly. 'You can't bring him
back though, can you?' she asked, almost accusingly.

'No, I can't,' agreed Hardcastle, then mumbled, 'and I'm
very sorry for your loss.' He was not very good at uttering
words of condolence, even though he had been obliged to visit
the recently bereaved on many occasions during his service.

'He suffered terribly from asthma, you know,' said Mrs
Somers.

'Chronic, it was,' said Mrs Perkins, reappearing with a tray
of tea. Hardcastle suspected that it had already been made
when he and Marriott arrived. 'I can vouch for that.'

'It stopped him from joining the army, you know,' continued
Mrs Somers, 'and I thought he'd be safe enough working at
the bank. You expect to hear of men getting killed at the Front,
but not when they work in a bank in London. Why did it have
to happen?' She looked at the two detectives as though
imploring them to work some sort of miracle.

'Were you aware of anyone who might've wanted to murder
your husband, Mrs Somers?' asked Marriott, accepting a cup
of tea from Mrs Perkins. It sounded a crass question to pose,

but sometimes the answer to such a question had solved a murder. Nevertheless, the police had to consider that a motive for murder was not always the most obvious one. Not that there was much doubt in the minds of either Hardcastle or Marriott, that Herbert Somers had been the victim of a random robbery at the hands of a soldier called Stacey.

'No. He was well liked, both at the bank and by the neighbours here in Tatnell Road.'

'I can testify to that, Inspector,' put in Mrs Perkins. 'Bert Somers was a lovely man. He'd do anything for anybody would Bert. And he was a great help to those round here who'd lost husbands or sons at sea, or at the Front. Being at the bank, he knew how to write letters to the Admiralty and the War Office about pensions and that sort of thing.'

Hardcastle realized that there was little to be gained by prolonging this painful interview, and he hurriedly finished his tea. 'If you can think of anything that might help us, Mrs Somers, you only have to tell a policeman – any policeman – and it will reach me.' He turned to Mrs Perkins. 'Thank you for the tea.'

And with that he and Marriott left the grieving widow to the tender ministrations of Mrs Perkins, her neighbour and friend.

From Tatnell Road, Hardcastle and Marriott rushed to St Mary's Hospital in Paddington.

Despite having told Hardcastle that he was to start the post-mortem examination at six o'clock that evening, Dr Bernard Spilsbury had almost finished by the time the two detectives arrived.

'No doubt about it, Hardcastle,' said Spilsbury as he washed his hands. 'It was the blow to the back of the head with the revolver you found at the scene that killed your victim.'

'I understand from his widow that he suffered from chronic asthma, doctor,' said Hardcastle. 'I wondered whether that would have made a difference.'

'Not at all. That would not have been a contributory factor in the man's death. I'll let you have my report in due course, Hardcastle.'

'I'm obliged to you, doctor.'

* * *

At ten o'clock the following morning, Hardcastle received Dr Spilsbury's report, neatly typed, into the death of Herbert Somers. He started to read it aloud for Marriott's benefit, stumbling over the less familiar words. 'Death was due to intracranial haemorrhage, accumulating in the subdural, and accelerated by the attendant . . .' He flung the report down on his desk. 'What in hell's name is he talking about, Marriott? Here you read it. See if you can make any sense of it.'

Marriott picked up the report and skimmed through it. Replacing it on Hardcastle's desk, he looked up. 'All we really need to know, sir, is that Somers died as a result of a blow to the skull with the butt of an army pistol.'

'Well, I knew that, and that's what he told us yesterday,' muttered Hardcastle testily. 'Why the bloody hell didn't the good doctor say so?'

'Yes, sir.' Marriott, knowing how inadvisable it was to encourage one of the DDI's criticisms, confined his response to monosyllables. He could have said that that is exactly what Dr Spilsbury's report stated, but decided that the safer course was to keep that opinion to himself.

A PC knocked on Hardcastle's open door. 'Excuse me, sir.'

'Yes, what is it, lad?'

'A telephone call from Colonel Frobisher, sir. He has some information for you, when you care to call on him.' The PC stepped into the office and laid a message flimsy on Hardcastle's desk.

'Ah,' exclaimed Hardcastle, 'perhaps we'll hear something that might help us to push this enquiry along a bit further. And not before time, either. Come, Marriott.' He seized his hat and umbrella, and swept out of the office, followed by Marriott.

As Hardcastle and Marriott arrived at the APM's office, a mounted troop of Life Guards entered Horse Guards Arch to change the guard. Their ceremonial scarlet tunics, silver-coloured helmets and breastplates, white breeches and knee boots, had been replaced by sombre khaki with puttees. And no ceremony had attended the guard change since the outbreak of war.

'I've traced your man Stacey for you, Inspector,' said Frobisher.

'Splendid, Colonel. I hope he's not too far away.'

'No. You'll doubtless be relieved that he's in Aldershot,' said the APM. 'I spoke to the officer in charge of Army Service Corps records, and he confirmed that Private Edward Stacey, with the same regimental number that was inside the cap, is in his fourth week of training at Buller Barracks on Queen's Avenue. He's one of Lord Derby's conscripts apparently. He tried pleading that he was a conscientious objector, but the tribunal turned him down.'

'Don't surprise me,' muttered Hardcastle, who had no high opinion of 'conchies' as he called them.

'I arranged for Captain Hector McIntyre of the Gordon Highlanders – he's one of my military police officers – to take Stacey into custody as soon as I learned he was the man you wanted,' continued Frobisher. 'You'll find him in the guardroom at Salamanca Barracks. McIntyre is expecting you.'

'But I thought you said he was at Buller Barracks, Colonel.' As ever, Hardcastle was finding difficulty understanding the military.

'That's where his training battalion is stationed, Inspector, but I thought it advisable to have him removed from among his own comrades. Anyway, Salamanca Barracks is where Captain McIntyre has his offices. When are you thinking of going down there?'

'I'll go and talk to him immediately, Colonel.' Hardcastle rubbed his hands together. 'With any luck we'll get a cough from Stacey, and have the case all done and dusted by nightfall.'

'A cough?' queried Frobisher, as unfamiliar with Hardcastle's argot as Hardcastle was with that of the military.

'A confession,' explained Hardcastle.

'I see. I'll have you met at Aldershot Station. You'll find a military policeman there to take you to Salamanca Barracks.'

'What about the revolver, Colonel?'

'No luck there, I'm afraid, Inspector, and I doubt there will be. As I said the last time you were here, the number of revolvers that are lost on the battlefield makes it almost impossible to keep track of them.'

'A pity, that. It might have led me to Somers' killer, not that I think there's any doubt that the man Stacey was responsible. I wonder how he got hold of a revolver, though,' mused

Hardcastle. 'However, I'm obliged to you for your assistance, Colonel.'

Leaving Colonel Frobisher's office at Horse Guards Arch, Hardcastle strode out to Whitehall and hailed a cab to take him and Marriott to Waterloo Station.

Fortunately, Hardcastle's rank entitled him to travel second class, otherwise he and Marriott – also travelling second class, because he was with the DDI – would have had difficulty in finding a seat in a train crowded with soldiers going to Aldershot and sailors on their way to Portsmouth.

As Frobisher had promised, a red-capped military police corporal was awaiting the detectives' arrival at Aldershot Station. It was as well: there were queues of officers waiting for the inadequate number of taxis.

'Inspector Hardcastle, sir?' asked the corporal, as he saluted.

'Yes.'

'Very good, sir. I've orders to take you to Salamanca Barracks. Captain McIntyre is expecting you.' The corporal conducted Hardcastle and Marriott to a highly polished Vauxhall staff car bearing military police insignia. The journey took but ten minutes.

THREE

Salamanca Barracks consisted, in the main, of two tall, long buildings facing each other. The ground floor of each, once stables, had been converted into a number of offices. Each bore mystifying signs in a military terminology that Hardcastle did not understand, nor had any desire to.

Eventually, the military police corporal showed them into an office at the far end of one of the buildings. 'Captain McIntyre's office, sir,' he said.

'Hector McIntyre, Inspector.' The tall Gordon Highlanders officer crossed the room and shook hands with the DDI and Marriott. He was wearing a kilt of the Gordon tartan, with a sporran that came to his knees. But his tunic, with its cutaway skirt, was the same drab khaki as everyone else had worn since the war began. It was relieved only by medal ribbons and a brassard bearing the letters MP. 'I've got your man locked up here as Colonel Frobisher ordered.' He glanced at his watch. 'But I daresay you'd care for a bite to eat, or perhaps a wee dram, eh, Inspector? Or even both,' he added with a chuckle.

'That would be most acceptable, Captain,' said Hardcastle, warming immediately to the military policeman.

'Aye, good,' said McIntyre. 'I always find interviewing prisoners on an empty stomach is nae good for the constitution.' He laughed loudly, and picked up his chequered glengarry and swagger cane. 'Follow me, gentlemen.'

McIntyre led the two detectives across a vast parade ground where several squads of men, under a fierce-looking sergeant, were being drilled. The recruits were brought to attention, and the sergeant saluted. McIntyre acknowledged the compliment by languidly touching his glengarry with his swagger cane. Finally the trio reached the officers' mess on the far side.

After several tots of malt whisky, and a splendid lunch, the MP officer escorted Hardcastle and Marriott back across the barrack square to the guardroom.

The regimental police sergeant leaped to his feet and saluted as McIntyre strode in.

'These two gentlemen are from the civil police, Sarn't, and they've come to have a word with Stacey.'

'Very good, sir.' The provost sergeant took a large bunch of keys from a hook on the wall, and led the three policemen down a dank corridor. Opening the door of a cell, he screamed at the occupant. 'On your feet, lad, officer present.'

Edward Stacey carved a pitiful figure. Not yet nineteen years of age, his hair was shorn, and he was dressed in canvas fatigues, the trousers of which he clutched as he stood up. The provost sergeant had wisely removed anything that the unfortunate youth might use to hang himself, and that included his belt and his bootlaces. The death of a soldier who had committed suicide in a guardroom inevitably led to a court of enquiry, and even the possibility of a court martial for whoever was in charge of him at the time.

'These officers are from the civil police and they're here to ask you some questions in connection with a serious crime,

Stacey,' said McIntyre. 'You will answer them truthfully. D'you understand?'

'Yes, sir.' Stacey was shaking visibly. He seemed to have no idea why he had been placed in close arrest, and certainly appeared to know nothing about this serious crime to which the military police officer was referring.

'Where were you yesterday morning, lad?' asked Hardcastle.

'Here, sir.' Stacey stared at Hardcastle as though the DDI had asked a fatuous question.

'No, you weren't,' put in McIntyre. 'You weren't arrested until last evening.'

'No, sir, I meant I was here in Aldershot, at Buller Barracks. We was doing weapon training all morning.'

'Is that so?' Hardcastle produced the cap bearing Stacey's name and number. 'Is this yours?' he asked, handing the cap to the prisoner.

Stacey looked inside the cap, and then glanced up, a mystified expression on his face. 'Yes, it's mine, sir, but how did you get hold of it?' he asked as he returned the cap.

'It was picked up by a North Staffordshire Regiment officer at Victoria Station at about quarter past ten yesterday morning. He claims to have been pursuing a soldier who we believe had just murdered the cashier in a military money-exchange booth,' said Hardcastle. 'What have you to say about that?'

'I lost it, sir.' Stacey really had no idea what this aggressive policeman was talking about.

'You lost it? And you expect me to believe that?'

'It's the God's honest truth, sir. I never had nothing to do with no murder. I was here all day. Well, at Buller Barracks, like.'

'Did you report the loss of your cap, Stacey?' asked McIntyre, who was leaning against the jamb of the cell doorway, his arms folded.

'No, sir.'

'Why not?'

'I'd've had to pay for a new one, sir.' To Stacey that seemed a logical answer.

'So how did you expect to appear on working parade this morning without a cap, eh? If you hadn't been put in close arrest last night, that is.'

'I'd've managed to borrow one, sir. One of the lads is off sick, and I thought—'

'And you thought you'd steal someone else's before you had to pay for another, I suppose, laddie.' McIntyre turned to Hardcastle. 'I'm sorry, Inspector, I shouldn't have interrupted.'

'That's all right, Captain McIntyre, but I need to have a word with you outside.'

When the three policemen were in the cell passage, with the door of Stacey's cell firmly closed, Hardcastle asked, 'D'you think there's any truth in this story, Captain?'

'It's easily checked, Inspector. If Stacey was attending weapon training yesterday morning, then the sergeant-instructor will be able to confirm it. It's a pity Colonel Frobisher didn't tell me why you wanted to see Stacey. It might have saved you a journey if what the lad says turns out to be true.'

'How soon can we check his story?' asked Hardcastle.

'In the time it takes us to get from here to Buller Barracks, Inspector, and find the sergeant weapon training instructor.'

The sprawling blocks of Buller Barracks in Queen's Avenue lay a mile away from Salamanca Barracks. It was said that, following the Crimean War, Florence Nightingale had condemned them, along with all the other barracks in Aldershot, as unfit for soldiers to live in, but the advent of the Great War had put paid to plans for what would have been an ambitious rebuilding programme.

Sergeant Finch, a veteran of the Boer Wars, was found instructing a squad of recruits in one of the wooden class-rooms that had been hurriedly constructed to cope with the influx of recruits that this latest war – and Lord Kitchener's pointing finger – had brought about.

The appearance of Captain McIntyre in the doorway imme-diately produced a roar from Finch for the recruits to come to attention.

As the young soldiers leaped to their feet, one unfortunate who was seated behind a Lewis gun, managed to knock it over in his haste.

'Mind what you're doing with that bloody thing, you stupid oaf,' roared Finch. 'We can get plenty more soldiers, but Lewis guns are hard to come by. Do it again and I'll tear off your arm and beat you to death with the soggy end.' He swivelled on his left heel, crashed his ammunition boots on the wooden floor to assume a position of attention, and saluted. 'Sah!' he yelled.

'Stand easy, lads,' said McIntyre, and beckoning to Finch, he said, 'Just step outside, Sarn't Finch.'

'Sah!' yelled Finch again, and followed the military police officer into the corridor.

'These two gentlemen are from the civil police, Sarn't Finch.'

'Yes, sir. Very good, sir.'

'They want to know about Private Stacey. He tells me that he was under training with you yesterday morning.'

Finch unbuttoned one of his tunic pockets and withdrew a sheet of paper. After a moment or two spent in perusing the document, he looked up. 'Yes, sir. Correct, sir. An idle man, sir.'

McIntyre smiled. To sergeant-instructors all recruits were idle men. 'Did he say anything about having lost his cap, Sarn't Finch?'

'No, sir, but the men don't wear headdress for these here lectures. That'd be a matter for his platoon sergeant, sir.'

'And you're absolutely certain that he was here yesterday morning.'

Finch contrived to look mildly offended without being insubordinate. 'He was definitely here, sir, and he should've been here today. I've marked him absent.'

'He's locked up in my guardroom at the moment, Sarn't Finch, but it looks rather as though you'll be getting him back shortly.'

'Very good, sir,' said Finch. 'I don't know what you banged him up for, but I daresay a couple of circuits of the barrack square with his rifle at the high port won't do him no harm, and that's a fact, sir.'

'Well, Inspector, it looks rather as though Stacey is not the man you want,' said McIntyre, when the three of them were walking back to McIntyre's staff car.

'It certainly looks that way, Captain,' said a disappointed Hardcastle, 'but I'm still wondering how our man at Victoria Station came to be in possession of Stacey's cap.'

'That seems to point to some other soldier in his platoon

having purloined Stacey's cap, but I wonder why,' said McIntyre.

'So do I, Captain,' said Hardcastle. 'So do I.'

But as it turned out, it was not that simple.

The problem of Stacey's cap was still vexing Hardcastle by the time he and Marriott alighted from their train at Waterloo Station.

Clearly in an irritable mood, the DDI marched out to the station forecourt, and hired a taxi.

'Scotland Yard, cabbie,' he snapped, and then, turning to Marriott, added, 'Tell 'em Cannon Row, and half the time you'll finish up at Cannon Street in the City,' he said.

'Yes, sir,' said Marriott wearily. Hardcastle had offered this advice on almost every occasion that he and the DDI had travelled back to the police station.

On the Friday morning, Hardcastle received a telephone call from Captain McIntyre.

'Inspector, I had another word with Stacey after you'd left, and persuaded him to tell me the circumstances under which he lost his cap. He was reluctant to tell me at first, but I explained to him that either he came clean or I'd hand him over to you.' McIntyre's statement was followed by a deep chuckle.

'What did he have to say, Captain?' Hardcastle was somewhat puzzled by the call. He thought that a lost service cap was a matter for the army, rather than for him. As far as the DDI was concerned, Stacey was not the man for whom he was looking in connection with the death of Herbert Somers, even though he thought that he was somehow involved. Even unknowingly.

'Apparently on the evening of Sunday the eighth – that's three days before the murder that you're investigating – he went absent.'

'How long was he absent?' asked Hardcastle, his interest immediately aroused.

'Not long. In fact, only a matter of hours. You see, Inspector, recruits are confined to barracks until they've completed ten-weeks training, but most of the barracks here are wide open, as you'll have seen. There are no brick walls, or anything of that sort. It's easy enough for a soldier to walk out without going anywhere near the guardroom, or being spotted by an officer or NCO. Mind you, they'd have been crimed by their company commander if they'd been caught and brought up before him.'

'How does this affect the issue, Captain?' asked Hardcastle, wondering why the provost officer should be telling him this.

'He went down to a pub in Aldershot with some of his pals, and was stupid enough to leave his cap on a hook. Well, the army code is that you never steal any personal property from a comrade, but army property is fair game for a thief. When Stacey left the pub, his cap was gone, and there wasn't another one there. That means it's unlikely to have been a case of another soldier picking up the wrong cap by mistake and leaving his own in its place, if you see what I mean.'

'Do you know which public house Stacey was in?' asked Hardcastle, even though that appeared to be irrelevant.

'I'm afraid not. There are over a hundred pubs in the Aldershot area, Inspector, and Stacey can't remember which one he was in. Probably three sheets to the wind by the time he got back to barracks. It looks to me very much as though the man who took Stacey's cap did it deliberately. Perhaps he'd lost his own and didn't feel like paying for a replacement.'

That did not accord with Hardcastle's view of the reason for the theft, but he let it pass.

'God knows how Stacey got back to barracks without a cap,' continued McIntyre. 'My patrols are everywhere, but I've looked through the reports, and there's nothing to indicate any military policemen checking a man for not wearing his headdress. Or for being absent without authority.'

'I seem to remember you asking him how he would appear on parade without a cap. Did you question him further about that, Captain McIntyre?'

'Aye, I did that. As he said when you interviewed him, he would have borrowed one from a laddie who was sick and excused duties.'

'But wouldn't he have had to appear on parade before going to the weapon training class that Sergeant Finch mentioned?'

'Yes, as far as I know. I can only assume that he did what he said he was going to, and borrowed one.'

'From what you're saying, I get the impression that it was one of Stacey's mates who stole his cap. But that begs the question of how his mate got to the pub without a cap,' Hardcastle added thoughtfully.

'Yes, that's the conclusion I came to.'

'Of course,' Hardcastle went on, 'he might not have gone to the pub *without* a cap. Perhaps the thief, whoever he is, stole the cap in order to commit the robbery at the money-exchange booth, and thereby implicate Stacey.'

'That sounds like a possibility, Inspector. I can make some enquiries, if that would be helpful. I'll get one of my sergeants to find out from Stacey which of his pals he went drinking with. You never know, but that might just turn up your murderer for you.'

Hardcastle laughed. 'D'you think Stacey will tell your sergeant?'

Now it was McIntyre's turn to chuckle. 'Believe me, Inspector, my sergeants can be very persuasive when the mood takes them.'

'Thank you for your help, Captain McIntyre.' Hardcastle decided that he would not enquire too deeply into the army's interrogation methods, preferring not to imagine the sort of pressure a military police sergeant would exert in order to extract the facts from Stacey.

'If there's anything further I can do, you know where I am.'

'Thank you,' said Hardcastle. 'Perhaps you'd keep me informed.'

The following day Hardcastle received a further telephone call from Captain McIntyre.

'An interesting development, Inspector,' he began. 'It seems that Private Stacey's cap wasn't the only item of kit that went missing. Another soldier in Stacey's platoon reported having a tunic stolen, and a third man a pair of trousers. Also, as I promised, I've had a list from my sergeant of those members of Stacey's platoon who were drinking with him the night that the lad lost his cap.'

'Are you suggesting that these soldiers lost a tunic and a pair of trousers in a pub, Captain McIntyre?' enquired Hardcastle impishly.

There was a guffaw of laughter from the other end. 'It's an

intriguing thought, Inspector, but no, they appear to have had them stolen from their barrack room.'

'It would seem, then, that someone living in that barrack room stole those items of uniform for the purpose of carrying out a robbery at Victoria Station, a robbery that resulted in murder. Either that or someone else entered the barrack room with the same aim in mind. The question is why should they have done so? If the idea was to implicate Stacey – who's now been rowed out of my investigation – it only serves to narrow the field of enquiry.'

There was a long pause before McIntyre replied. 'I suppose it looks to be the case,' he said eventually. 'What do you want to do about it, Inspector?'

Hardcastle also paused before answering. 'I think I'll have to come down to Aldershot and have a word with them, Captain. When do you suggest?'

'It's Saturday today,' said McIntyre, 'and this afternoon the men are involved in interior economy ready for the commanding officer's inspection on Monday. After that they'll be playing football, visiting the canteen, or even sleeping. As for tomorrow, well, that's taken up with church parades in the morning, and in the afternoon they're allowed to do more or less what they want to do within the confines of the barracks.'

'Interior economy?' queried Hardcastle. 'What on earth is that?' Once again, the DDI was mystified by army terminology.

'Pressing uniforms, and cleaning equipment and barrack rooms,' said McIntyre. 'So I would suggest you come down on Monday morning. I'll send a car to Aldershot Station in time for you to call at my office at, say, ten o'clock. Then I'll take you to Buller Barracks and introduce you to the commanding officer of the training battalion. As a matter of courtesy, you understand.'

'Very well, I'll see you on Monday.' Finishing his conversation with McIntyre, Hardcastle turned to his sergeant. 'We're being buggered about by the military once again, Marriott.' The DDI leaned forward to pick up his pipe, and began to fill it with tobacco. 'This is turning out to be a bit of a dog's dinner,' he continued, and relayed the details of his last conversation with the military police officer.

Marriott was always amused at his chief's description of

any enquiry as a dog's dinner, although this was sometimes varied to a dog's breakfast. 'It looks as though someone stole the cap, the tunic and the trousers so he could carry out the robbery, sir,' he said, repeating what Hardcastle had said to McIntyre.

'Yes, it does, but why?' Hardcastle applied a match to his pipe and leaned back thoughtfully.

'Perhaps he's a civilian, sir. Someone who didn't want to be recognized among all the other soldiers at the railway station.'

Hardcastle scoffed at that suggestion. 'If some civilian can walk into a barracks in time of war and steal bits of uniform, it don't say much for their security. No, Marriott, it's got to have been a soldier. But it was obviously a soldier who didn't know that Stacey would have a copper-bottomed alibi for the time of the murder.'

'I agree, sir, but apart from anything else, surely a soldier would've saluted an officer – that Lieutenant Mansfield who saw the murderer running away – rather than risk getting caught for something as silly as that after having done a murder, sir.'

'I'd've thought so, Marriott, but like I said, it's a dog's dinner. Still, thanks to the military police, there's nothing we can do until Monday. Take the rest of the weekend off, and give my regards to Mrs Marriott.'

'Thank you very much, sir.' It was rare for the DDI not to work right through Saturday and Sunday when he was engaged in a murder enquiry. 'And mine to Mrs H.'

Hardcastle did not, however, leave immediately. As usual, he managed to find some reports to scrutinize, criticize and correct, but at about half past two, he descended the stairs and walked through the front office of the police station.

A police constable was donning a large cardboard placard that read: POLICE NOTICE – TAKE COVER.

'What's that all about, lad?' asked Hardcastle.

'Air raid, sir,' said the PC, who thought – although he did not say so – that the placard made perfectly clear what was happening. 'Didn't you hear the maroons?'

'Maroons? What maroons?'

'Three of them were set off from Southwark Fire Station, sir, at fifteen-second intervals. It's the new scheme for warning of an air raid. It usually means the raiders are about twenty miles away from us.'

'Well, I'm going home, lad. Bound to be a false alarm, and we've had more than enough of them lately.'

The PC looked doubtful. 'You'd be better off staying here in the basement, sir. Much safer, like.'

'It'll take more than Fritz in one of his infernal flying machines to stop me from going home, lad, bombs or no bombs,' said Hardcastle, and donning his bowler hat, he marched purposefully out of the police station.

'I s'pose being a DDI he thinks he's exempt from getting killed, Sergeant,' said the PC to the station officer. 'His umbrella won't be much help.'

'You watch your bloody tongue when you're talking about Mr Hardcastle, lad,' said the sergeant. 'Now get out on the streets, and start blowing your whistle.'

FOUR

Hardcastle walked out to Victoria Embankment to catch a tram to his home in Kennington. To his surprise there was one waiting at the stop, but it had been abandoned by the driver, the conductor and the passengers, doubtless to seek shelter from the air raid.

Hearing the deep engine note of an aircraft, he looked up at the sky and saw a huge German Gotha bomber, its distinctive Maltese crosses clearly visible on its vast wings and its tail fin. Well, that took less than twenty minutes to get here, he thought, mindful of what the PC had said about the warning maroons.

There was smoke funnelling from the aircraft's port engine, which probably accounted for it flying so low, and it was surrounded by puffs of white smoke from the anti-aircraft gun battery in Hyde Park. As Hardcastle watched, spellbound almost, he saw a long, black cylindrical object fall from the aircraft to splash, harmlessly, into the river.

Suddenly, as if from nowhere, a tiny Sopwith Pup fighter plane appeared above the lumbering bomber. There were coloured streamers fixed to its wing struts indicating, did

Hardcastle but know it, that the pilot was a flight commander. Executing a daring manoeuvre, the aircraft dived underneath the German machine, coming down so low that Hardcastle thought it might finish up in the water of the Thames. But suddenly the British pilot, so close that Hardcastle was able to see his helmeted head, lifted the nose of his aircraft so that he was in a position to attack the Gotha from beneath. Almost immediately, he saw flames spurting from the Sopwith's Lewis gun a split second before he heard its rat-a-tat-tat.

Moments later, as the British aircraft wheeled away, smoke began to issue from the Gotha's starboard engine and it started a slow, involuntary descent. Both the aircraft's engines had now stopped, and the huge machine glided lower and lower in a silence so sudden that it was almost eerie. It proved to be one of the few successes achieved by the defence forces.

Astounded at having witnessed this aerial combat, Hardcastle still had time to hope that the crippled German bomber would crash on the south side of the river and, thus, become the responsibility of the Lambeth Division of the Metropolitan Police. Divisional CID officers were responsible for the initial interrogation of prisoners of war before handing them over to the military.

Half an hour later, as Hardcastle waited at the tram stop, a policeman cycled along Victoria Embankment bearing a placard on his chest that read ALL CLEAR. At the same time, the DDI spotted a Boy Scout on Westminster Bridge sounding a call on his bugle. He remembered reading a police order that stated it was one of several efforts by the authorities to indicate that the raiders had passed.

Eventually, the tram driver, his conductor, and a few passengers returned to their tram.

'Think it'll be safe enough to get under way now?' asked Hardcastle acidly.

'Can't afford to take a chance, guv'nor,' said the conductor, tugging at his moustache. 'One of our single-deckers got a direct hit the other day, not a few yards from here. The crew and all the passengers were killed,' he added mournfully.

Hardcastle's tram crossed Westminster Bridge and moved into Westminster Bridge Road. As it passed the Bethlehem Royal Hospital on the corner of Lambeth Road and Kennington Road, it was evident that the DDI's hope had come true. In the hospital grounds was the smoking wreckage of the Gotha bomber, now surrounded by firemen and policemen. The DDI later learned from George Lambert, his opposite number on L Division, that all three members of the crew – pilot, observer and rear-gunner – had perished.

As a result of the delay caused to his tram by the air raid, it was past four o'clock by the time that Hardcastle let himself into his house in Kennington Road. It was the house into which the Hardcastles had moved immediately following their marriage twenty-four years ago, and was not a great distance from number 287, where the famous Charlie Chaplin had once lived.

Alice Hardcastle was sitting in an armchair in the parlour, knitting cap comforters for the soldiers in the trenches. Resting her knitting on her lap, she looked up as her husband entered the room.

'You're early, Ernie. Run out of things to do at your police station?' It was usually about seven o'clock, at the earliest, before Hardcastle made an appearance at home, even on a Saturday.

'For the moment,' said Hardcastle, who made a point of never discussing cases with his family. He was still irritated that his enquiries were being held to ransom by the military. 'Where are the girls?'

'Kitty's on duty,' said Alice. For some time now, Kitty Hardcastle had been working as a bus conductress. Against her father's wishes, she had taken the job with the London General Omnibus Company 'to release a man to join the army', she had said. 'Maud's gone out shopping up West, and Walter's at the post office.'

'He seems to spend a lot of time there,' muttered Hardcastle, seating himself in the armchair opposite Alice.

'Well, of course he does. Being a telegram boy means that he's always taking those little yellow envelopes to the bereaved. I must say I wouldn't care for his job. Have you ever noticed how the curtains twitch whenever a telegram boy cycles down the road? They're all terrified that it's their man who has been killed. That Mrs Wainwright from across the road has never been the same since her husband was killed on the first day of the Battle of the Somme. And that was over a year ago. And it was Wally who took the telegram. He asked her if there was a reply – which he has to do because it's the regulations – and she just burst into tears.'

'I saw an air raid today,' commented Hardcastle conversationally, deciding to change the subject, albeit slightly.

'Oh, really?' said Alice as she resumed her knitting. 'I thought I heard the maroons go off.'

'I saw one of those big German Gothas drop a bomb in the river. It didn't do any damage.'

'Their eyesight never was much good, Ernie,' said Alice. 'Have you noticed how many Germans wear glasses?'

'And then one of ours came from nowhere and shot it down.'

'Where did it crash?'

'On L Division's ground.'

'Pah!' snorted Alice, putting down her knitting again. 'How d'you expect me to know where that is?'

'I saw it in the grounds of the Bethlehem Hospital. Still on fire, it was.'

'You could have said that in the first place, Ernie. I'm not in your precious police force, and I don't know where L Division is.'

'L Division is where we live, Alice,' rejoined Hardcastle, scoring a point. At least, in his own mind. 'Anyway, it's that precious police force, as you call it, that pays me enough to put our food on the table, my girl.'

Alice carefully pushed her knitting needles into the ball of wool she was using, and placed them on a side table. 'I suppose that's a heavy hint that you'll be wanting a cup of tea,' she exclaimed as she stood up.

'I'm not too happy about our young Kitty being on the buses,' said Hardcastle, ignoring his wife's comment, and returning to their previous conversation. 'My tram conductor told me that one of their trams got a direct hit the other day. Everyone on it was killed.'

'Well, you won't stop Kitty, Ernie. Direct hits on trams or not. She's got a will of her own, that girl.' And with that comment, Alice disappeared to the kitchen to make the tea. 'Just like her father,' she called over her shoulder.

I might be a DDI at work, thought Hardcastle, *but it doesn't count for much at home.*

Alice returned with a tray of tea things. 'I was lucky enough to get some of your favourite ginger snaps today,

Ernie.' She poured the tea, and sat down opposite her husband. 'I wouldn't be surprised if there wasn't more of those air raids,' she said. 'Mr Squires reckons that if there was ever another war, it'd all be with just aeroplanes.'

'Huh!' snorted Hardcastle. 'What the blue blazes does he know about warfare?' Squires was the red-faced and self-opinionated grocer whose shop was at the end of Kennington Road, and which was patronized by Alice Hardcastle.

'And he says that those tanks they had at the Somme would be the weapon of the future, with no more men dying in the trenches.'

'Does he indeed?' said Hardcastle. 'Well, my girl, Field Marshal Haig reckons that once this war is over, tanks will be done with, and aeroplanes, too, I wouldn't wonder. He said that the army will use cavalry again in the future, and as he's a field marshal, I should think he knows more about it than Mr Squires the grocer.'

A fretful Hardcastle had spent Sunday reading the *News of the World*, and mooning about the house, occasionally doing the various odd jobs that Alice had lined up for him.

When Monday morning came, he could not get to work fast enough, and arrived at the police station at eight o'clock.

Following his usual practice, he sat down at the station officer's desk and examined the crime book.

'The winter patrols nicked a couple of tea leaves breaking into a house in Esterbrooke Street, sir,' said the station officer. 'DS Wood's dealing with them. Up at Bow Street Court this morning.'

'Good,' said Hardcastle, idly wondering why aspirant detectives continued to be called winter patrols in the height of summer. Satisfied that none of the other entries in the crime book were of immediate interest to him, he stood up.

'Another raid on Saturday, sir,' said the station officer. 'One of our lads brought down a Fritz bomber. Landed in the grounds of the Bethlehem Hospital in Lambeth Road, so I heard.'

'I know. I saw it when I was on my way home,' said Hardcastle curtly, and went upstairs to his office, calling for Marriott on the way.

'Did you hear about the raid on Saturday, sir? Must've been about the time you left.'

'Yes, I saw it, Marriott,' said Hardcastle wearily. He could envisage a day of people asking the same question.

Unabashed, Marriott continued. 'The bomber was brought down on L Division's ground apparently, sir. I hope it wasn't anywhere near your house.'

'No, it wasn't,' said Hardcastle, 'and I can tell you that Mrs Hardcastle would've been extremely annoyed if it had been. She had the curtains down last week and washed them.' And following that somewhat lame attempt at humour, the DDI took out his pipe and began to fill it. 'We'll get off down to Aldershot, then, Marriott, and see what these leery soldiers have got to tell us about the mystery of their missing kit.'

Hardcastle, a stickler for timekeeping, had ensured that he and Marriott arrived at Aldershot railway station at ten minutes to ten. Once again a military police corporal was waiting with a staff car, and, at ten o'clock precisely, Hardcastle and Marriott walked into Captain McIntyre's office at Salamanca Barracks.

'I've arranged for you to meet Lieutenant Colonel Valentine Fuller at a quarter to eleven, Inspector. He's the commanding officer of the battalion where Stacey is undergoing training. In the meantime, gentlemen, perhaps you'd care for a cup of coffee.'

'Thank you,' said Hardcastle. He did not want a cup of coffee, and would much have preferred to get on with the job. As a seasoned detective, he knew that the farther away one got from a crime, the less chance there was of solving it. It seemed to him that the army was a bit lackadaisical in its approach, and he hoped that it adopted a more purposeful attitude to prosecuting the war on the other side of the Channel. But he should have known that was the case; senior officers at Scotland Yard never seemed to possess the same urgency as those in the front line of policing.

Once the unnecessary – in Hardcastle's view – social niceties of coffee and biscuits were completed, McIntyre took the DDI and Marriott out to his staff car, and together they drove up Queen's Avenue to Buller Barracks.

'Colonel, this is Divisional Detective Inspector Hardcastle of the Metropolitan Police, and his assistant, Detective Sergeant Marriott.'

Lieutenant Colonel Valentine Fuller was at least sixty years of age, if not older. He had a grey complexion, a drooping grey moustache and a stooped posture. As he crossed his office to shake hands with Hardcastle, the DDI noticed that he had a pronounced limp.

'Valentine Fuller, Inspector,' said the colonel in what proved to be a deceptively soft and croaking voice. 'I'm what they call a "dugout". I retired from the army in the year ten, but I was called back in 1914 to replace a fitter officer who went off to the war and got himself killed.' Fuller punctuated this comment with a brief, bitter laugh. 'Incidentally, the limp is thanks to some damned fool of a subaltern who shot me in the leg on a tiger shoot in India years ago. He wisely resigned his commission sometime later, and went off to do something with stocks and shares in the City. The last I heard of him he was a millionaire. Do sit down, gentlemen.'

Hardcastle, Marriott and McIntyre took seats on the hard-backed chairs that the army provided for the colonel's guests. The DDI glanced around the austere office, taking in the photograph of a group of officers wearing tropical kit and pith helmets. In front of them was a dead tiger.

Fuller noticed Hardcastle's interest. 'Taken at Poona in oh-one,' he commented. A faraway look came into his eyes. 'Those were the days,' he said. 'Now, Inspector, how may I help you?'

Hardcastle explained the circumstances surrounding the murder he was investigating.

'Well, surely, that's a matter to be dealt with by the military, ain't it, eh what?' Fuller appeared to be somewhat nonplussed by the DDI's presence in his office, and glanced at the military police officer. 'General court martial, eh what, McIntyre? I mean the cashier at this, er, booth or whatever it was, was quasi-military, so to speak, and if the man's killer was a soldier, well, there you have it.'

'Not so, Colonel,' said McIntyre. 'The Army Act is quite clear on the subject. It states categorically that if one soldier kills another soldier in England, even on military property, and even in time of war, it is still a matter for the civil police. And, in any event, this murder was on Victoria railway station, and the cashier was a civilian.'

'Really?' Fuller sounded disbelieving, but he had never been very conversant with *King's Regulations* or the *Manual of Military Law*. 'Well, in India that sort of thing would have been dealt with by a field general court martial, eh what?'

'I agree, Colonel,' said McIntyre patiently, 'but we're not in India, sir.'

'Oh, well, I suppose you military police wallahs know about these things,' mumbled Fuller. 'So what d'you want me to do about it, eh, Inspector?' he said, directing his question to Hardcastle with a raised eyebrow.

'I should like to interview the soldiers that Captain McIntyre has identified as having been with Private Stacey the night his cap was stolen.'

'Very well. If you think that'll help.' Fuller shook his head, stood up, and limped across to open the door of his office. In a surprisingly loud voice, he bellowed, 'Sarn't-major.'

'Sir!' came a distant reply from down the corridor.

Moments later, the regimental sergeant-major appeared on the threshold. Magnificently turned out in immaculate service dress with a highly polished Sam Browne belt, he snapped to attention with a crash of his black glass-like ammunition boots and saluted. Both his highly burnished brass crown-in-laurel-leaves rank badge and his regimental cap badge shone in the shaft of sunlight coming through the commanding officer's window.

'You wanted me, sir?'

'Yes, Mr Punchard. These gentlemen are from the civil police. They wish to ask some of our recruits questions regarding a matter that I'm sure they'll tell you about.' Fuller turned to Hardcastle. 'RSM Punchard will take care of everything, Inspector. Anything you need, he'll deal with.'

'Thank you, Colonel, most kind,' murmured Hardcastle. But secretly he was infuriated by the indolent attitude of army officers who seemed unable to grasp the urgency of the matter with which he was dealing. He was not altogether surprised at Fuller's stance, but felt that McIntyre – a military police officer – should have had a greater awareness of what the police were trying to do. And a greater sense of urgency.

'Perhaps you'd be so good as to accompany me, gentlemen,' said RSM Punchard. Tucking his pace stick under his left arm, he gave the colonel another quivering salute, turned and marched out of the commanding officer's office.

Hardcastle, Marriott and McIntyre accompanied RSM

Punchard across the vast parade ground that, he told them, was called W Square.

'Why is that?' asked Hardcastle unwisely.

'All the barrack squares in Aldershot are given letters,' said Punchard. 'God knows why. You see, Mr Hardcastle, I was a Coldstream Guardsman, and I was trained at Caterham Barracks, the Guards depot. We knew how to do things there. I haven't always been in Ali Sloper's Cavalry.'

Once again, Hardcastle was mystified by army terminology. 'What on earth is Ali Sloper's Cavalry?' he asked.

It was Captain McIntyre who provided the answer. 'It's an army nickname, Inspector,' he said with a laugh, 'using the initials ASC, which really means the Army Service Corps.'

'I see,' said Hardcastle, determined that he would ask no more questions about military customs and terminology.

FIVE

The four soldiers, who had admitted being with Stacey on their illegal visit to an Aldershot pub, had been assembled in one of the classrooms, along with Stacey himself, now released from custody.

'Privates Stacey, Ash, Joliffe, Stone and Paterson,' said the RSM, scowling at the five conscripts, all of whom were standing rigidly to attention. 'Right, my lucky lads, this here is a detective inspector from Scotland Yard, come to ask you some questions. You will tell him the truth. Understood?' he added, screaming the last word at them.

In unison, the recruits shouted, 'Yessir!'

Hardcastle did not bother to correct the RSM's statement that he came from the Yard; indeed, it tended to reinforce his authority. He turned to McIntyre. 'I think it might be best if Sergeant Marriott and I interviewed these soldiers alone, Captain. In that way they might tell me more than if you and Mr Punchard were present.'

McIntyre grinned. 'You may well be right, Inspector,' he said, 'but they are already facing charges for being out of barracks without a pass. Not that they would've got one.'

Once Captain McIntyre and RSM Punchard had left, Hardcastle took out his pipe and began to fill it with tobacco. 'You might as well sit down, lads,' he said to the soldiers. 'I'm Divisional Detective Inspector Hardcastle, and this is Detective Sergeant Marriott.'

'D'you mind if we smoke, sir?' asked Private Ash.

'Not at all,' said Hardcastle, lighting his pipe.

It was not the most ideal of places to conduct interviews, but Hardcastle had already decided that these five young conscripts had had nothing directly to do with Herbert Somers' murder.

'I'm investigating a murder that took place on Victoria Station during the morning of Wednesday the eleventh of this month,' Hardcastle began, and sensed that he had immediately captured the young soldiers' attention. At least, the four newcomers; the DDI had told Stacey about the murder on his previous visit. 'And I understand that the five of you went drinking in a pub in Aldershot on the Sunday before that. Is that correct?'

After a brief pause, during which time he glanced at the others, Stacey nodded. 'That's right, sir.'

'When did you notice that your cap was missing, Stacey?'

'It must have been about half past ten, sir,' said Stacey. 'I'd hung me cap on a hat peg near the door, but when I went to get it, it'd gone.'

'And was there another cap left there that no one claimed?' Hardcastle had already been told that no other cap had been left there, but, as was his usual practice, he was confirming the facts.

'No, sir. I had a good look round, but it'd gone, and there wasn't no other there.'

Marriott looked up from the notes he was making. 'One of you had a tunic stolen. Which one of you was that?'

'Me, Sergeant,' said Private Ash, raising a hand.

'You have more than one tunic, do you?'

'Yes, Sergeant. We've all been issued with two tunics and two pairs of trousers.'

'When was it taken?'

'It was on the Monday morning that I noticed it had gone adrift, Sergeant, but I don't know when it was took.'

'When did you last see it?'

'Saturday afternoon,' said Ash. 'It was my best tunic, and I'd took it down to give the buttons a polish. But on Monday morning I noticed it'd been nicked.'

'Have you any idea who took it?' continued Marriott.

'No, Sergeant.'

'And who was it who lost a pair of trousers?'

'Me, Sergeant.' Private Joliffe raised a hand.

'And when did you notice them missing?'

'The same as Charlie Ash, Sergeant. I'd seen 'em on the Saturday, but they was gone on the Monday. It was only Charlie saying as how his tunic had been nicked, that made me have a look to see if I'd lost owt.'

'At what time did you notice that your trousers were missing, Joliffe?'

'After we'd come in from working parade, Sergeant. Like I said, on the Monday at about half past eight, I s'pose. We'd come back to get changed for physical training.'

'And you?' asked Marriott, pointing at Ash.

'The same.'

'As a matter of interest, Stacey,' asked Hardcastle, 'how did you get back to barracks without being seen, especially without a cap? I mean you'd've been spotted easily enough, surely?'

'We had to keep a lookout for the monkeys, sir. They're usually on horseback.'

Hardcastle took his pipe out of his mouth and glared at the young recruit. 'I hope you're not taking the piss, my lad. What's all this about monkeys on horseback, eh?' He glared at the unfortunate Stacey.

But it was Private Paterson who provided the answer. 'They're military policemen, sir,' he said. 'They're always called monkeys in the army, and some of them patrol on horseback. With bloody great lances,' he added.

'I see,' said Hardcastle, only slightly mollified. 'And did you see any of these so-called "monkeys on horseback"?'

'Only the once, sir,' continued Paterson. 'In Queen's Avenue, but we dodged behind the post office till they'd gone past, then we legged it back to barracks.'

'How many people have access to your barrack rooms, Paterson?' asked Marriott.

'Do what, Sarge?' Paterson looked mystified by the question.

Marriott phrased it in a different way. 'When you're out of the barrack rooms, are they locked?'

'No, Sergeant. They ain't got no locks, and in any case the officers and NCOs go round doing snap inspections when we ain't there.'

Marriott glanced at Hardcastle. 'It doesn't look as though we're going to get any further with this, sir.'

'No, Marriott. It looks as though someone went into the barrack room while these lads were on parade, and took the tunic and the trousers.' Hardcastle stood up and walked to the door. 'I think we're done here, Captain McIntyre,' he said.

'Was it any help?' asked McIntyre.

'Not much. It looks as though someone stole the clothing while those lads were on parade or about the barracks somewhere.'

'They'll still be charged for the loss.' RSM Punchard sniffed. 'Someone's been smoking in there,' he said.

'Me, Mr Punchard,' said Hardcastle mildly.

'Mr Punchard,' said Marriott, 'these men said they were issued with two sets of uniform.'

'That's correct, Mr Marriott.'

'Does that include two caps?'

'No, they only gets the one cap.'

Hardcastle was in a foul mood for the whole journey back to London. 'Well, that was a waste of bloody time, Marriott,' he said.

'I agree, sir. Just about anyone in the barracks could have swiped those bits of uniform, and according to the RSM there's about a thousand men under training, plus the permanent staff and the officers.'

When Hardcastle and Marriott returned to Cannon Row, there was a message awaiting the DDI.

'Excuse me, sir.' DC Henry Catto hovered in the doorway of Hardcastle's office.

'Yes, what is it, lad?'

'Mr Fitnam from V Division telephoned with a request for you to speak to him.'

'What does he want?' Hardcastle settled behind his desk and filled his pipe.

'He didn't say, sir, but he did say it was important.'

'Yes, all right, Catto.' Hardcastle knew that when Arthur Fitnam, the DDI of V Division said it was important, then it was. 'Looks like we're off again, Marriott.' The DDI sighed, stood up and walked down to the front office of the police station.

'All correct, sir,' said the station officer, an elderly station-sergeant.

'Can you get me Mr Fitnam at V Division on that thing?' asked Hardcastle, gesturing at the telephone.

'Certainly, sir.' The station officer, clearly more adept at using the telephone than was Hardcastle, quickly made the connection. After a short delay, DDI Fitnam came on the line.

'Arthur, it's Ernest Hardcastle on A. I'm told you've got something important to tell me.' For a few minutes, Hardcastle listened intently to what his V Division opposite number had to say. When their conversation had finished, the DDI replaced the receiver on its little hook and turned to the constable on station duty. 'Run up to my office, lad, and tell Sergeant Marriott we're going to Wandsworth.'

'Very good, sir,' said the PC.

'And while you're about it,' added Hardcastle, 'ask him to bring down my titfer and gamp.'

A few moments later, Marriott appeared with the DDI's hat and umbrella. 'Something on, sir?' he asked.

'Mr Fitnam's got a murder on his hands that he thinks might be of interest to us, Marriott.'

'I'm sorry to drag you all the way down here, Ernie, but I think there's a tie-up between your murder and the one I've got going here. I saw the brief details of your topping in this morning's *Police Gazette*.'

Hardcastle laughed. 'I always enjoy a trip to the country, Arthur, you should know that. But what about this murder of yours?' It was one of the DDI's little jokes that A Division was at the centre of things, whereas V Division, in his jocular view, was almost bucolic. It was not the case, of course, as Hardcastle would be the first to acknowledge. The Wandsworth Division had more than its fair share of villainy.

'It took place in Kingston upon Thames during the night of Wednesday the eleventh. That's the same day as your murder at Victoria. A patrolling PC found the dead body of a young woman lying in the centre of Cambridge Road. At first it looked as though she had been run over, which turned out to be true, but on closer examination it was obvious that she'd been stabbed as well.'

'How does that have anything to do with my killing, Arthur?' asked Hardcastle.

'A baker's van was found abandoned in Kingston Road, which is what Cambridge Road becomes when you get nearer Malden,' continued Fitnam, ignoring Hardcastle's question. 'It took a few days, and we only got the results this morning, but it was apparent from the damage that it was the van that had hit the young woman, and there was blood on the front bumper. More to the point, though, a bloodstained knife was found in the van that almost certainly was the murder weapon. As far as we can work out, the van driver must've picked up this woman at some stage, and, for some reason, stabbed her. Despite that, it looks as though she made her escape from the vehicle, but was then deliberately run down by the driver. After he'd knocked her over in Cambridge Road, he must've driven on for about half a mile, and then abandoned the vehicle.'

'I still don't see what this has to do with my enquiry,' said Hardcastle.

'Ah, but just wait, Ernie. We later discovered that the van was stolen from a bakery in Cowleaze Road, Kingston. And that is what made me think of you.'

'I wasn't a baker, but I do like a decent slice of farmhouse,' said Hardcastle, tiring of the way in which Fitnam was spinning out his yarn. He made a point of taking out his watch and glancing at it.

'The lock-up where the van was kept wasn't broken into, Ernie. The padlock was undone with a key, and the doors locked again after the van was taken. And guess who used to work there as a baker's roundsman before he was conscripted for the army.'

'Indulge me,' said Hardcastle, taking out his pipe and filling it. He was growing weary of Fitnam's lengthy dissertation.

'A lad called Edward Stacey who, the baker told me, is now in the Army Service Corps at Aldershot. And the same Edward Stacey was mentioned in your entry in the *Police*

Gazette in connection with your Victoria Station topping. So it's just a case of going down to Aldershot and nicking him.' Fitnam leaned back with a look of triumph on his face. 'There, what d'you think of that, eh?'

A smile spread slowly across Hardcastle's face, and he shot a sideways glance at Marriott, who was also smiling. 'I'm sorry to disappoint you, Arthur, but Stacey was in the custody of the military police all that night from six o'clock in the evening. At my request.' It had, of course, been Colonel Frobisher who had ordered Stacey's arrest, but Hardcastle saw no point in complicating the story. 'So the entry in *Police Gazette* was out of date by the time you read it. The lad Stacey has been rowed out of my enquiry.'

'Well, I'll be damned!' exclaimed Fitnam, and leaned back in his chair. 'Trust you to bugger up my investigation, Ernie.'

'Nevertheless, it interests me, Arthur,' said Hardcastle, and went on to explain about the missing cap, tunic and trousers.

'It looks as though someone's got it in for young Stacey, then,' said Fitnam thoughtfully. 'I wonder who he's upset.'

'Who was the woman, sir?' asked Marriott. 'Has she been identified?'

'Yes, skipper, she was a local tom called Ivy Huggins,' said Fitnam. 'She was well known to police, and had been arrested quite a few times. Her usual haunt was the Richmond Road, so I reckon that's where she was picked up. Incidentally, Cowleaze Road – where the bakery is – is a turning off Richmond Road.'

'I wonder how the killer got hold of Stacey's keys,' mused Hardcastle, 'unless it was someone else who'd worked there. Or even the baker himself.'

'Thanks, Ernie,' said Fitnam sourly. 'What I thought was an easy job to solve has now become very complicated.'

'Be so good as to keep me informed, Arthur,' said Hardcastle, as he and Marriott rose to leave.

'I don't know what I'll have to inform you about, Ernie,' said Fitnam mournfully.

As usual, Hardcastle arrived at the police station at exactly eight thirty. Following his customary practice, he examined the crime book, noting that DC Carter had arrested a pick-pocket on Trafalgar Square the previous evening. Climbing the stairs to the first floor, he put his head round the door of the detectives' office. 'Marriott, a moment of your time.'

'Yes, sir. Good morning, sir.' Marriott put on his jacket and followed the DDI into his office.

Hardcastle sat down behind his desk, and spent a few silent moments scraping out the bowl of his pipe. He opened a drawer and took out a chicken feather that he then drew through the stem of the pipe. Noticing Marriott's puzzled expression, he said, 'Can't get proper pipe cleaners these days, but fortunately my neighbour keeps chickens. Apparently the wire they used to make pipe cleaners has been diverted to the munitions factories to make shells to pound the enemy with. Talking of which, did you see the report in yesterday's linen drapers about Fritz using mustard gas at somewhere near Wipers?'

'Yes, I did, sir,' said Marriott. 'They reckon that two thousand men were affected, and eighty-seven died. I just hope my brother-in-law's not among them.'

'Using gas ain't playing the game in my book.' The DDI spoke as though the war were a cricket match. 'There was also a bit in the *Daily Mail* about the King changing the Royal Family's name from Saxe-Coburg to Windsor. Seems a funny business.'

'Apparently the King thought Saxe-Coburg sounded too German, sir,' said Marriott.

'Well, the Royal Family *are* Germans, aren't they?' said Hardcastle, in a tone that suggested the whole exercise had been pointless. 'Anyway, sit down, m'boy. Smoke if you want.'

'Thank you, guv'nor.' Recognizing that Hardcastle was about to indulge in one of his little chats about the Somers case, Marriott adopted the less formal mode of address. He took out a packet of Gold Flake cigarettes and lit one, dropping the dead match into Hardcastle's ashtray.

'Those things won't do you any good, m'boy,' said Hardcastle. 'You ought to consider taking up a pipe.' It was something that Hardcastle said every time he saw his sergeant smoking a cigarette.

'Yes, I've thought about it,' said Marriott. 'I just can't seem to get the hang of it.' Which is what he always said in reply.

'Something a bit funny is going on down at Aldershot, m'boy,' mused Hardcastle, having at last got his pipe alight satisfactorily. 'You know how to use that telephone thing in the front office, don't you?' It was one of the DDI's little foibles that he pretended ignorance of the telephone and its workings. In fact he was thoroughly conversant with it, and even had one on his desk, but often said that he didn't keep dogs to bark himself. 'Nip downstairs and give Captain McIntyre a call. Ask him to have a word with young Stacey, and see if he ever lost any keys.'

When Marriott returned, he said, 'He'll let us know as soon as possible, guv'nor.'

'You didn't say anything about Mr Fitman's murder of a prostitute at Kingston, I hope.'

Marriott grinned. 'No, sir. It doesn't do to tell these military policemen too much.'

'True,' said Hardcastle. 'Before we know where we are, he'll be trying to solve it for us. And there's nothing worse than having these amateur coppers interfering in a murder. Mind you, it could be worse; at least we haven't got MI5 poking their noses in.' The DDI still resented the interference of MI5 when he was trying to solve a murder last year, and he still blamed them for attempting to draw him away from the real killer.

'It strikes me, sir, that someone at Buller Barracks purloined the cap, tunic and trousers for the purpose of carrying out the robbery and murder at Victoria. The puzzle is why did he then go on to murder a tom.'

'If it was the same man, Marriott.'

'Bit of a coincidence if it wasn't, sir.'

'Yes,' said Hardcastle thoughtfully, 'and I don't like coincidences. But it's no coincidence that Ivy Huggins plied her trade in Richmond Road within spitting distance of the bakery where Stacey worked before the army grabbed him.' He placed his pipe in the ashtray, and rubbed his hands together. 'On second thoughts, Marriott, we'll go back to the barracks and make a few enquiries of our own.'

'D'you want me to let Captain McIntyre know, sir?'

'No, I don't, Marriott. I think we'll make our own way. I reckon that RSM Punchard is about the only bloke down there who knows what's going on.'

SIX

Observing Hardcastle's immaculate appearance, bowler hat and tightly rolled umbrella, the cab driver at Aldershot Station leaped from his taxi, and opened the door.

'Buller Barracks guardroom, cabbie,' said Hardcastle.

'Off to the Front to give old Fritz a thrashing, sir?' asked the driver.

'No,' said Hardcastle, 'I've come to sort out the British Army.'

'Blimey!' exclaimed the driver, thinking that he must have a general in his cab.

The guardroom at Buller Barracks appeared to have been built along the lines of an Indian bungalow, complete with a veranda. A smartly dressed sergeant stood in front of the door at the top of a short flight of steps, a brassard on his right arm bearing the letters 'RP'. A cross-strap from his right shoulder to his left hip supported the weight of the revolver on his belt. Sighting Hardcastle alighting from his cab, the sergeant snapped to attention and saluted.

'Can I help you, sir?' he asked.

'I'd like a word with RSM Punchard,' said Hardcastle.

'Very good, sir. Who shall I say it is?'

'Divisional Detective Inspector Hardcastle of the Metropolitan Police.'

'Ah, right, guv'nor,' said the regimental police sergeant, relaxing now that he knew Hardcastle was not an army officer. 'Shan't keep you a tick,' he added, and went into the guardroom. Shortly afterwards a soldier came out and doubled across to the headquarters block. 'I've sent a runner for him, gents. Doubtless, Mr Punchard will be with you directly.'

Five minutes later, the ramrod figure of the regimental sergeant-major came marching towards the two civil police officers.

'Good day to you, Mr Hardcastle, and what can I do for you?' Punchard noticed that the regimental provost sergeant was listening. 'You can stop earwigging, Sarn't Webster.

Get about your duties a bit *jildi*. And if you mention to anyone
that I've had a visit from the civil police, I'll have them tapes
off your arm quicker than you can ask the way to Wipers.'

'Sir!' yelled the abashed Webster, and retreated to the inside
of the guardroom.

'I take it you don't want your visit here advertised, Mr
Hardcastle?'

'It would be better if it wasn't,' said Hardcastle.

Punchard glanced at his watch. 'Thirty minutes after twelve
pip emma,' he said. 'Whatever your business, Mr Hardcastle,
I daresay you could stand a wet in the sergeants' mess before
we get down to brass tacks.'

'Splendid idea,' said Hardcastle, even more impressed by
the RSM's appreciation of priorities than he had been the first
time he met him.

'I presume the colonel don't know you're here.' Punchard
had quickly surmised that Hardcastle's unannounced arrival
at the guardroom, in the absence of Captain McIntyre, meant
that few people knew he was there.

'I certainly didn't tell him I was coming,' said Hardcastle,
'nor Captain McIntyre, but I thought that if I wanted any
information, you were the man to talk to.'

RSM Punchard preened himself slightly. 'There's nothing
as how goes on in these here barracks that I don't know about,
Mr Hardcastle,' he said, 'and that's a fact.' And with that pithy
comment, he took his pace stick from under his arm, and set
off at a brisk pace, followed by the DDI and Marriott.

Halfway to the mess, Punchard spotted a figure some
hundred yards away. 'That man there!' he roared, pointing
with his pace stick.

The figure stopped, and came to attention.

'You're ambling about like a constipated clergyman. Get
into quick time when you're moving about the barracks.'

Without further interruption, the RSM and the two
policemen arrived at the sergeants' mess.

Leaving his cap, pace stick and Sam Browne in the entrance
hall, Punchard waited while Hardcastle and Marriott deposited
their hats and umbrellas there. He marched into the anteroom
and invited the two detectives to take seats at 'my table' near
the bar. Hardcastle noticed that there was a small card on the
table that read 'RSM'.

'Well, now, Mr Hardcastle,' said Punchard, once the steward had served each of them with a pint of beer. 'What can I do for you?'

Hardcastle summarized what he knew, so far, of the death of Herbert Somers. He went on to tell the RSM of his theory about the murderer being someone at the barracks who had stolen the items of clothing for the purpose of committing the murders.

'I hope I can speak to you in confidence, Mr Punchard,' continued the DDI.

'Your secret's safe with me, Mr Hardcastle,' said Punchard as he drained his pint of beer.

Hardcastle turned to Marriott. 'Tell Mr Punchard about the murder at Kingston, Marriott.'

Marriott told the RSM about the stolen van, taken from a lock-up garage, and that Stacey had previously worked at the bakery from which it had been taken. He also added what was known about the murder of the prostitute Ivy Huggins.

Punchard beckoned to the steward and ordered three more pints of beer before answering. 'A pretty kettle of fish, Mr Hardcastle, and that's a fact. But Stacey couldn't have done it, as I'm sure you know.'

'I've sent a message to Captain McIntyre asking him to find out if Stacey had lost any keys, as it was his keys that were used to open the garage where the van was kept. But it'll probably be a few days before I get an answer.'

Punchard chuckled. 'Very likely, Mr Hardcastle. But I can get the answer sweated out of the little bastard in seconds. Officers tend to pussyfoot about, if you take my meaning.' He turned in his seat and crooked a finger at a young lance-sergeant.

The sergeant was at the RSM's side in an instant. 'Yes, sir?'

'Double across to the guardroom and ask—' Punchard paused. 'As you were. The man I want has just come in.'

At that moment, Sergeant Webster, the regimental police sergeant, had entered the anteroom, presumably intent on having a pint before going in for lunch.

'Sarn't Webster.'

'Sir?' Webster hurried to the RSM's table.

'You'll have to delay your lunch and your pint for a minute

or two, Sarn't Webster. Go and find Stacey in B Company's lines or the cookhouse, and ask him if he's lost any keys lately. Well, since he was conscripted. He's a leery little sod, so don't take any old fanny from him.'

'Yes, sir.' Sergeant Webster looked mildly affronted at the RSM's implication that he would have difficulty in extracting information from recruits. Apart from which, he was irritated at having been deprived of his beer, albeit briefly, and that would spur him on to getting an answer quickly.

'And not a word to anyone else about it. It's confidential police business. And don't tell him or anyone else that the civil police are here making enquiries. Understood?'

'Yes, sir,' said Webster, and hurried away.

Punchard turned to the two detectives. 'I daresay you could do damage to some lunch, Mr Hardcastle, and you too, Sergeant Marriott.'

'Most kind,' murmured Hardcastle, and he and Marriott rose to follow the RSM into the dining room.

They had just finished the main course, and were about to embark on the dessert, when Sergeant Webster returned.

'I've just had a word with Stacey, sir, and he says that he thinks he had his keys swiped about the same time as he lost his cap, although he can't remember exactly when he noticed they was gone. Does that make sense to you, sir?'

'Thank you, Sarn't Webster,' said the RSM, without answering the RP sergeant's question. 'You can go and get your pint now.' As Webster left, Punchard turned to the DDI. 'Well, there you have it, Mr Hardcastle, but how does that help?'

'It means,' said Hardcastle, as he polished off the last of the excellent plum duff pudding that the sergeants' mess cook had prepared, 'that someone in this barracks was able to enter the room where Stacey was quartered, and nick his keys, and, by the looks of it, a tunic and a pair of trousers. I reckon he also had the lad's cap from the boozer they were in. And that that someone then went on to murder the cashier at Victoria Station, and top the prostitute in Kingston. All I need to know is who could have left the barracks last Wednesday, carry out two murders, and his absence wouldn't have been noticed.'

Punchard led the way back to the anteroom, and, without asking the detectives if they wanted any, ordered three glasses of Cockburn's old port which, Hardcastle knew, cost at least three shillings a bottle. 'It's not that easy, Mr Hardcastle,' he said, answering the DDI's last question. 'As I said, last time you was here, we've got nigh-on a thousand men under training here.'

'Would any of them be able to disappear for twenty-four hours without being noticed?'

'Certainly not,' said Punchard vehemently, as though the suggestion were a slight on his professional competence. 'But there's the permanent staff to consider.' He paused in thought for a moment or two, calculating. 'There's some forty-six officers, plus numerous warrant officers, sergeants and corporals. And there are a few private soldiers in the stores and elsewhere. All in all, you're probably looking at nigh-on two hundred personnel who can more or less come and go as they please when they're not on duty.'

'Ye Gods!' exclaimed Hardcastle, as he grasped the full impact of the daunting task now facing him. 'I wonder if it's possible to narrow it down a bit.'

'How?' Punchard took a sip of his port.

'To those who would have legitimate access to the barrack room where Stacey, Ash and Joliffe were billeted. That'd be a start.'

RSM Punchard lit his pipe, and gave the question some thought before replying. 'Well,' he began slowly, 'there's the colonel. He can go anywhere, as can the second-in-command and the adjutant.' He smiled. 'And I can go anywhere, too, Mr Hardcastle. Then there are B Company's officers. That's the company that Stacey's in. There's the company commander, and his second-in-command. Added to that, there are the company sarn't-major, a platoon commander, a platoon sergeant, and his corporal deputy. But quite frankly any of the permanent staff can more or less go anywhere without question.'

Hardcastle took out his pipe, and began slowly to fill it as he mulled over the problem facing him. 'I think we can rule out the colonel, and probably the more senior officers, but that's about all.' Taking out a box of Swan Vestas matches, he lit his pipe, drawing on it with a degree of satisfaction. 'Would you know if any revolvers are missing, Mr Punchard?'

'Revolvers.' The RSM savoured the word. 'The only people

issued with revolvers are the officers, the regimental policemen, and one or two animal transport personnel. But what has that to do with your case?'

Hardcastle explained about the army revolver that had been used to strike Herbert Somers, and cause his death. 'It was left at the scene,' he added.

'How very careless,' said Punchard, to whom the loss of a firearm came third only after mutiny and desertion in the face of the enemy. 'I could make some enquiries of the armourer, but it could take some time. It would mean an inventory check, and asking all the officers to produce their weapons.'

'I don't really see any other way round it,' mused Hardcastle.

'I'd have to get the colonel's permission, of course,' said the RSM. 'But then he'd have to know you'd been down here talking to me. And I gather you wouldn't want him to know that.' He looked thoughtful for a moment or two. 'Might I make a suggestion, Mr Hardcastle?'

'Certainly, Mr Punchard. Anything that might help.'

'If that request – a perfectly legitimate one in the circumstances – were made by a military police officer, the colonel wouldn't be able to refuse.'

'Good,' said Hardcastle. 'I'll have a word with Captain McIntyre directly.'

'It's possible, though, isn't it, Mr Punchard,' said Marriott, 'that the theft of the tunic and the trousers was coincidental? I recall that Captain McIntyre said something about soldiers not hesitating to steal military property, but fought shy of taking personal possessions.'

'Very true, Sarn't Marriott, very true.' Punchard stood up. 'I'll arrange for some transport to Salamanca Barracks where Captain McIntyre has his office.'

'Most grateful,' murmured Hardcastle.

'I didn't realize that you were coming back today, Inspector,' said McIntyre. 'I'd've arranged to have you met at the station.'

Hardcastle waved a hand of dismissal. 'We took a taxi,' he said, without disclosing that the taxi had taken him and Marriott to Buller Barracks in order to speak to RSM Punchard. 'Didn't want to trouble you.'

'Well, now you're here, what can I do for you?'

Hardcastle explained, once again, about the revolver that

had been used to bludgeon Herbert Somers to death, and went on to expand his theory that the murderer was, in his view, someone with access to Buller Barracks, and to B Company's lines in particular.

'I'd like to be satisfied that none of the officers, or anyone else who's been issued with a revolver, were responsible.'

'You want me to check the sidearms of every officer at Buller Barracks, Inspector?' asked McIntyre incredulously.

'Thank you, Captain, that would be most helpful,' said Hardcastle, cunningly choosing to take McIntyre's question for a statement of intent.

'It's a bit of a tall order,' said McIntyre. 'I'd have to get Colonel Fuller's permission.'

'Of course,' murmured Hardcastle. 'Perhaps you'd explain to the colonel that to do it the gentleman's way would be better than obtaining a search warrant from the Bow Street magistrate.' But the DDI did not, for one moment, imagine that the Chief Metropolitan Magistrate would grant a warrant to search the whole of Buller Barracks. But he was betting that McIntyre, with his comparatively limited knowledge of criminal law, would not know that.

'Mmm!' McIntyre fingered his moustache. 'Are you suggesting that an officer carried out this murder?'

'Good heavens, no,' exclaimed Hardcastle, who had not dismissed the possibility, 'but maybe that one of the officers had his revolver stolen.'

'But such a loss would have been reported immediately, Inspector. It would be most unusual for something like that to go astray.'

'Well, a cap, a tunic, and a pair of trousers did,' commented Hardcastle drily. 'I think it was you who said that military property was fair game for a thief, but a thief would never take a soldier's personal belongings.'

McIntyre dithered. Whatever powers he might possess as an officer in the military police, he would not wish to upset a colonel whose co-operation he might need in the future. 'I'll see what I can do, Inspector,' he said with a sigh.

'I'm much obliged, Captain McIntyre,' said Hardcastle. 'By the way,' he continued, forbearing to mention his conversation with RSM Punchard, 'there's no need to ask Stacey if he lost any keys. I've decided that they don't have any bearing on my enquiries.' He pulled out his watch, glanced at it, gave it a brief wind, and dropped it back into his waistcoat pocket. 'We'll not waste any more of your time. Must get back to the Smoke. There are things to do.'

'It's a bloody quandary, Marriott, and no mistake.' A frustrated Hardcastle took off his spats and shoes, and began to massage his feet. 'We're having to wait for the damned army to get its act together at every turn.'

Marriott could not but agree with his chief. 'I wonder if Mr Fitnam's made any progress, sir,' he said, and immediately regretted it. He knew what would happen next. But he was irritated at Hardcastle's habit of massaging his feet, and had spoken without thinking. Had Hardcastle not been the DDI, Marriott would have suggested that he consulted a chiropodist as clearly he had something wrong with his feet.

Hardcastle took out his watch and glanced at it, before dropping it back into his waistcoat pocket. 'Probably not, but it's time we paid him a visit, Marriott. I suppose we ought to let him know what progress we've made. Which is damn all.' He replaced his shoes, and buckled on his spats.

To Marriott, it appeared that there was little need to go to Wandsworth, but he knew that, being unable to further his enquiries, the DDI would only sit and fret. And that meant that he would start looking round the detectives' office for something to do. And that usually spelled trouble.

Arthur Fitnam, the divisional detective inspector of V Division, looked distinctly glum as Hardcastle and Marriott entered his office.

'If you've come to ask me if I've caught the bugger, Ernie, the answer's no. How are you getting on with *your* topping?'

Hardcastle related what he had learned so far, which, as he had told Marriott, was very little. 'I'm certain that someone in that barracks was responsible, Arthur,' he said, and went on to tell the V Division DDI about his discussion with RSM Punchard.

'It seems that almost any one of about twelve hundred assorted soldiers could have done it, Arthur, and I'm not too happy about Punchard's claim that none of the recruits was responsible. It's all very well him saying that he'd know if any of the recruits went adrift, but I'm not so sure. Would you know where every one of twelve hundred constables were at any given time?'

'More than likely half of them would be in a boozer somewhere, I expect, Ernie,' said Fitnam cynically.

'Well, I'm damned sure I wouldn't know.' Hardcastle had started to look as gloomy as the V Division DDI.

'I don't envy you the task, Ernie,' said Fitnam. 'I was hoping you'd nicked the bloke, because I'm sure that you'd have solved my problem at the same time.'

'Did you get any fingerprints from the van that your murderer abandoned?'

'Yes, we got some, but none that mean anything. Charlie Collins reckons they're probably Stacey's anyway. But that doesn't mean that he killed Ivy Huggins, because any smart barrister will say Stacey had legitimate access to the vehicle. Even though Stacey's been in the army for a few months, Charlie says that they've found prints years later. Anyway, you've rowed him out of it.' Fitnam pulled a file across his desk, and thumbed through a few folios. 'The blood on the knife that was found in the van matches Ivy Huggins's blood group, but that's no good until we find out who wielded the weapon. Not that it will help much: she was blood group O, the commonest type. There were some fingerprints on the knife, too. Unfortunately, Charlie Collins said that they don't match any in his collection, but they do tally with some of those in the van. In fact, Collins said that there are two different sets in the van, so I reckon one set are Stacey's and the other our murderer's. There was a glimmer of hope, though, for both of us, I suppose. Collins said that some of the prints in the van match those he found on the revolver that was left at your scene. But until we catch the bugger and take his prints, we shan't know.' He pushed the file away. 'I suppose that officer who saw your murderer running away couldn't give a better description, could he, Ernie?'

'All he said was that he only really saw the back of him, as he ran off, Arthur,' said Hardcastle, and paused in thought. 'But he must've seen his face because he said he challenged the man for not saluting, and then he ran away. And he couldn't've saluted him with his back to him, anyway. Although, right now, I wouldn't put anything past the army.'

'Perhaps we could try speaking to Lieutenant Mansfield again, sir,' suggested Marriott. 'Now he's had time to think about it, he might've remembered something.'

'Maybe,' said Hardcastle. 'I suppose it's worth a try. We haven't got anything else.'

'I was wondering if we could get someone to take Stacey's fingerprints, Ernie,' said Fitnam. 'At least it would eliminate some of those found in the van.'

'Good idea, Arthur. Have a word with Captain McIntyre. He's the military police officer at Aldershot who's been helping me. In a manner of speaking. Marriott will give you his telephone number. Not that he's been much help. But if he can get a set of Stacey's dabs, perhaps Charlie Collins would be able to eliminate some of the prints found in the van.'

'I can see I'll have to go into this business of fingerprints more thoroughly, Ernie.'

'Good idea, Arthur. I reckon they're here to stay.'

SEVEN

The police station matron placed a cup of tea on Hardcastle's desk, and put a plate of biscuits beside it. 'Managed to get some ginger snaps today, sir,' she said.

'Splendid, Mrs Cartwright. You've made my day.' Hardcastle put down his pipe and rubbed his hands together. 'On your way out pop your head round the detectives' office door, and ask Sergeant Marriott to see me, would you?'

A few moments later, Marriott appeared. 'You wanted me, sir?'

'Yes, Marriott,' said Hardcastle, dunking a ginger snap in his tea. 'Have you got an address for that officer we saw at Victoria Station? The chap who claimed to have seen our murderer running away.'

'It's in the office, sir. I'll fetch it.'

Marriott returned holding his daybook, the book into which he entered all the useful information he might need or, more to the point, which his DDI might demand. 'Officers' Mess, St John's Wood Barracks, sir. It's in Ordnance Road.'

'What's he doing there? I thought St John's Wood Barracks was where the artillery lived.'

'So it is, sir,' said Marriott, who was better acquainted with military matters than the DDI. 'It's where they billet units of the Royal Horse Artillery including, I believe, the Rough Riders' battery. They are horsemen skilled in riding unbroken, or rough, horses.'

'Yes, all right, Marriott, I don't want a bloody history lesson. What was that lieutenant's name?' As usual, Hardcastle was asking a question to which he already knew the answer.

'Geoffrey Mansfield, sir.'

'Yes, that's the chap. But I thought he said he was in the North Staffordshire Regiment, not the Gunners.'

'Yes, he did, sir, but he also said he was on leave, so I suppose he lodged there because he's probably hard up. Subalterns don't get paid all that much. And, if you remember, sir, he said he was meeting his fiancée.'

'Who have we got in the office?'

'There's only Catto at the moment, sir.' As was his duty Marriott knew the whereabouts of all the detectives at Cannon Row Police Station, and what they were doing at any given time.

'I suppose he'll have to do.' Hardcastle replaced his teacup carefully in the saucer. 'Catto!' he yelled.

Detective Constable Henry Catto hovered uncertainly in the doorway of the DDI's office. 'Yes, sir?'

'Well, don't stand there like a dying duck in a thunderstorm, Catto. Come in.'

'No, sir. Er, yes, sir.' Catto moved closer to Hardcastle's desk.

'D'you remember that army officer who reckoned he saw our murderer running away?'

'Yes, sir. Lieutenant Geoffrey Mansfield of the North Staffordshire Regiment.'

Hardcastle raised his eyebrows in surprise. 'You're coming on a treat, Catto,' he said. 'Get up to St John's Wood Barracks in Ordnance Road—'

'Where's that, sir?' asked Catto, interrupting.

'In St John's Wood, Catto,' snapped Hardcastle. 'Where the hell did you think it was? Timbuktu? Just listen, will you?'

'Yes, sir.' Catto was usually a confident and competent detective, but always became uncertain of himself in the DDI's presence, almost to the point of becoming a quivering mass of indecision.

'Lieutenant Mansfield gave his address as the officers' mess there. Get up there a bit *jildi*, and ask him if he can give a better description than the useless information he gave us at the time. And don't take all day about it.'

'Yes, sir,' said Catto, and fled to do Hardcastle's bidding.

'I don't know, Marriott,' said Hardcastle. 'You'll have to do something about Catto. He never seems to know what he's about.'

'I'll have a word, sir,' said Marriott, who had no intention of so doing. He knew Catto's worth, and knew that it was only the DDI who had such a debilitating effect on him.

An hour and a quarter later, Catto reappeared in Hardcastle's office.

'Well?' barked the DDI.

'He's not there, sir.'

'Who's not where? I've told you before about sloppy reporting, Catto. I won't have it. There are God knows how many names I'm dealing with in this damned enquiry.'

'Lieutenant Mansfield's not at St John's Wood Barracks, sir,' replied Catto nervously.

'What d'you mean, he's not there?'

'I had a word with the guard commander, and he said that he'd never heard of him. He said they were all Royal Horse Artillery there, and there was no reason why there should've been an infantry officer staying there.'

'Is that it?'

'Yes, sir.' Catto waited for the inevitable rebuke.

'Did you enquire at the officers' mess?'

'No, sir. I thought that what the guard commander said would be right.'

'When I send you to make an enquiry in a murder investigation, Catto, I don't expect you to take the word of a bloody sergeant. And I suppose the guard commander *was* a sergeant, was he?'

'No, sir. He only had two stripes. A corporal would that be, sir?'

'They're called bombardiers in the artillery,' said Marriott quietly.

Hardcastle sighed. 'It's true what they say, Marriott,' he said, ignoring his sergeant's latest exposition of military knowledge. 'If you want a job done properly, do it yourself. Come, Marriott, we'll have to go there ourselves.'

Hardcastle was in a foul mood by the time he and Marriott arrived at St John's Wood Barracks.

The guard commander stood up from behind his desk as the DDI crashed open the door.

'Sir?'

'I want to see whoever's in charge of the officers' mess, Bombardier.' Although Hardcastle was often withering about Marriott's frequent explanation of military terminology, he was, nonetheless, quick to take advantage of it when it suited him.

'Might I ask who you are, sir?'

'Divisional Detective Inspector Hardcastle of the Metropolitan Police, and I don't have time to waste.'

'Ah, that'll be the mess sergeant you want, Inspector.'

'No, it is *not* the mess sergeant I want. It's an officer. I'm sick and tired of dealing with sergeants, and it seems to me that I can only get an answer from someone who knows what he's doing. Not that I'm sure an officer will give me what I want anyway. Not in my experience so far.'

'One moment,' said the guard commander. He turned to one of the off-watch sentries. 'Here, you, gunner, double across to the officers' mess, and tell the mess sergeant there's a policeman here wanting to see an officer about mess business, and be quick about it.'

While he waited, Hardcastle turned and stared out of the window of the guardroom, tapping irritably at the side of his leg with his umbrella and watching a gun team hitching a field gun to its limber. 'D'you know, Marriott,' he said, without turning, 'I sometimes wonder if we shall ever win this bloody war.'

'Yes, sir,' said Marriott, and received a glance of sympathy from the guard commander who had quickly worked out that Marriott was Hardcastle's subordinate.

Eventually the sentry returned. 'If you come with me, sir, I'll show you across to the PMC's office.'

'What the hell is a PMC?' demanded Hardcastle crossly,

believing he was being treated to yet more of what he termed army hocus-pocus.

'The president of the mess committee, sir,' said Marriott, trying to stave off any further show of bad temper on the DDI's part. 'He's usually a major or a captain. He's responsible for the good running of the mess.'

Hardcastle grunted. 'Well, let's hope we can get a half sensible answer from him.'

'Archibald Grayson, Inspector.' The booted and spurred captain crossed his office, and shook hands with Hardcastle and Marriott. 'I'm the battery commander of A Battery. How may I help you?'

'I understand you're President of the Mess Committee, Captain Grayson,' said Hardcastle, who had quickly mastered this latest piece of army terminology.

'That's so. Do take a seat, gentlemen.' Grayson was a tall, fair-headed officer, immaculately attired in khaki service dress tunic and sand-coloured breeches. Above his left breast pocket was the ribbon of the India General Service Medal, preceded by the Distinguished Conduct Medal. It was an indication, did Hardcastle but know it, that Captain Grayson had received the award prior to becoming an officer, and had, therefore, been commissioned from the ranks.

Hardcastle related briefly the circumstances of Herbert Somers' murder, and his desire to trace one of the witnesses, namely Lieutenant Geoffrey Mansfield of the North Staffordshire Regiment who had claimed to be staying at the barracks.

Grayson opened a drawer in his desk and withdrew a slender book. 'Mess accounts,' he said, glancing briefly at the DDI. 'Yes, there is a record of a Lieutenant Mansfield, North Staffs, having booked into the mess for the night of Tuesday the ninth of this month, for an indeterminate period.'

'But did he actually stay here, Captain Grayson?'

'Ah, that I can't tell you. One of the army's regulations is that officers on furlough from the Front must leave an army address with their commanding officer so that they can be recalled should the necessity arise. The officer in question must then, in turn, leave details with the PMC of that local mess of any private address at which he might stay. To be perfectly honest, Inspector, it's a rule that's more often honoured in the breach. He certainly didn't leave any such address with me.'

'Is there anyone here who might know?' Hardcastle was beginning to become frustrated at what he saw as military intransigence.

'One moment.' Grayson lifted the receiver from the 'candle-stick' telephone on his desk, jiggled the rest, and asked for the officers' mess sergeant. 'He'll ring me back as soon as they find him, Inspector. Won't be long. I hope.'

Marriott's long experience of working with Hardcastle told him that the DDI was becoming increasingly frustrated at the casual way that the army appeared to deal with police enquiries. The army, however, had a war to prosecute, and that, in Marriott's view, probably took precedence. However, he attempted to fill the conversational void.

'Are you back from France, Captain Grayson?' he asked.

'Good God, no. As a matter of fact, I've only just returned from India. I finished up commanding a screw gun battery at Chitral on the North West Frontier,' explained Grayson. 'The irony is that although we're fighting the Hun, I was wounded by a Pathan, of all people, and was repatriated to England.'

Hardcastle was not greatly interested in Captain Grayson's experiences, and had no intention of asking what a screw gun battery was. He had been treated to long, and meaningless, explanations about the army before.

The telephone rang, and the PMC snatched at the receiver. 'Captain Grayson. Ah, Sergeant Broad, did we have a Lieutenant Mansfield of the North Staffs staying in the mess?' After a few moments spent in conversation, he turned again to Hardcastle. 'It seems that a room was assigned to Mr Mansfield, but was never used, Inspector. I rather imagine that Mansfield has a young lady somewhere with whom he might have stayed. On the other hand, he might've stayed at a hotel.'

'I suppose that's possible,' said Hardcastle grudgingly. 'He did say that he was at Victoria Station to meet his fiancée.'

'I daresay that's the answer, then,' said Grayson. 'The North Staffs have their depot at Lichfield in Staffordshire. And if his fiancée's place was in London, or the south somewhere, he wouldn't've wanted to travel the one hundred and fifty-odd miles from Lichfield.'

'But if he didn't intend to stay at the mess he booked into, what difference would it have made which one it was?'

'I've no idea, Inspector.' Grayson laughed. 'But you're the detective, not me.'

Hardcastle's bad mood had not lifted by the time he and Marriott returned to Cannon Row Police Station.

'Well, we didn't get much more out of that trip, Marriott.'

'No, sir,' said Marriott.

Hardcastle took his pipe from the ashtray, looked at it, and put it back again. 'Get a telegraph message off to the Staffordshire Constabulary. Ask them to make enquiries at the North Staffs depot at Lichfield, and find out where this Lieutenant Mansfield is now.'

'Very good, sir.' Marriott departed without much hope that he would get an answer to the DDI's query. The police had had dealings with the military before regarding the whereabouts of individuals, and it took time. And more often than not the answer was inconclusive.

At breakfast on that Thursday morning, Hardcastle opened his copy of the *Daily Mail* and propped it against a bottle of HP Sauce. He read that on the previous Tuesday, there had been an uprising in Petrograd, encouraged by some hothead called Leon Trotsky. And this coincided with the news that the Russians had started to retreat from the Eastern Front.

Leaving the newspaper, Hardcastle spent the next few minutes tucking into his breakfast. Despite the shortages, his wife was still able to provide him with his usual fried eggs, bacon, two slices of fried bread, and a couple of sausages, two slices of toast and marmalade, and three cups of tea. He justified such a large meal by claiming that he could not go to work on an empty stomach. Hardcastle never asked his wife how she managed to get enough to feed the family, given the strictures imposed by the general shortages and rationing. He was, however, cynical enough to believe that the grocer, knowing that she was a policeman's wife, gave her preferential treatment because of it.

'This is bad,' said Hardcastle, glancing once again at the newspaper. 'Very bad indeed.'

'What is, Ernie?' Alice Hardcastle began to clear away the plates and cutlery from the breakfast table.

'Now that the Tsar's abdicated, it could develop into a full-blown revolution, Alice. If that happens, the Russians will likely capitulate, and that means that all the enemy troops on the Eastern Front will come west to fight Britain and France. Thank God the good old Americans have joined in.'

'I daresay it'll turn out all right in the end, Ernie,' said Alice, forever the optimist.

'Well, I hope you're right, Alice, my girl. If not, we're going to be in serious trouble.' Hardcastle folded the newspaper, took off his glasses and stood up. He glanced briefly at his watch. 'I'd better be going,' he said.

'We've got a reply from Staffordshire, sir.' Marriott greeted Hardcastle with the news as the DDI reached the top of the stairs.

'Have we now? Come in.'

Once the DDI was settled behind his desk, Marriott referred to the telegraph form in his hand. 'It seems that the Staffordshire Constabulary doesn't cover Lichfield, sir. They passed our enquiry to the Lichfield Borough Police. The chief constable himself went to the barracks.'

'Ye Gods!' exclaimed Hardcastle, pausing in the act of filling his pipe. 'They can't have much to do up there. Either that or the chief's angling after an invitation to a regimental dinner.'

Marriott smiled, but did not respond to Hardcastle's acerbic comment. He had never known his DDI to have a good word to say about any other police force, his severest condemnation being reserved for the City of London Police whose square mile of jurisdiction lay in the centre of the Metropolitan Police District.

'Well, don't keep me in suspense, Marriott. What did the bold chief constable have to say about it?'

'It seems that Lieutenant Mansfield is back in France, sir. His leave expired on Saturday the fourteenth of July. It also says that his leave – a week altogether – was spent in London at his fiancée's parents' house in Bayswater, and that Mansfield had informed the adjutant at Lichfield Barracks.'

'Did they give a name and address for this young lady?'

'Yes, sir. Her name is Isabella Harcourt, and she lives with her parents in Westbourne Terrace.'

Hardcastle spent a few seconds getting his pipe alight before answering. 'Keep a note of it, Marriott. On reflection, I doubt that young Mansfield could've given us any more, but we may have to see him again. Certainly when it comes to a trial. If there is one,' he added gloomily.

EIGHT

At half past eleven, Captain McIntyre telephoned from Aldershot to say that Lieutenant Colonel Fuller, the commanding officer of the Army Service Corps training battalion, had reluctantly agreed to a check of his officers' sidearms. It would, however, take some time, but McIntyre promised to let Hardcastle have the result as soon as possible.

'The bloody war will probably be over by the time we get an answer to that, Marriott,' said Hardcastle. 'I wouldn't mind betting that that dugout colonel is going to make it as difficult as possible. I suppose because men are being killed in their thousands at the Front, one dead body at Victoria Station don't carry much weight with him.'

But no sooner had the DDI expressed that pessimistic view of the army than there was a knock at his office door.

'There's a military gentlemen downstairs wishing to see you, sir,' said the station officer, a youngish sergeant.

'Who is it, skipper?'

'He says he's RSM Punchard, sir, of the Army Service Corps. He says it's important.'

'Send him up,' said Hardcastle.

The ramrod figure of the training battalion's RSM appeared in Hardcastle's doorway a few moments later.

'Good morning, Mr Hardcastle.'

'Good morning to you, Mr Punchard,' said Hardcastle, shaking hands with the RSM. 'Take a seat.'

Punchard placed his cap on the hatstand in the corner of Hardcastle's office, and, noticing that the DDI was smoking, withdrew a pipe from the inner recesses of his tunic and held it aloft. 'D'you mind?' he asked.

'Not at all, carry on. Perhaps you'd care for a cup of tea.'

'That would be most welcome, Mr Hardcastle, thank you.'

Hardcastle glanced at Marriott. 'Be so good as to organize that.'

'Yes, sir.' Marriott crossed to the detectives' office and told one of its occupants to arrange for three cups of tea.

'Now, Mr Punchard,' began Hardcastle, once Marriott had rejoined them, 'I don't suppose you've made the journey up here because you like being in the Smoke. Or has the War Office decided to offer you a commission?' he added flippantly.

'Not me,' said Punchard. 'I'd rather be top dog in the sergeants' mess than a spare part in the other place. Anyhow, they're making any young fool a second lieutenant these days, and often do, but regimental sergeant-majors are hard to come by. No, Mr Hardcastle, I'm stuck where I am, thank the Good Lord. However, to get down to business, I thought it best to come up here to see you in person rather than trusting to the telephone. You never know who's listening.'

'You managed to get away without any questions being asked, then.'

Punchard bristled slightly at that. 'What an RSM does and where he goes is no business of anyone else, Mr Hardcastle, except the colonel, and between you and me he's not that much interested. I come and go as I please.'

'Yes, I suppose so,' said Hardcastle, who never quite understood the status of warrant officers in the army. There was no comparable rank in the Metropolitan Police, although, having witnessed a few army warrant officers exercising their authority, the DDI often wished there were.

'I have a piece of information that I think might be of interest to you, Inspector.' Punchard took a slim notebook from his breast pocket and flicked it open. 'When officers are commissioned into the ASC, they have to attend a regimental officers' course at Buller Barracks, to learn about what the Corps does. I had a word with the chief clerk of the battalion . . .' The RSM paused. 'Name of Fred Welch, SQMS Welch to be exact.' Seeing the puzzled look on Hardcastle's face, he explained that SQMS meant staff quartermaster sergeant, and that Welch was a warrant officer.

'I see.' Hardcastle nodded. He did not need to know the precise rank of the battalion's chief clerk, but imagined that Punchard thought it would add weight to his statement.

The RSM was interrupted by the arrival of Mrs Cartwright, the station matron, who appeared in the doorway carrying a large tray. 'I've got your tea, sir,' she said to the DDI.

'Thank you, that was very good of you,' said Hardcastle, dropping a sixpence on the tea tray.

'But I'm afraid there ain't any biscuits today.'

'Never mind, Mrs C.'

'I give 'em all to my boy Jack, you see. He was off to the Front again yesterday. He's a bombardier now.' Mrs Cartwright was clearly very proud of her son.

'I hope he keeps safe,' said Hardcastle.

'He says as how he'll be all right. He's in the Royal Garrison Artillery. And he's a long way behind the lines, he says.'

'He should be all right there, ma'am,' volunteered Punchard, running a thumb up the inside of the cross-strap of his Sam Browne belt.

Once Mrs Cartwright had departed, the RSM continued. 'Fred Welch told me that out of the twenty officers who'd finished the course, four of the young gentlemen never arrived at the units they was posted to.'

'How on earth can that happen?' asked an incredulous Hardcastle. 'D'you mean they've deserted?'

'Your guess is as good as mine, Mr Hardcastle, but just because they've got a pip on their cuffs don't mean they don't run. You'd be surprised how many officers have slung their hook since this caper with Fritz started.'

Hardcastle pulled a sheet of paper across his desk. 'Do you have the names of these officers, Mr Punchard?'

Punchard referred to his notebook again. 'They was all posted on Friday the sixth of July, Mr Hardcastle. The course ended on the preceding Wednesday, and they was given forty-eight hours' leave. There was a Mr Adrian Nash who was posted to 143 Mechanical Transport Company at Boulogne, Mr Wilfred Bryant should have gone to 1 Corps Troops Column BEF . . .' The RSM looked up. 'God knows where they are; apart from being somewhere in Flanders, the last time I heard tell of 'em. Anyhow, then there's Mr Bertram Morrish who should have gone to 233 Supply Company at Fort William in Scotland, and Mr Ashley Strawton to 64 Ambulance Company at Cairo with General Allenby's lot. But, like I said, none of 'em turned up.'

Hardcastle put down his pipe, leaned forward, and linked his hands on the desk, his interest suddenly aroused. 'Can your colleague be sure of that?' he asked.

'Most certainly,' said Punchard. 'The training battalion sends a signal to the receiving units advising them of the officers' impending arrival. But the orderly room got signals back asking if there'd been a mistake, because the officers hadn't arrived.'

'Do you know anything about these officers, Mr Punchard?'

'Only brief details, Mr Hardcastle,' said the RSM, studying his notebook again. 'For a start they're all nineteen years of age, except Morrish who's twenty-two. Nash was a clerk with the Metropolitan Water Board, and worked at their offices in the City. He was conscripted under Lord Derby's scheme, and I suppose he talked a bit posh so the upshot was he was commissioned. Bryant was a shop assistant at the Army and Navy Stores in Victoria, Morrish was straight out of university – Cambridge, I believe – and Strawton was a footman in some big house, God help us.' He shook his head in an expression of disbelief, and then paused to apply a match to his pipe. 'Mind you, like I said just now, they're giving commissions to almost anyone these days. You see, Mr Hardcastle, the average life of an infantry subaltern in the trenches is about six weeks, so they're obviously running a bit short. Still, these young whippersnappers won't come to much harm where they're going, except perhaps the chap who's gone to the ambulance company in Cairo.'

'Do you happen to have home addresses for these officers, Mr Punchard?'

'I'm afraid not,' said Punchard, referring again to his notebook. 'But I should be able to get them from Fred Welch. I'll telephone them to you, if you think that'll be of assistance.'

'Thank you, Mr Punchard, that would be most helpful. Incidentally, what exactly does this officer training consist of?'

The RSM gave that question some thought before answering. 'Well, there's a lot of classroom stuff, tactics and that sort of thing. Not that the ASC needs to know a lot about that. Then there's lectures about the functions of the ASC, and they do a driving course. And they also shadow the permanent staff officers. I s'pose it teaches them how to inspect the common soldiery,' he added with a scoff.

'Would that mean that these officers would have access to some of the barrack rooms?' asked Hardcastle thoughtfully.

'Very likely,' replied Punchard. 'They learn how to be proper little bastards, going round bollocking people for not saluting, having dust in the welts of their boots, dirty brasses, and generally getting in the way of the warrant officers and NCOs.'

Hardcastle stood up and shook hands with the RSM. 'Thank you very much for that information, Mr Punchard. I'll follow it up and let you know the outcome. I suppose they've been posted as deserters already.'

'Of course they have, Mr Hardcastle. Like I said before, just because they're officers don't stop 'em being shot for running.'

For some time after the departure of Punchard, Hardcastle sat behind his desk pondering the magnitude of what the RSM had told him. His enquiry had taken on an almost impossible task. The four officers who had not arrived at their designated units, and were possibly now wanted for desertion, put them at the top of the DDI's list of suspects. But, from what the RSM had said, they could be anywhere from Fort William to Cairo. Had one of them stolen items of clothing – Stacey's cap, Ash's tunic and Joliffe's trousers – and used them to carry out the robbery at Victoria? There was little doubt in Hardcastle's mind that the murderer had also stolen Stacey's keys. But which one? Then again, perhaps it was none of them.

'I suppose, as a matter of courtesy, we ought to have a word with Colonel Frobisher before we go making enquiries about officers who're adrift, Marriott. Don't want to tread on any toes. Mind you, the military don't care about treading on mine when it suits them.' And with that, Hardcastle seized his hat and umbrella. 'Come, Marriott.'

Lieutenant-Colonel Frobisher looked up warily when Hardcastle and Marriott were shown into his office at Horse Guards Arch in Whitehall.

'Inspector?'

'Good day, Colonel.' Without wasting any time on social niceties, Hardcastle related what he had heard from RSM Punchard about the ASC officers who had failed to arrive at their official destinations. 'Can you confirm that these officers are absent without leave, Colonel?'

'I'll soon find out, Inspector.' Frobisher struck the polished brass table bell on his desk, and Sergeant Glover, the colonel's chief clerk, appeared.

'Yes, sir?'

'Mr Hardcastle will give you a list of ASC officers who were recently posted from Buller Barracks, Aldershot, Sergeant. However, they didn't turn up at the units to which they were posted. Can you tell me if they have been posted absent?'

'One moment, sir.' Glover took Hardcastle's list, and disappeared to return a minute or so later with a file in his hand. 'Yes, sir. All were posted from Number One Training Battalion ASC at Aldershot on the sixth of July, but failed to report. We were advised of their absence on the twelfth, sir.'

'Thank you, Sergeant Glover.' Frobisher turned to Hardcastle. 'May I ask where you got your information, Inspector?'

'A reliable informant, Colonel,' said Hardcastle cagily. He was unwilling to reveal the training battalion's RSM as his source for fear that it might involve Punchard in disciplinary proceedings of some sort. He was not to know, however, that that was extremely unlikely. As Punchard had hinted, RSMs were a law unto themselves.

'Of course, Inspector, it might all be an administrative blunder of some sort. I'm sorry to have to say that this sort of thing is happening all the time. They'll probably have turned up at entirely different units, all because a clerk at the Aldershot despatching unit got the number of the respective companies wrong on the movement orders, or sent the signals to the wrong units. If, on the other hand, they'd arrived at the wrong unit, that unit should query why they'd got an officer they weren't expecting.'

'Does that happen often, sir?' asked Marriott.

'I'm afraid so, Sergeant Marriott, and more often than not, the receiving unit will hang on to the man, because they're always short of subalterns. And we only get to hear of it months later. To give you but one example, we had a case of an officer who was listed as having failed to report to a unit at Arras when for four months he had been with a different battalion of his regiment with General Hamilton at Gallipoli in the Dardanelles. And a bloody disaster that turned out to be,' he added mournfully. 'Lost a lot of good men in that fiasco, many of them seasoned Australian troops.'

'I suppose you wouldn't have the home addresses of these officers, Colonel.' If the information were to hand, it would save Hardcastle awaiting the result of RSM Punchard's promise to find them for him from the records at Aldershot.

Frobisher glanced at his chief clerk. 'Sergeant Glover?'

'Yes, we have them, sir. That's normally the first place we'd look for a deserter. I'll have a list prepared.' Glover returned to his office.

'Would you have any objection to my making enquiries of these officers' families, Colonel?' asked Hardcastle, steering Frobisher back to the present. As a police officer, he had the power to arrest a deserter without resort to the army, and would have made enquiries whether the colonel liked it or not. But he saw no harm in being courteous about it.

'By all means, Inspector. If you find any of the young bounders perhaps you'll let me know. But what's your interest?'

'It's a bit of a long shot, but it's possible that one of them was responsible for the murder of the cashier at Victoria Station that I told you about before, and a prostitute in Kingston upon Thames.'

'Good God!' exclaimed Frobisher. 'D'you really think so?'

'No, but it's a stone that we mustn't leave unturned, so to speak,' said Hardcastle enigmatically. He and Marriott stood up. 'Thank you for your assistance, as usual, Colonel. I'll inform you of any developments.'

Back at his police station, Hardcastle stared glumly at the sheet of paper that Sergeant Glover had given him, before handing it to Marriott.

'I don't know, Marriott,' he said eventually. 'We could be running all over the bloody place in search of this lot. Bryant lives in Fulham, Morrish in Norwich, Nash in south-east London, and Strawton in Carlisle. And, if what Colonel Frobisher said is true, it might all be some administrative balls-up anyway.'

'We could start with those closer to home, sir,' suggested Marriott. 'Bryant and Nash don't live too far from Victoria Station, and I somehow doubt that the chap from Norwich or the fellow from Carlisle would risk doing a robbery in an area they didn't know too well.'

'Maybe you're right, Marriott.' Hardcastle pulled his watch from his waistcoat pocket. 'What's Nash's correct address?'

'Twenty-five Stanstead Road, Forest Hill, sir. I've had a look at the map, and the road's only a short walk from the railway station.'

'Better make a start, then.' With a sigh, Hardcastle stood up, seized his hat and umbrella, and made for the door.

NINE

For the most part, the houses in Stanstead Road were occupied by bank clerks, middle-ranking civil servants, and those in lower managerial positions. They were terraced and each pair of houses shared a porch, the front doors of which were side by side.

'Would you be Mrs Nash by any chance?' asked Hardcastle, raising his bowler hat.

'Yes, I'm Rose Nash.' The woman appeared to be about forty years of age, and was wearing a floral pinafore apron over a black-and-white check day dress. She looked enquiringly at the two men on her immaculately whitened doorstep.

'We're police officers, madam,' said Hardcastle, 'and we'd like to talk to you about Adrian Nash. I understand he's your son.'

Rose Nash paled and put a hand to her mouth. 'Oh God!' she exclaimed. 'He's not been killed, has he?'

'Not to my knowledge, Mrs Nash,' responded Hardcastle.

'Well, what, then? You gave me quite a turn.'

'I think it might be as well if we came in, Mrs Nash,' said Hardcastle. Marriott had noticed that the adjacent front door had opened slightly, and he had touched the DDI's arm to draw attention to what was probably a nosey neighbour engaging in a little eavesdropping.

Rose Nash showed the two detectives into the front parlour, a fussily furnished room. The paintwork was brown, as was the three-piece suite, and there were brown velvet curtains that tended to darken a room already made gloomy by heavy net curtains. The mantelshelf and several small tables were cluttered with bric-a-brac and personal photographs of people in stiff poses; presumably they were of the Nash family.

'I'm Divisional Detective Inspector Hardcastle, ma'am, and this is Detective Sergeant Marriott.'

'What's this about Adrian?' asked Rose Nash, having invited the police officers to sit down. She whipped off her apron, and dropped it behind the settee, out of sight, before sitting down herself.

'I understand from the military authorities that your son is absent without leave, Mrs Nash.'

'Absent? How ridiculous. He's serving in France. He's just been granted a commission, you know. Why on earth would he absent himself, now that he's an officer?' Mrs Nash was obviously very proud of her son. 'We had the military police here a day or two ago asking the same silly questions. I sometimes wonder how we're going to win the war if that's the way the army carries on.'

'Be that as it may,' said Hardcastle, although he was inclined to share Mrs Nash's view about the lack of military efficiency. 'But I have it on good authority – namely the military police – that he did not arrive at his unit in Boulogne.'

'Well,' said Mrs Nash, with a measure of hauteur, 'I suggest they've got it wrong, and I'm surprised that a detective inspector . . . That is what you said you were, isn't it?'

'Yes, ma'am,' said Hardcastle.

'Yes, well, I'm surprised that you're wasting your time on this ridiculous business. I'm sure you have more important things to do.'

It was obvious to Hardcastle that he was not going to get an admission from Adrian Nash's mother, much less to be told where her son was now – even if she knew – and he tried another tack. 'When did you last see him, Mrs Nash?' he asked.

'The fifth of July, a Thursday,' replied the woman promptly. 'My husband and I saw him off at Waterloo Station. He was going to Southampton to embark on the night troopship to Boulogne.'

'Is your husband in the army, Mrs Nash?' asked Marriott.

'No, he's an engineer with the water board. It's a reserved

occupation. Rather like yours, I imagine,' said Rose Nash tartly.

'Your son worked there, too, didn't he?' enquired Hardcastle. RSM Punchard had said so, but the DDI always liked to make sure of his facts.

'Yes, but he was a clerk. They said that his job wasn't essential to the war effort, and he was conscripted. Personally, I didn't think he was well enough. He had a lot of illness as a youngster, you know, apart from the usual childish maladies, but the army passed him fit. Anyway, he was lucky enough to get a commission – no more than he deserved, of course – and looked very smart in his new uniform.'

'D'you happen to have a photograph of him?' asked Hardcastle.

'No. We wanted him to have a portrait done at that photographic studio at Lea Green, but he said we were making too much fuss.' Mrs Nash pointed at one of the framed photographs on a small shelf. 'I'm afraid that's the only one we have,' she said. 'That was taken the year he started at grammar school.'

Hardcastle stood up and moved nearer to the print, peering closely at it, but it was not well done – probably taken by an amateur photographer – and was a rather fuzzy photograph of a ten-year-old who could have been anybody. It was certainly of no use as a means of identifying the absentee officer. If, in fact, he was absent rather than merely being misplaced by the army.

'Have you by any chance received a letter from your son, Mrs Nash?' asked Marriott.

'Not since he went on active service, no. But I'm told such letters take a long time to get through.'

'Well, we'll not trouble you any further, Mrs Nash,' said Hardcastle. 'I've no doubt that the army has made a mix-up, and that your son will turn up right as rain.'

'I'm certain of it,' snapped Rose Nash.

'I hope you understand that we have to follow up this information.'

'Yes, I suppose so,' said Mrs Nash grudgingly, and showed the two detectives to the door.

'Well, that was a waste of time,' muttered Hardcastle, as he and Marriott walked back to the railway station.

'D'you think he might be our man, sir?'

'He was at Buller Barracks at the right time, Marriott, but then so were dozens of others, including the other three absentee officers. And as Colonel Frobisher said, it's quite likely that they've been the victim of shoddy paperwork.'

'But he didn't want to have his photograph taken, sir.'

'No, he didn't, and I find that interesting, Marriott. When you think about it, almost every house we've been to since the war started has a photograph of any serving man of the house in his uniform. Especially if he's an officer.'

All in all, Marriott thought that Adrian Nash's shyness about being photographed was irrelevant, but decided not to say as much.

The Bryants' house in Jervis Road, Fulham, was a semi-detached property with clean windows and a newly whitened doorstep.

'Would you be Mr Bryant, by any chance?' enquired Hardcastle of the man who answered the door.

'Yes, I'm John Bryant. Who are you?'

'Divisional Detective Inspector Hardcastle of the Whitehall Division, Mr Bryant. This is Detective Sergeant Marriott.'

'The police! What can I do for you?'

'There's nothing to worry about, sir, but we'd like to talk to you about your son Wilfred.'

'He's not here. He's in the army. You'd better come in, gentlemen.'

Once in the sitting room, which proved to be in as clean and tidy an order as the Somers' residence in Lewisham, John Bryant invited the two detectives to take a seat. 'Now, what is it you want to know about young Wilfred? He's not in any trouble, is he?'

'Not to my knowledge, sir, no,' said Hardcastle.

'It's a strange coincidence, you calling today, because we had the military police here a few days ago. They wanted to know if we'd seen Wilfred lately. They talked some nonsense about him being missing. Well, that gave me quite a start, I can tell you. The boy's only just been posted, although he wasn't allowed tell me where he was going, but I suppose it was France somewhere.'

'It's partly in that connection I've called, Mr Bryant,' said Hardcastle.

'Really? Well, what the hell d'you think I can do about it?' John Bryant was beginning to sound annoyed.

'We think there's probably been a mix-up at the War Office, sir,' said Marriott, seeking to placate Wilfred Bryant's father and stem any possible show of irritability by his DDI. 'I'm afraid we have to follow up these enquiries, although we have much more important things to do.'

'Yes, I suppose you do,' said Bryant, his irritation slowly lessening. 'But we said goodbye to him on the . . .' He paused as he tried to recall the date. 'The fifth of July, I think it was. He'd only been given forty-eight hours embarkation leave, and he had things to do in that time.'

'Does he have a lady friend?' asked Hardcastle.

'I believe so. He talked of some young lady he'd got to know while he was working at the Army and Navy Stores in Victoria Street, but I don't think anything came of it. Once he'd volunteered for the army and got his commission, he seemed hell bent on soldiering. I think he might be tempted to make a career of it.'

If he lives that long, thought Hardcastle, as he stood up. 'As my sergeant said, sir, it appears to be a mix-up with the army. No doubt you'll get a letter from him soon. If you do hear he's safe and sound perhaps you'd let me know at Cannon Row Police Station. Saves the paperwork getting the better of us.'

'Certainly I will,' said Bryant, as he escorted the two policemen to the front door.

Hardcastle paused on the threshold. 'Do you happen to have a recent photograph of your son, Mr Bryant?'

'Not yet. He had a studio portrait done in his new uniform, but I haven't got it back from the photographer yet. But why d'you want a photograph?'

'So that I can see what he looks like,' said Hardcastle. 'Good day to you, Mr Bryant.' And with that, he and Marriott strode off down the road before Bryant could enquire more deeply into Hardcastle's interest in a photograph.

But Marriott could not understand his chief's obsession with photographs. It would be no good, in his opinion, showing Lieutenant Mansfield a posed portrait of an officer in the hope that he would be able to identify the private soldier he saw running away. And of whom, presumably, he had but a fleeting glimpse.

*   *   *

'We've been wasting too much time, Marriott,' said Hardcastle as the two CID officers reached the end of Jervis Road. Marriott agreed, but said nothing. And then the DDI made a surprise announcement. 'As we're not far away, I think we'll pay a visit to this Jack Utting who managed to get himself knocked over by a bicycle the day before the murder. If he's finished work.'

Marriott was amazed. 'What d'you hope to get out of him, sir?' he asked.

'Watch me, and you'll learn, Marriott,' said Hardcastle mysteriously. 'What's his address?'

'I don't know, sir. Mr Richards gave *you* the piece of paper with it on.'

'Ah, so he did.' Hardcastle ferreted in his pockets until he found the note of the details that the Cox and Company's bank manager had provided. 'Here we are.' He hailed a taxi. 'Gloucester Street, cabbie. It's off Belgrave Road, just by the junction with Denbigh Street.'

'I know where it is, guv'nor,' muttered the cabbie. 'It's my job.'

A man who appeared to be in his mid-twenties answered the door of the house in Gloucester Street, Pimlico, and stared at the two men on the doorstep.

'Yes?'

'I'm looking for Mr Jack Utting,' said Hardcastle.

'That's me,' said the man. 'Who are you?'

'We're police officers, Mr Utting. I'm Divisional Detective Inspector Hardcastle of the Whitehall Division, and this is Detective Sergeant Marriott.'

Utting appeared a little perplexed, if not unnerved, by this announcement. 'What's it about?'

'I'm investigating the murder of your colleague Herbert Somers at Victoria Station a week ago last Wednesday.'

Utting shook his head. 'That was terrible,' he said. 'I was supposed to be on duty that day.'

'So I understand,' said Hardcastle, 'and I want to ask you some questions about it.'

'Oh, I see. You'd better come in, then,' said Utting, and led the way into the parlour. 'My wife's out doing some shopping at the moment, but I can make you a cup of tea if you like.' He seemed anxious to please, something that did not escape the DDI.

'No thank you, Mr Utting,' said Hardcastle, sitting down in one of Utting's armchairs. 'Been married long?'

'No. About seven months, as a matter of fact.'

Hardcastle nodded. 'I hope you're feeling better now,' he said. 'I understand you were off sick.'

'Yes, I had a bilious attack, and just couldn't face going in on that day.'

'But you've been back to work since, I suppose?'

'Yes, I'm quite all right now, as it happens.'

'A quick recovery, then,' said Hardcastle with a smile. He saw fit not to mention that Utting had told the bank manager that he had been knocked over by a cyclist the day before the murder.

'Yes, I was able to go back to work the day after poor Somers was killed.'

'I wanted to ask you about that, Mr Utting. Were you aware of anybody who might have had the robbery of your kiosk in mind?'

'I'm not sure I know what you mean, Inspector.' Utting appeared to be puzzled by the question.

'Well, I'd wondered if you'd seen anyone loitering near the booth for a few days before the murder. Or whether anyone asked you any questions about the hours you worked, or how the money got to Victoria Station from the bank. That sort of thing.'

'No, nothing like that. The most we had to deal with were a few impatient soldiers who'd just come home on leave and wanted to get their money changed as quickly as possible. But there was always an army copper nearby to keep an eye on things.'

Hardcastle nodded amiably, despite thinking that the military police had not kept 'an eye on things' the day that Somers was murdered. 'It was just a long shot, Mr Utting. The police have to explore every avenue when they're looking into a murder.' He stood up. 'Well, I'll not detain you any longer. And thank you for your assistance.' He paused at the door to the sitting room. 'If you do think of anything that might help, perhaps you'd let me know at Cannon Row Police Station. It's just off Whitehall, next to Scotland Yard.'

'Yes, of course,' said Utting, hastily ushering the two detectives to the front door.

'You've finished work for the day, I take it?' Hardcastle turned in the doorway.

'Yes,' said Utting. 'There aren't any more troop trains coming in until tomorrow.'

'Why didn't you mention what Mr Richards had told us, sir?' asked Marriott, when they were in a cab returning to Cannon Row. 'About Utting supposedly having been knocked down by a bicycle.'

'We don't have to tell suspects everything we know, Marriott,' said Hardcastle, leaning back against the leather of the cab's seat. 'Interesting though. There's more to that Mr Utting than meets the eye,' he added.

'D'you regard Utting as a suspect, then, sir?'

'You know me, Marriott. Everyone's a suspect until I'm happy they ain't.'

And that, Marriott knew only too well, was the truth. 'You didn't ask him where he was on the day he took off, sir.'

'Of course not, Marriott. We'll ask his wife, and that won't give him any time to make up an alibi.'

It was obvious to Marriott that his chief was becoming increasingly frustrated at the lack of progress in the investigation into the murder of Herbert Somers. And the DDI's almost daily telephone calls to his opposite number at Wandsworth revealed that Arthur Fitnam was no further forward in discovering the identity of Ivy Huggins's murderer. The only factor was that the fingerprint evidence pointed to the same killer being responsible for both murders.

Hardcastle crossed the corridor to the detectives' office. 'Marriott, bring in that telegraph message that we got from the police at Lichfield.'

'Right, sir.' Marriott quickly donned his jacket, and, moments later, appeared in the DDI's office with the document.

Hardcastle lit his pipe, and then studied afresh the information that the Chief Constable of Lichfield had sent.

'I thought so!' exclaimed Hardcastle. 'I knew there was something we'd missed, Marriott.'

'What's that, sir?' Marriott was accustomed to the DDI

including him in the blame for some omission when, in fact, it was Hardcastle's own shortcomings that had been responsible for an error.

'This message says that Lieutenant Mansfield informed the adjutant at Lichfield Barracks *before* going to his fiancée's place in Westbourne Terrace, Bayswater.'

'That's how I understood it, sir.'

Hardcastle tossed the message on to his desk and stared at Marriott. 'Now why should he have booked a room at St John's Wood Barracks – which he never used – if the adjutant at Lichfield knew that he was going to spend his leave with his lady friend? As far as I understood it, from what Captain Grayson at St John's Wood said, officers on leave only need to book in at *one* barracks, not two. And why St John's Wood? That's miles from anywhere.' He spoke as though it were at the North Pole. 'Why not a barracks nearer to Bayswater, like Chelsea Barracks or Hyde Park Barracks, for instance? You're my military expert, Marriott. Why did he do that?'

'I've no idea, sir. It certainly seems a strange thing to do.' Marriott forbore from pointing out that St John's Wood Barracks was probably the nearest to Westbourne Terrace, whereas Chelsea and Hyde Park Barracks were on the other side of Hyde Park from there. Not that it mattered a great deal, and he had no desire to set the DDI off on another tirade about the army. 'There was something else, sir.'

'What?'

'No one at St John's Wood Barracks seemed to have seen Mansfield.'

Hardcastle pondered that proposition for a mere second before issuing another order. 'Marriott, telephone that Captain Grayson, and check how Mansfield informed them.'

It took Marriott about a quarter of an hour to discover the truth of the matter. 'It appears that Captain Grayson received a telephone call from Lieutenant Mansfield, sir, but that he never saw him in person. Grayson said that it was quite normal practice.'

'Sounds a bit sloppy to me.' Hardcastle took out his watch, glanced at it, and returned it to his waistcoat pocket. 'We'll go and have a word with this fiancée of his, Marriott. See what she has to say.'

'Very good, sir.' Marriott had no idea what Hardcastle hoped to discover by visiting a witness's fiancée, but he recognized the DDI's mood. If there were nothing to do, he would find something, even if it were inconsequential.

TEN

The house in Westbourne Terrace, where the Lichfield police had reported that Lieutenant Mansfield's fiancée lived, was an elegant residence, and clearly the quality of the property indicated that its occupants were not without a substantial income.

A trim housemaid answered the door. 'Good morning, sir.' She gave a brief bob at the sight of the two men on the doorstep.

'Good morning,' said Hardcastle. 'We're police officers. Is Miss Isabella Harcourt at home?' Recalling the alarm with which Mrs Nash had greeted his arrival at Stanstead Road when he called about her absentee son Adrian, he quickly added, 'But tell her there's nothing to worry about.'

'If you care to step inside, sir, I'll enquire.'

Hardcastle gazed around the opulent entrance hall. 'There's a bit of sausage and mash here, Marriott,' he remarked, while they were waiting. 'I wonder what Miss Harcourt's old pot and pan does for a living.'

A moment or two later, the maid returned. 'If you'd be so good as to step into the drawing room, sir, Miss Isabella will be down shortly.'

To Hardcastle's surprise, the woman who entered the room a few minutes later was about forty-five years of age. Her jet-black hair was drawn into an elegant chignon, and there was a distinctly foreign appearance about her olive skin, high cheekbones and large black eyes. Her red silk frock shone in the light cast from the windows. *Surely*, thought Hardcastle, *this woman could not be young Mansfield's fiancée.* Attractive and well groomed though she was, she was old enough to be his mother.

'I am Miranda Maria Harcourt,' the woman announced.

There was the trace of a Spanish accent, and her statement would have sounded haughty if it had not been accompanied by a smile. 'I understand that you are from the police, and that you wish to speak to my daughter.'

'That's correct, ma'am. I'm Divisional Detective Inspector Hardcastle of the Whitehall Division, and this is Detective Sergeant Marriott.'

'Please sit down, gentlemen.' Mrs Harcourt indicated a sofa with a wave of her hand before seating herself opposite the two detectives. 'Would you be so good as to tell me what this is about? My daughter is not in any trouble, I hope.'

'No, she's not,' said Hardcastle. 'We're are trying to trace Lieutenant Mansfield, who, I understand, is your daughter's fiancé.'

'Is it Geoffrey who's in some sort of trouble, then?' Mrs Harcourt inclined her head in a questioning manner, and gave the impression that, if he were in trouble with the police, then he would be an unsuitable match for her daughter and, in consequence, would not be asked to call again.

'No, not at all, and to the best of my knowledge he's quite safe.'

'Then why are you interested in tracing him?'

Hardcastle explained, as briefly as possible, that Mansfield had witnessed a man running away from the scene of a murder at Victoria Station. 'I was hoping that he might be able to add a little more to the statement he gave us at the time, but we've been unable to get in touch with him since then.'

'I see.' Mrs Harcourt rose from her chair, causing the two detectives to struggle to their feet. 'I'll call my daughter, Inspector. It's possible, I suppose, that Geoffrey mentioned something of it to her. I doubt that he would have omitted to do so.'

'Funny business, sir,' said Marriott, once Mrs Harcourt had left the room. 'Isabella's mother wanting to know what it was all about before we were given permission to talk to her daughter.'

'Foreign,' said Hardcastle dismissively. 'Always have a queer way of carrying on.'

The young woman who entered the room moments later was obviously Miranda Harcourt's daughter. Isabella Harcourt possessed her mother's beauty and poise, and also her smile, but it was warmer and open.

'I'm Billie Harcourt,' she announced.

Momentarily nonplussed, Hardcastle did not immediately answer. 'I thought your name was Isabella,' he said eventually. 'So it is,' said the young woman, 'but then it got shortened to Bella, and finally to Billie.' She smiled again. 'Which I much prefer,' she added. She arranged herself in the chair that her mother had just vacated. 'Please sit down, gentlemen. My mother tells me that you are anxious to trace Geoffrey.'

Once again, Hardcastle explained what had happened at Victoria Station. 'I was hoping that Lieutenant Mansfield might have remembered something that came to him afterwards, but, as I told your mother, we're having some difficulty in tracing him.'

Billie Harcourt was unable to disguise her surprise at Hardcastle's comments. 'This is all most extraordinary, Inspector. Geoffrey didn't mention any of this to me,' she said. 'I wonder why.'

'Perhaps he thought it might worry you or your parents if he told you about it, miss,' suggested Marriott.

'I doubt that it would,' said Billie. 'My father is a diplomat and many years ago served in Spain at our embassy there. That's where he met and married my mother. Madrid was quite a violent place in those days, so I understand. I remember my father telling me that it was not uncommon to see a dead body in the street.'

'Good gracious!' exclaimed Hardcastle, expressing a shock he did not feel.

'And what with the air raids here,' continued Billie Harcourt, 'I'm afraid we're all growing regrettably accustomed to violence.'

'So, Mr Mansfield mentioned nothing to you of this business?'

'No, nothing at all. I somehow doubt that he would not have told me all about it. It sounds a very exciting thing to have seen. After all, murders don't happen every day, do they?'

Hardcastle did not regard any murder as 'very exciting'. He turned to Marriott. 'What was it that Lieutenant Mansfield said?'

'He said that he was waiting to meet his fiancée, sir. That's why he was on the railway station.'

'Meet me from where?' Billie Harcourt seemed even more puzzled by this statement.

'He didn't say, miss,' said Marriott. 'Other than to suggest you would be arriving by train.'

'But I didn't go anywhere by train while Geoffrey was on leave, so I don't know what he meant by that.'

'Do you happen to have a photograph of Lieutenant Mansfield, Miss Harcourt?' asked Hardcastle.

'Yes, I do. It was taken just after he was commissioned.' Billie Harcourt stood up, but as the two CID officers were about to follow suit, she said, 'Please, don't get up.' She left the room, and returned a few moments later clutching a silver frame. 'There, Inspector.' She handed the photograph to Hardcastle. 'Handsome, isn't he?'

Hardcastle studied the photograph of a young officer in uniform, and then passed it to Marriott without comment.

Marriott looked at the print carefully, but he too said nothing.

'Thank you, miss.' Hardcastle returned the photograph to Billie Harcourt. 'Am I to understand that your fiancé is now back in Flanders with the North Staffordshire Regiment?'

'Yes, he is.'

'I see. Well, I don't think we'll need to trouble you again, Miss Harcourt. I'm sorry if we've wasted your time. No doubt the military police will be able to speak to him on our behalf.'

'It's still rather strange he didn't mention it though,' said Billie, as she showed Hardcastle and Marriott to the front door.

It was not until the two detectives had left the house that Hardcastle spoke again. 'Well, Marriott?'

'That photograph wasn't the Lieutenant Mansfield we spoke to at Victoria Station, sir.'

'No,' agreed Hardcastle, 'it wasn't.'

Clearly deep in thought, the DDI had remained silent for the journey back to Cannon Row Police Station, and, in fact, did not speak until he was seated behind his desk.

'We've got to put our thinking caps on, Marriott.' Hardcastle took off his spats and shoes, and began to massage his feet. That done, and his shoes and spats replaced, he filled his pipe and lit it.

'Why should a man claim to be someone else when he was only a witness, sir?' queried Marriott. 'It makes no sense.'

'No, it doesn't make sense, Marriott. Unless there are two Lieutenant Mansfields in the North Staffordshire Regiment. I wouldn't have thought that likely, but there are so many men under arms these days that I suppose it's possible.'

Marriott considered carefully what he was about to say next, but eventually gave voice to his thoughts, hoping that the DDI would not express his usual opinion about the incompetence of provincial police forces. 'Is it possible that the Chief Constable of Lichfield got it wrong, sir?' he asked warily.

'I wouldn't put anything past some of these country coppers, Marriott. All sheep stealing and incest up there, I wouldn't wonder.' Hardcastle sighed. 'Well, I suppose we'll have to go to Lichfield, and sort out the problem ourselves.'

'I'll check the train times, sir.' Marriott thought it unwise to point out that, far from dealing with bucolic crime, Lichfield was a cathedral city, and doubtless beset with problems similar to those encountered here in the capital. 'I suppose it means waiting until Monday, sir,' he added hopefully.

Hardcastle raised his eyebrows. 'I hope you're not suggesting that the army doesn't work on a Saturday when there's a war on, Marriott.'

At two o'clock that afternoon, Hardcastle had a surprise visitor.

'There's a Captain McIntyre of the Military Police downstairs, sir,' said the PC on station duty. 'He wishes to see you.'

'Send him up, lad,' said Hardcastle, wondering why McIntyre should be paying a personal visit rather than resorting to the telephone.

'I was in London seeing Colonel Frobisher on official business, Inspector, so I thought I'd catch you in your lair, so to speak.'

'Take a seat, Captain McIntyre.' Hardcastle paused, and then withdrew the bottle of whisky he kept in the bottom drawer of his desk. 'I daresay you could use a tot of whisky,' he said.

'Never known to refuse a dram, Inspector,' said McIntyre, tossing his glengarry carelessly towards Hardcastle's hatstand. And missing.

Hardcastle poured two substantial measures of whisky, and set a glass in front of the military policeman. 'Cheers!'

McIntyre raised his glass in brief salute. '*Slàinte!*' he said, as he made the Gaelic toast of good health. He placed the glass carefully on the desk. 'Colonel Fuller assures me that none of his officers' revolvers are missing, Inspector.'

'Can we be certain of that, Captain?'

'To be perfectly honest,' said McIntyre, drawing back his kilt and placing his hands firmly on his bare knees, 'I wasn't too happy about it. He told me that he'd assembled all his officers in the mess, and asked if any of them had lost a revolver. None had.'

'You mean he didn't check them physically, or had someone do so?' Hardcastle was astounded. In a similar situation, he would have made sure that the weapons were produced, no matter what the rank of those involved.

'I'm afraid so, Mr Hardcastle.' The DDI noticed that there was an element of apology in the provost officer's statement. 'Colonel Fuller has an old-fashioned faith in the integrity of officers. But I'm afraid I don't, not since I've had dealings with some of the ragtag and bobtail that are being commissioned these days.' McIntyre raised his hands in a gesture of hopelessness. 'But there's nothing I can do about it.'

Hardcastle now realized why McIntyre had arrived in person to give him the result of the firearms check; he doubted whether he had an appointment with Colonel Frobisher at all. 'And the armoury?'

'I spoke to the regimental quartermaster, and he assured me that no revolvers are missing. And when the RQM says that, it's true.'

'Oh, well,' said Hardcastle, draining his glass. 'I doubt that it makes a great deal of difference. Thank you for letting me know, Captain McIntyre.'

It was close to midday on Saturday by the time that the two detectives arrived at the North Staffordshire Regiment's depot.

'Halt. Who goes there?' As he quoted the time-honoured formula for greeting strangers, the sentry at the barrack gate raised his rifle to the high port, and stared at Hardcastle. 'Can I help you, sir?' he asked.

'I want to see whoever's in charge here, lad,' said Hardcastle, holding his warrant card in front of the sentry's face.

'You'd better go into the guardroom and see the sergeant, sir.' The sentry lowered his rifle.

The wooden floor of the guardroom shone with years of polish. In the centre of this impeccable oasis of military efficiency stood a soldier, his uniform immaculate, his red sash indicating that he was a full sergeant. 'Gentlemen?'

'I'm Divisional Detective Inspector Hardcastle of the Metropolitan Police, Sergeant, and this here's Detective Sergeant Marriott.'

The sergeant of the guard allowed himself a brief smile. 'Bit off your patch, aren't you, gents?' he said.

'A bit of an expert on policing, are you, Sergeant?' exclaimed Hardcastle.

'I was a copper in Sheffield until this lot started,' said the sergeant. 'Who have you come to see?'

'Someone who can tell me about one of your officers,' said Hardcastle.

'Ah!' The sergeant brushed briefly at his trimmed moustache. 'I think that Captain Murdoch might be your best bet, Inspector. He's the adjutant. He's the one man who knows everything about anything hereabouts, apart from the regimental sarn't-major, of course. One moment, and I'll get a runner to show you the way.' He paused as a late thought occurred to him. 'I suppose you've got your briefs with you, have you, gents?'

Hardcastle laughed, and he and Marriott produced their warrant cards.

The office into which Hardcastle and Marriott were shown was the usual stark army accommodation.

Hardcastle introduced himself and Marriott.

'Peter Murdoch, gentlemen,' said the young captain, as he shook hands with the two detectives. 'How may I help you?'

Once again, Hardcastle explained about Lieutenant Geoffrey Mansfield, and the mystery that had now developed about him.

'Interesting,' said Murdoch, waving a hand towards some chairs to indicate that the two CID officers should sit down. 'I had no less a personage than the Chief Constable of Lichfield here a few days ago making enquiries about this same officer.'

'I know. He was here at my request,' said Hardcastle, 'but it now looks as though the Lieutenant Mansfield I spoke to

at Victoria Station was an impostor. Although why he should
have adopted a false identity beats me.'

'I'm afraid I can't help you there, Inspector,' said Murdoch
with a laugh.

'Unless, of course, you happen to have two officers called
Geoffrey Mansfield in your regiment.' But Hardcastle doubted
that it was likely.

'I'm pretty certain that we don't,' said Murdoch, as he stood
up. 'And I know Geoffrey Mansfield quite well. I'm sure he
would have mentioned it if there had been another Mansfield.
But I'll just have a word with the orderly room quartermaster
sergeant. He'll be able to tell me in a trice.' He opened a door.
'Mr Wilson, be so good as to find out how many officers by
the name of Mansfield we have in the regiment.' Sitting down
again, the adjutant said, 'He won't be a moment. Has everything at his fingertips, does our Mr Wilson.'

Five minutes later, during which time Captain Murdoch
launched into a depressing analysis of the progress of the war,
ORQMS Wilson returned.

'We only have the one, sir,' said Wilson. 'Lieutenant
Geoffrey Mansfield, currently serving with the fourth battalion
in or around Arras. At least, that's unless they've moved again.'

'Thank you, Mr Wilson,' said Murdoch, and turned his attention to Hardcastle. 'A strange business, Inspector. Incidentally,
I told the Lichfield policeman that Mansfield had registered
here when he returned from the Front on leave.'

'So I understand,' said Hardcastle, 'but I've also been told
that he lodged his details at St John's Wood Barracks in
London. What's more, he booked a room in the mess there
for the period of his leave, but according to the officer we
saw, he never made use of it.'

'That's easily explained, Inspector,' said Murdoch. 'I
suggested that he registered at a barracks nearer to where his
fiancée was living.'

'Why should you have done that?' asked Hardcastle, a
bemused expression on his face.

'If he was suddenly recalled before his leave was up, it
would be easier for him to obtain travel warrants, and that
sort of thing, from, say Wellington Barracks, Chelsea Barracks
or even St John's Wood Barracks. It would save him travelling all the way up here to Lichfield.'

'I see,' said Hardcastle, not really seeing at all. Not for the first time, he failed to understand why the army had to work in such a convoluted way. He thought that Mansfield could have called in at any barracks to obtain travel documents, whether he was registered there or not. 'Can you tell me the date of his return to the Front?' he asked, realizing that he should have posed that question to Billie Harcourt.

'Just a moment.' Once again, Murdoch walked to the communicating door and relayed Hardcastle's request to the chief clerk. Returning to his desk, he said, 'Lieutenant Mansfield embarked from Southampton on the morning of Tuesday the tenth of July.'

'Are you sure about that, Captain Murdoch?'

'Quite sure, Inspector.'

'But the Chief Constable of Lichfield told us that he went back on the fourteenth of July.'

'He must have got it wrong,' said Murdoch. 'I quite definitely told him the tenth of July.'

'So, there we have it,' muttered Hardcastle vehemently, much to Murdoch's surprise. 'Mansfield left the country the day *before* the murder at Victoria Station. Bloody country coppers,' added the DDI under his breath.

'So it wasn't Lieutenant Mansfield that we interviewed, sir,' said Marriott.

'Well, I knew that as soon as Billie Harcourt showed us his photograph, Marriott. And if the Chief Constable of this God-forsaken police force had done his job properly, we wouldn't have had to traipse all the way up here.'

Hardcastle was still in a foul mood by the time he and Marriott returned to Cannon Row Police Station.

'I'm damned if I know what's going on, Marriott.' Hardcastle filled his pipe, and lit it. 'Why the hell should an army officer give us a false name?'

'Perhaps he didn't want to get involved, sir. Or perhaps he wasn't an army officer at all.'

'Then why did he hang about? He could've pushed off without waiting for us to turn up and start asking questions.'

'To allay suspicion, sir?' suggested Marriott.

'Suspicion of what, for crying out loud?'

'He might've committed the murder himself, sir.'

Hardcastle shook his head in bewilderment. 'There are times, Marriott, when I wonder if you've learned anything about the investigation of murder.' But secretly, he thought that there might just be something in Marriott's bizarre comment.

'In view of what Captain Murdoch said about reporting to a barracks nearer home, sir, d'you think we should have enquiries made at Wellington and Chelsea Barracks?'

'I suppose so, Marriott, but I'm buggered if I'm going to do it. Tell Wood to run round all the barracks in the vicinity and check it. And tell him to speak to an officer, not the bloody guard commander.'

ELEVEN

Unable to pursue his investigation into the murder of Herbert Somers until at least the following day, Hardcastle fretted for the whole of Sunday. He spent half the morning reading the *News of the World*, which included an account of the Germans breaking through the Russian lines at Zloczov, a place of which he had never heard. He wandered out to the kitchen to search for this obscure place on the map provided by the *Daily Mail*, which, unwisely as it happened, he had pinned on the wall next to the cooker.

'What on earth do you want out here, Ernest?' said Alice. The use of Hardcastle's Christian name in full was an indication of his wife's impatience. 'You're just getting under my feet while I'm trying cook the Sunday lunch. If you're looking for something to do, I've been on at you for the past two weeks to put a new washer on this tap. And now the sink's turned brown where it's been dripping. But don't think of doing it now.'

Hardcastle muttered to himself, and retreated to the sitting room.

Despite the shortages, which had become worse as the war progressed, Alice Hardcastle had been able to produce roast beef and Yorkshire pudding, with roast potatoes and cabbage. For once, all the Hardcastles' children, Kitty, Maud and young

Walter, had been present for the meal. It was an unusual event because all three were engaged on shift work, and very often Hardcastle himself was involved in some enquiry that kept him from joining them.

'Did you hear about the tram that was hit by a bomb on Victoria Embankment, Pa? Everyone on it was killed.' Kitty's choice of becoming a bus conductress had been decried by her father on the basis that it was both unladylike and dangerous.

'Yes, I did,' said Hardcastle tersely. 'It's time you gave up that job.'

'You know why I took it, Pa,' said Kitty, embarking on a now familiar set of reasons. 'It's released a man to join the army. It's patriotic. Anyway, these days you can get killed just walking down the street. A bomb might even hit this house.'

'I don't know why you can't do what your sister's doing,' said Hardcastle testily. 'That's woman's work.' His other daughter, Maud, had taken voluntary work as a nurse, and was based at one of the large houses in London that had been given over to the care of the war wounded. Although only nineteen years of age, Maud's nurse's uniform coupled with her harrowing tales of wounded soldiers – some of whom had died while she was tending them – had caused her to grow up very quickly.

'And I suppose you're still working overtime, Wally.' Realizing that, as always, he had lost his argument with his eldest daughter, Hardcastle turned his attention to Walter. Now seventeen, he was a telegram boy working out of the local post office.

Walter, whose job had also matured him beyond his years, looked at his father. 'I delivered ten telegrams yesterday telling folk that one of the men of the family had been killed,' he said. 'And that's only for the area covered by my post office.'

'Thank God you're too young to join up, Wally,' said Hardcastle, as he finished carving the joint.

'Only another six months, and I can go,' said Wally enthusiastically. Despite his experience of delivering harrowing news to the bereaved, he still maintained a romantic view of the war. In his mind, it was all derring-do and winning medals. 'I rather fancy the navy.'

'Please God, the war will be over by then,' said Alice. She

was convinced that, if Walter joined the forces, he would be dead within weeks. But her wish was granted. Although Walter applied for the Royal Navy on his eighteenth birthday in January 1918, the fatherly chief petty officer at the recruiting centre had told him that the war was nearly over, and they had enough men. 'Get on with delivering your telegrams, lad,' he had said. 'That's important war work.'

'Don't forget what happened to Arthur, Mrs Crabbe's boy,' said Hardcastle. 'He put up his age and enlisted. On his first day in the trenches he was killed by a sniper. One of his pals wrote and told the boy's mother how he'd died. And her husband had been killed the year before.'

'I know,' said Walter moodily, 'I delivered the telegrams. Both of them.' He skewered a piece of meat, and put it in his mouth. 'On the other hand I might join the police. I rather fancy the City of London force.'

'Over my dead body!' exclaimed Hardcastle, nearly choking.

'Don't talk with your mouth full, Wally,' said his mother.

Although Hardcastle was a loving husband and father, he was nonetheless pleased to be back at work on Monday morning. After inspecting the crime book, he went upstairs to his office to find that Marriott was waiting for him.

'Good morning, sir.'

'Morning, Marriott. You got something for me?'

'Yes, sir. A message from Colonel Frobisher. He's double-checked the information about Second Lieutenant Nash, and—'

'Who the hell's Nash?' demanded Hardcastle, looking up from the task of filling his pipe.

'Second Lieutenant Adrian Nash is the Army Service Corps officer who failed to arrive at his new unit in Boulogne, sir. We went to see his mother at Forest Hill.' Marriott suspected that his chief was playing another of his little games in pretending not to know who Nash was.

'Oh, that Nash. Yes, I remember. What about him?'

'Colonel Frobisher has had his clerk check with Buller Barracks, and there was definitely no mistake in the movement order that required Nash to report to 143 Mechanical Transport Company. So he's adrift, sir. And then there was Bryant whose people live at Fulham . . .' Marriott glanced up.

'We saw his parents too, sir. But Bryant hasn't arrived either. The colonel also checked the other two – Morrish and Strawton – and they still seem to be unaccounted for as well.'

Hardcastle finished filling his pipe, lit it, and dropped the match into the ashtray. He expelled a long plume of smoke, and leaned back with a satisfied smile on his face. 'I do believe things are coming together, Marriott,' he said. 'Any one of those officers would've been in a position to steal those items of clothing that went missing from Stacey's barrack room. Give Captain McIntyre a call, and ask him if he'd be so good as to ask Stacey if there were any officers in the pub where he lost his cap.' After a further moment's thought, he shot forward in his chair. 'Where do Mansfield's people live?'

'Er, I don't know, sir. We never thought to ask.' Marriott was unconcerned that he was including the DDI in this lapse. He regarded it as a just return for all the occasions that the DDI had blamed Marriott for his own shortcomings. But Hardcastle chose not to notice.

'Mmm! Perhaps it would be as well to find out. Get one of the men to look into it.'

'But what do we hope to learn, sir?' asked Marriott, who could not understand why Hardcastle attached so much importance to the Mansfield family, particularly as it had been proved that Geoffrey Mansfield was not the man they had spoken to at Victoria Station.

'Think about it, Marriott. It's no coincidence that the officer we saw at Victoria Station claimed to be Lieutenant Geoffrey Mansfield of the North Staffordshire Regiment. It means that whoever he was must've known Mansfield, and knew which regiment he was in. I don't believe that he just conjured that name out of thin air.'

'But we'll not find anything out from Mansfield's parents, surely, sir.'

'We shan't know until we ask, Marriott. On the other hand, this tale about Mansfield going back the day before the murder might be all my eye and Betty Martin. I know what that officer at Lichfield said about Mansfield going back from leave on the tenth of July, but I'm more inclined to believe the Chief Constable of Lichfield when he told us that Mansfield had gone back on the fourteenth. I know I don't think much of country coppers, but policemen don't usually make a mistake about dates. I'm beginning to have grave doubts about the efficiency of the military machine, Marriott. And despite what Frobisher and Punchard said, I'm still not convinced that our four officers are adrift. In fact, I'm certain they'll turn up somewhere.'

'But where do we start, sir?' asked Marriott, once Hardcastle had finished his diatribe about the army. He was still unsure that his DDI was steering the enquiries in the right direction. But he had known Hardcastle for long enough to know that he frequently went off at a tangent, and had solved many a murder as a result of having done so. 'We can't travel to the places where they were supposed to have been posted.'

Hardcastle had no intention of leaving England. But instead of responding to Marriott's statement, he said, 'Have you got a telephone number for that chap we saw in Lichfield, Marriott? The adjutant, I think he called himself.'

'Captain Murdoch, sir. Yes, we have.'

'Good. Speak to him on the instrument and find out Mansfield's home address.' He put his pipe in the ashtray. 'Let's just hope his people don't live in Cornwall or the Hebrides, or some equally wild sort of place.'

'Yes, sir.' Marriott glanced at the telephone on the DDI's desk and wondered why his DDI did not make the call himself. But then he recalled what Hardcastle had said about not barking yourself if you had dogs to do it for you.

Nearly three-quarters of an hour had passed before Marriott was able to report back to the DDI.

'Well?' Hardcastle looked up expectantly.

'Lieutenant Mansfield's family lives in Twickenham, sir.'

'At least that's in the Metropolitan Police District,' muttered Hardcastle.

'His father, Major Oscar Mansfield, is an instructor at the Royal Military School of Music, and he and his wife live in officers' quarters at the school.'

'How do we get there?' Hardcastle stood up, and seized his hat and umbrella.

'Train from Waterloo, sir,' said Marriott, prepared, as ever, for the question he knew the DDI would ask.

'Good. And get someone to have a look in the records of

births and marriages at Somerset House. See what he can find out about the Mansfields. Who's available?'

'There's Catto, sir.' Marriott could not understand why the DDI was taking so much interest in the Mansfield family. The photograph of her fiancé that Billie Harcourt had shown them proved conclusively that Lieutenant Geoffrey Mansfield was not the officer to whom they had spoken at Victoria Station.

'Not Catto,' said Hardcastle, who, unreasonably, had no great faith in the young detective. 'Send a sergeant.'

'There's Bert Wood, sir.'

'He'll do.'

Once Marriott had instructed DS Wood, he returned. 'There's a message from DI Collins, sir.'

'Oh, and what does he have to say?'

'He says that Mr Fitnam at Wandsworth got Captain McIntyre to take Stacey's fingerprints, and that they match some of those found in the van.'

'Well, what a surprise,' said Hardcastle, and leading the way downstairs, strode out into Whitehall and hailed a taxi.

The cacophonous sound of musical instruments being tuned greeted the two detectives as they arrived at Kneller Hall.

The pompous custodian manning the main gate loftily enquired their business – to which he did not get an answer – and then directed them to Major Mansfield's quarters.

Hardcastle was surprised that a private soldier answered the door.

'Yes, sir?'

'You're not Major Mansfield, are you?' asked the DDI, thinking that he had been directed to the wrong house, despite the custodian's air of efficiency.

'I'm Major Mansfield's batman, sir. Private Hobbs is my name.'

'Good,' said Hardcastle. 'We're police officers, and we'd like a word with Major Mansfield.'

'It's not about the lieutenant is it, sir?' asked the soldier, a worried expression on his face. 'He hasn't been killed, has he?'

'He's quite safe, as far as I know,' replied Hardcastle. 'It's an enquiry about another matter.' The DDI did not intend to tell this man why he was there.

'I think the major's across in one of the band blocks, sir, but Mrs Mansfield's here.'

'Perhaps a word with her, then,' said Hardcastle.

'Won't keep you a moment, gents.' Leaving the detectives on the doorstep, the soldier retreated to another part of the house. He returned moments later. 'If you come this way, sir, Mrs Mansfield's in the parlour.'

The woman who rose from a chintz-covered settee was in her late forties or early fifties. Her blonde hair was swept up in the prevailing fashion, and Hardcastle's immediate impression was that she was – or had been – an actress.

'I'm Carrie Mansfield,' said the woman, a quizzical expression on her face. 'Hobbs tells me you're from the police.'

'That's correct, ma'am. Divisional Detective Inspector Hardcastle of the Whitehall Division, and this here is Detective Sergeant Marriott.' The DDI indicated his sergeant with a wave of the hand.

'Do sit down, both of you, and tell me how I can help you.'

'Your son, Lieutenant Mansfield—'

'But he's all right, isn't he?' asked the officer's mother. 'Hobbs told me that you haven't come about him.'

'As far as I'm aware, your son is quite safe, ma'am, but I have come about him, in a manner of speaking. While he was on leave, Lieutenant Mansfield witnessed a man leaving a money-changing kiosk in Victoria Station where a man had been murdered.'

Marriott was amazed at Hardcastle's statement. Not sharing the DDI's doubts about the army's efficiency, or lack of it, he was satisfied that their enquiries had proved conclusively that Geoffrey Mansfield was not the man they were seeking. Added to which Billie Harcourt's photograph of her fiancé confirmed that he was not the 'witness' they had spoken to at Victoria Station. But he knew that Hardcastle was capable of deviousness when it suited him, or more particularly, when it suited the enquiry that he was conducting.

'Really? He never mentioned it.'

'He stayed here for a while, did he, then?'

'No, he was staying with his fiancée – a Miss Isabella Harcourt – at Westbourne Terrace in central London. But he brought Isabella to see us on the second day of his leave. A charming girl. She has a Spanish mother, you know.'

'When did he come on leave, Mrs Mansfield?' asked Hardcastle, casually glancing around the room, and, in particular, studying a series of framed photographs on top of a bookcase.

Marriott could not understand why Hardcastle was persisting with this fiction, and did not visualize that anything the woman might say would be of any assistance in discovering who had murdered Herbert Somers, the Victoria Station cashier.

'It must've been the end of June, I suppose, and he went back—'

But the conversation was interrupted by a disturbance in the hall.

'That'll be my husband,' said Carrie Mansfield.

The door to the sitting room opened, and a portly man entered. He was wearing khaki uniform with a major's crown insignia on the cuffs, not yet being one of those officers who wore his rank on his shoulder straps, known to the rank and file as 'wind-up' badges.

'I'll have to get a new lead trombonist, Carrie. The one I've got's bloody hopeless, and—' Major Oscar Mansfield paused as he caught sight of the two detectives. 'Oh, I'm sorry, love. I didn't know you'd got company. I didn't want to disturb Hobbs, so I let myself in.'

'These gentlemen are from the police, Oscar.'

'It's not about Geoff, is it?' A brief look of concern crossed Mansfield's face, as he unbuckled his Sam Browne belt and handed it to Hobbs, who had suddenly appeared in the doorway.

'No, Major, it's not,' said Hardcastle, and introduced himself and Marriott. 'I was just explaining to your wife about the murder I'm investigating.' The DDI repeated what he had told Mrs Mansfield.

'Sounds a bit of a rum do, Inspector.' Major Mansfield rubbed his hands together and advanced on a side table upon which was a collection of bottles and glasses. 'Can I tempt you to a drink, Inspector?'

'That's very kind, sir,' said Hardcastle. 'A drop of Scotch wouldn't go amiss.'

Mansfield busied himself pouring drinks, and then turned to face the detectives. 'I'm surprised young Geoff never laid hands on this chap. He's pretty good at hand-to-hand fighting, so I've heard. And he was a useful rugby player. Got a Military Cross, you know. In Arras, that was. Anyway, what did you want to see him about? Need him at the trial, do you?'

'That'll be in the future,' said Hardcastle, fervently hoping that there would indeed be a trial, but knowing full well that Lieutenant Mansfield would not be required to give evidence. 'But right now I was wondering if he could add anything to what he told us at the time.'

'Well, you'll have to nip across to Arras if you want to have another chat with him. But keep your head down,' added Mansfield, with a chuckle.

The DDI permitted himself a brief smile. 'I doubt that Mrs Hardcastle would be too keen on that,' he said, as he stood up. 'But I daresay I can arrange for the military police to obtain a statement from him. Well, thank you both. I'll not take up any more of your time.' He added, as if it were an afterthought, 'When did your son return to the Front from leave, Major?'

'The tenth of July.'

Hardcastle expressed surprise. 'Oh, I'd heard that he was in England until the fourteenth. Never mind, I must've got it wrong.'

'I hope you catch the bugger, whoever he is,' said Oscar Mansfield, as he shook hands with Hardcastle.

'Never fear, Major,' said Hardcastle. 'He'll be taking the eight o'clock walk sooner rather than later.'

After Hardcastle and Marriott had left, Major Mansfield looked at his wife. 'That's a damned queer business,' he said. 'I read about that murder, and it was on the eleventh of July, the day after Geoff went back off furlough. It strikes me the police don't know what they're doing.'

TWELVE

The two detectives were at Twickenham railway station before Hardcastle spoke.

'That Oscar Mansfield seems a rough and ready sort of bloke for a major, Marriott.'

'Commissioned bandmaster, sir. Worked his way up from the ranks. That's how most of them become a director of music.'

'You're full of useless information, Marriott, but did you notice them pictures on the bookcase?'

'Yes, sir, but what about them?'

'See anyone you knew?'

'I can't say as I did, sir.'

'Well, Marriott, there was a photograph of a young floozy in a wedding dress clutching hold of a young man.'

'Yes, I did notice that, sir.'

'Well, Marriott, a pound to a pinch that young man was Jack Utting. If he ain't, then Kaiser Bill's my uncle. And Utting was the bloke who took a day off on the day that Herbert Somers was topped. If you remember, Utting told the bank manager that he'd been knocked down by a bicycle, but he told us that he'd had a bilious attack. I think we need to have another word with Master Utting, Marriott.'

'It looks as though the Chief Constable of Lichfield did make a mistake over the date of Mansfield's return from leave, sir.'

'Yes, it looks that way, Marriott, but then you know what I think about country coppers.'

That afternoon, another avenue of enquiry was closed with a telephone call from Captain McIntyre, the military police officer at Aldershot.

'I've had a word with Stacey, Inspector, and he cannot recall whether there were any officers in the pub the night he had his cap stolen. But I doubt there would've been. Officers tend to stay away from the pubs of Aldershot. Especially those patronized by the common soldiery.' McIntyre emitted a short laugh. 'They might get involved in a fight, and that would never do,' he added.

The revelation that Jack Utting could, in some way, be related to Geoffrey Mansfield caused Hardcastle to ponder what he was to do next.

'If Utting is Mansfield's brother-in-law, Marriott, it might begin to shed some light on this murder of ours.'

'That's assuming that the young woman in the photograph was Mansfield's sister, sir.'

'Yes, that's true, but I can't see why else they'd have that snap on their bookcase,' mused Hardcastle. 'Unless they're in the habit of going about taking pictures of weddings. Anyone's wedding. Is Wood back yet?'

'Yes, sir. He's in the office.'

'Fetch him in, then, and we'll see what he's learned. If anything.'

Detective Sergeant Herbert Wood entered Hardcastle's office clutching a sheaf of paper.

'Sit yourself down, Wood, and tell me what you've found out.'

Wood took a seat, and spent a moment or two sorting through his papers before looking up.

'Jack Utting, born the fifth of May 1892, was married to Nancy Utting, née Mansfield, on the sixth of January this year, sir. Nancy Mansfield was born on the twenty-first of February 1897, and is shown as an actress, and she's the daughter of Oscar and Carrie Mansfield.'

'Ha! You see, Marriott, I was right about that photograph,' exclaimed Hardcastle, banging the top of his desk with the flat of his hand. 'Seek and ye shall find, Marriott.'

'Did you think there was a connection between the killer and Lieutenant Mansfield, then, sir?' asked Marriott.

'Of course I did. There had to be.' In truth, Hardcastle had not had the faintest inkling that the Mansfield family might be somehow associated with the murder. 'Yes, go on, Wood,' he said, turning to his other sergeant.

'Jack Utting also has a sister, sir, name of Cora, but I couldn't find any marriage for her. Mind you, she's only eighteen. She was born on the twenty-third of June 1899.'

'This is beginning to get interesting, Marriott,' said Hardcastle, rubbing his hands together.

'What do we do now, sir?'

'We go and see Utting again, and give him a bit of a firm talking to.' Hardcastle glanced at Wood. 'Well done, Wood. You might just have helped to solve our topping for us.'

'Are you going to let Mr Fitnam know, sir,' queried Marriott, once Wood had left the office.

'All in good time, Marriott, all in good time. I don't want to get his hopes up. You never know, but once we've shaken up Utting a bit, we might persuade him to confess.'

'Yes, sir.' Marriott was by no means convinced that, simply because Utting was married to Geoffrey Mansfield's sister, he had murdered Somers. He had to admit, though, that if Utting was not involved, it was a bizarre coincidence. But Marriott knew his DDI, and was bound to acknowledge that he was a master when it came to securing convictions for murder.

Half an hour later, Superintendent Hudson entered the DDI's office.

Hardcastle immediately stood up. 'Good morning, sir.'

'Good morning, Ernie,' said Hudson, taking a seat, and waving Hardcastle to do the same. 'I've had a telephone call from the Chief Constable of Lichfield.'

'Oh?'

'He told me that he was looking through the notes he made when he saw a Captain Murdoch at Lichfield Barracks on your behalf. Does that mean anything to you, Ernie?'

'Yes, sir. He was asked to make enquiries about Lieutenant Mansfield, the officer of the North Staffordshire Regiment who claimed to have seen the murderer of Herbert Somers running away from the kiosk at Victoria Station. But he seemed to have made an error over the date of Mansfield's return to the Front.'

'Yes, that's what he said. Apparently when he was going through his notes again, he found that he'd mistakenly told you that Mansfield had returned to the Front on the fourteenth of July when, in fact, he'd returned on the tenth.'

'I'd already discovered that, sir. But I wonder why he telephoned you and not me.'

Hudson laughed. 'The chief constables of small forces are very rank-conscious, Ernie. Lichfield's chief only rates as a superintendent by the Met's standards, so I suppose he preferred to speak to me.'

'Thank you for telling me, sir,' said Hardcastle, but refrained from expressing the opinion that he felt about the chief constable's slipshod approach to enquiries. 'I don't suppose they have many murders to deal with up there.'

The following morning, Hardcastle was in his office at eight o'clock, and sent for Marriott immediately. 'The sooner we have that chat with Jack Utting the better, Marriott. And there's no time like the present. Find out when he finishes his stint at the money-changing place at Victoria, will you? On the other hand, I suppose we could speak to him there. But it's best to ask the manager at Cox and Company. What was his name?'

Marriott grinned; Hardcastle was playing his usual game. 'Mr Richards, sir.'

'Yes, that's the fellow. But don't let on that we fancy Utting for the topping of Somers.'

'Certainly not, sir.' Marriott sighed inwardly. He had long since grown accustomed to Hardcastle telling him how to do his job, apart from which he thought that suspecting Utting of Somers's murder was tenuous to say the least.

But Hardcastle was in for a surprise when Marriott returned.

'I spoke to Mr Richards, sir, and he told me that Utting had resigned from the bank.'

'Resigned!' exclaimed Hardcastle. 'When?'

'Last Friday, sir. It was all quite irregular apparently. Utting didn't turn up for work on the Friday, but Mr Richards received a letter from him in that morning's post tendering his resignation with immediate effect.'

'Well, if that don't beat cockfighting. That'll be guilty knowledge, Marriott. You mark my words. Did you see this letter? What did it say? He's involved, Marriott, he's involved. I can feel it.' Hardcastle emitted the string of short sentences like the staccato firing of a machine gun. He stood up and began to pace around his office, puffing furiously at his pipe.

'Mr Richards got his secretary to make a copy of it, sir,' said Marriott, taking a sheet of paper from his pocket.

'Well, read it then. Read it.'

'It was brief, sir. Utting said: "I'm sorry to have to submit my resignation as from today, but my wife doesn't want me to work at such a dangerous job any more. Not after the murder of Mr Somers." And that's it, sir.'

'Dangerous? What's so bloody dangerous about being a bank clerk, eh, Marriott? What did Richards have to say about it all?'

'He was extremely annoyed, sir. He said that he'd be unable to give Utting a reference, because the bank's policy required a month's notice. He also mentioned that Utting's departure would involve him in a lot of unnecessary work.'

'Oh dear, it must be hard being a bank manager, worse than being in the trenches,' said Hardcastle sarcastically. 'No doubt he'll have to write a report for head office. Here we are investigating a murder, and he's carping about a bit of paperwork.'

'What do we do now, sir?' asked Marriott.

'We go and see the young bugger, Marriott, that's what we do. And we find out why he really left the bank.'

It was precisely ten o'clock when Hardcastle rapped loudly on the door of the Utting residence at Gloucester Street, Pimlico. There was no answer. He knocked again, louder this time.

'I've got a nasty feeling about this, Marriott.' Hardcastle walked on to the garden at the front of the house, and peered through the windows of the parlour. The room was devoid of furniture.

'The little bastard's done a flit, Marriott.' Hardcastle sounded exasperated.

'Look's like it, sir.'

'He's up to something, Marriott, you mark my words,' said Hardcastle, not for the first time.

The DDI turned from the window and saw a constable patrolling his beat on the opposite pavement.

'Here, lad, come over here a minute.'

The PC strolled across the road, irritated at being summoned peremptorily by someone he thought was a somewhat impertinent member of the public. 'And what are you all in a lather about, mister?'

'I'm DDI Hardcastle of A, lad, and I don't get in a lather, as you call it, about anything.'

'Oh, I'm very sorry, sir. I didn't recognize you,' said the now contrite PC, and saluted. 'All correct, sir.'

'Well, you might think so, lad, but I've got news for you. It looks as though the residents of this here house have done a moonlight flit.' Hardcastle pointed at Utting's house. 'What d'you know about the people who lived here?'

'Not very much at all, I'm afraid, sir. To the best of my knowledge the occupants have never come to the notice of police.'

'Well, they have now,' muttered Hardcastle. 'D'you know who owns this property?'

'It's one of the big insurance companies, sir. They own most of this street, if not all of it. It's the Mutual Life with offices in Baker Street.' The PC took out a small pad and scribbled down the address. 'There you are, sir,' he said, tearing off the slip of paper and handing it to the DDI.

'When you get back to the nick, ask the station officer to speak to the men who were on this beat from Thursday last. I want to know if any of them saw a furniture van being loaded outside number five. If any of 'em have, I want to hear about it *tout de suite*. Tell the station officer to pass any results to the DDI at Chelsea, and I'll speak to him later.'

'Very good, sir.' The PC saluted once more.

Hardcastle waved his umbrella at a passing taxi. 'Baker Street, cabbie,' he said. 'The Mutual Life Insurance Company's offices. It's not far from where Sherlock Holmes lived,' he added impishly.

The young clerk manning the counter in the front office of the insurance company looked up. 'Can I help you, sir?' he asked, running a finger around the inside of his celluloid collar. It sounded as though he was speaking through his nose.

'I'm a police officer,' said Hardcastle, 'and I want to know about a Jack Utting who occupies one of your houses in Gloucester Street. Number five it is.'

'I don't know as how I can release that information,' said the clerk. 'Anything to do with our clients is confidential.'

'Then you'd better get hold of someone who can tell me about it,' snapped Hardcastle. 'I'm investigating a murder and I don't have time to waste on pettifogging rules and regulations.'

'One moment, sir. I'll fetch the manager.'

'Good idea, and be quick about it,' said Hardcastle to the clerk's departing back. 'I haven't got all day.'

The man who appeared from a back office was about fifty, and was attired in the traditional black jacket and striped trousers of his calling.

'My clerk tells me you're from the police.'

'Yes, I'm Divisional Detective Inspector Hardcastle of the Whitehall Division, and I'm investigating a murder. I have reason to believe that a Jack Utting, resident at number five Gloucester Street might be able to assist me. However, when my sergeant and me visited the said premises, they was empty.'

The manager, who introduced himself as Nathaniel Green, raised his eyebrows. 'Empty? Are you sure, Inspector?' 'Well, there's no furniture in the front parlour. I had a look through the windows, and the cupboard's bare, so to speak.' 'This all sounds most irregular.' Green shook his head in bewilderment. 'I shan't keep you a moment, Inspector.' With that he turned on his heel, and made his way to a filing cabinet at the far end of the office.

'It strikes me, Marriott,' said Hardcastle, 'that Master Utting's doing a lot of irregular things just lately.'

The manager returned with a Manila folder in his hand. 'Mr Utting's paid up until the end of last month,' he said, 'but he still owes us for the period from the first of July.' He calculated mentally. 'That amounts to something in the region of three weeks' rent. We took up references from his employer and his previous landlady, and he seemed a perfectly acceptable tenant. He'd always paid his rent promptly until now. He works for a bank which is quite an acceptable profession from our point of view.'

'Not any more, he doesn't,' said Hardcastle, relishing the manager's discomfort. 'He packed it in last Friday.'

'Did he, indeed? He should have informed of us of any change of employment. It's in the agreement.'

'And I suppose he should've told you he was moving,' said Hardcastle. 'That'll be in the agreement, too, I imagine.'

'Perhaps you'd be so good as to give us Utting's previous address, Mr Green,' said Marriott.

'With pleasure.' Green flicked open the folder. 'He was resident at number seventeen Great Peter Street until the beginning of this year. That's when he moved into our Gloucester Street house.'

'That'll be when he got married, Marriott.' Hardcastle returned his attention to the manager. 'Thank you for your assistance, Mr Green. For some reason, your clerk didn't seem very happy at parting with that information.'

The manager lowered his voice. 'To be honest, Inspector, I'll be glad to see the back of him. I keep hoping he'll be called up for the army, but he tells me that he's got asthma and has trouble with his adenoids. That's why they won't take him.'

'If the war keeps going like it is, Mr Green,' said Hardcastle, 'they'll get to the point when they'll take anyone.' And he only just stopped himself from saying 'including you'.

'The trouble is,' continued the manager, 'that we're short-staffed as it is. If I sack him, I'll have difficulty in getting a replacement.' He sighed. 'I suppose I'll have to take a female, but the board of directors won't like it.'

The woman who answered the door of number seventeen Great Peter Street had a frown on her face.

'Yes, what is it? If you're selling something, I don't want it.' She began to close the door.

But Hardcastle put a foot against it. 'We're police officers, madam,' he said, raising his hat.

'Well?'

'We're making enquiries about a former tenant of yours, a Mr Jack Utting.'

'Oh, don't talk to me about him!' exclaimed the woman, and then contradicted herself by saying, 'You'd better come in.'

The front room of the house was furnished with several armchairs and a settee. The empty fire grate was filled with a newspaper folded into a fan shape, just like the one in the Somers' house, and the mantelshelf was cluttered with small ornaments.

'What d'you want to know about Jack Utting, then?' demanded the woman. She remained standing, her arms folded across her ample bosom.

'I take it you're the owner of these premises,' said Hardcastle.

'That I am. Mrs Freda Tolley's my name. Me husband went down with HMS *Hampshire*, the one old Kitchener was on, and left me with a load of debts. And the pension's nothing to write home about, I can tell you that.' She was clearly none too distressed at the demise of her husband. 'And this is a respectable house. Never had no trouble with tenants, least-ways not until that Jack Utting turned up.'

'D'you mind if we sit down?' asked Hardcastle.

'Suit yourself,' said Mrs Tolley, with a toss of her head, 'but the furniture ain't much to write home about. They're for the paying guests, and they don't pay enough to get the chairs done up proper.'

Hardcastle glanced at the settee, but seeing that its springs were almost through the upholstery, decided to remain standing.

'What was this trouble with Utting, then, Mrs Tolley?'

'It wasn't so much him as that floozy he eventually married. Well, I say married; the fact is they had to get wed. Put her in the family way, see. Or someone did.'

'D'you know her name?'

'Nancy Mansfield,' said Mrs Tolley promptly. 'At least she was until he made an honest woman of her. She reckoned she was actress.' The landlady sniffed contemptuously. 'She was full of airs and graces, was that one.'

'You say she was the trouble, rather than Mr Utting. What did you mean by that?'

Mrs Tolley tossed her head again. 'A scarlet woman if ever I saw one. She'd never think nothing of bringing home some theatrical Johnny and spending the afternoon in bed with him. When her husband was at work, like. Mind you, I don't think he gave a fig what she got up to. No better than a whore, I can tell you that. In fact, I wouldn't be at all surprised if you'd told me she made her living as a strumpet. She certainly looks the part.'

'Really?' Hardcastle made a mental note to have the prostitutes' register checked.

'Why didn't you throw them out, then, Mrs Tolley?' asked Marriott.

'What, and have empty rooms on me hands. It ain't easy to get tenants, you know, what with the war an' all. Them rooms what he left is still empty,' she added. She seemed to make a habit of contradicting herself.

'I understand that he left here in January, Mrs Tolley,' said Marriott, busily making notes.

'Straight after the wedding, such as it was. Glad to see the back of him, and that's the God's honest truth.'

'Not a very splendid affair, this wedding of theirs, then,' said Hardcastle, making the enquiry sound like casual conversation.

'No, it wasn't. They trotted off to the local registry office, and got spliced there. Not surprising, mind. I doubt they'd have got a preacher to tie the knot for 'em. Not with her nigh on six months gone, an' all.' Mrs Tolley primped at her hair.

'And to cap it all, he left owing a week's rent.' She paused as a thought occurred to her. 'Here, you don't know where he's gone, do you?'

'Unfortunately no, madam,' said Hardcastle. 'But we hope to catch up with him fairly soon.'

'Well, when you do catch up with him, perhaps you'd get hold of his last week's rent for me.'

'We're police officers, madam, not rent collectors,' said Hardcastle curtly, 'and we're investigating a murder.'

'That don't surprise me,' said Mrs Tolley, with a knowing nod. 'I always knew as how he'd come to no good. I always thought to meself that that Utting'd fetch up on the scaffold, and his whore of a wife with her throat cut.'

'I'm not for one moment suggesting that he *committed* the murder, Mrs Tolley, but he may be able to assist us.' Hardcastle sensed that it would be extremely unwise to trust this woman with his suspicions. If Utting did happen to return, Mrs Tolley would be falling over herself to tell him that he was wanted by the police. Not that Hardcastle's disclaimer would have done much to allay her suspicions. She was obviously the sort of woman who, having made up her mind about something, would not change it.

'Well, it wouldn't surprise me if he had murdered someone. Probably that tart of a wife of his if he's got any sense.'

'I understand you gave a reference to the Mutual Life Insurance Company, Mrs Tolley,' said Marriott.

'Well, of course I did. If he hadn't got that place, he'd likely have wanted to stay on here with their wretched kid. And I'd had enough of him, and that's a fact. I'd rather do without the money than have to put up with him and his cow of a wife.'

'Thank you for your assistance, Mrs Tolley,' said Hardcastle, as he and Marriott made for the front door.

The two detectives walked down Great Peter Street, Hardcastle's eyes searching for a cab. 'I don't think that woman knows what she wants, Marriott,' he said. 'One minute she says she was glad to see the back of Utting, and the next she's complaining about having empty rooms. There's no pleasing some people.'

'Very true, sir,' said Marriott, with a measure of heartfelt feeling.

THIRTEEN

It was nigh on four o'clock by the time a frustrated Hardcastle returned to Cannon Row Police Station.

'I don't know, Marriott,' he said, taking off his spats and shoes, and massaging his feet, 'we're getting no bloody where with this enquiry.'

Detective Constable Henry Catto tapped on Hardcastle's door. 'Excuse me, sir.'

'Yes, what d'you want, Catto?'

'A message from the DDI at Chelsea nick, sir.'

'Not a murder on his patch he wants clearing up, is it?'

'Er, no, sir. Not as far as I know.' Catto looked suitably bemused by the DDI's response. 'A PC on the Gloucester Street night-duty beat saw a van being loaded outside number five at about ten to twelve last Thursday evening, sir.'

'Did he now?' Hardcastle replaced his shoes and spats, and leaned forward to take his pipe out of the ashtray. 'Is that all?'

'The PC spoke to the van driver, and he admitted that he was moving the folk at that house, sir.'

'And I suppose this PC thought it was all right, someone shifting their furniture late at night, did he?'

Catto immediately felt sympathy for the unknown PC. 'Apparently, the van driver said that the man who lived at number five worked very late, and was only able to supervise his removal at that hour, sir.'

'Worked late my arse,' exclaimed Hardcastle. 'A likely bloody story, that is.'

By now, Catto was beginning to think that this unusual removal was somehow his fault, but that was the effect Hardcastle had upon him.

'There was something else, sir. The PC took a note of the removal company's details, sir.'

'Ah, that's better. Well, let's have them, Catto, and stop beating about the bush.'

'It was a Percy Tranter of Tachbrook Street, sir.'

'Right. Off you go, Catto.'

'You want me to make enquiries there, sir?' Catto was never quite sure how to interpret the DDI's instructions.

'Of course I don't, Catto. This enquiry requires experienced detectives, like me and Sergeant Marriott here.'

The woman who answered the door of Tranter's house looked nervously at the two detectives. Something in their appearance – and in her experience – led her to believe that their arrival did not bode well.

'Yes, what is it?'

'I'm looking for someone called Percy Tranter,' said Hardcastle.

'That'll be my husband. Who wants him?'

'We're police officers,' said Hardcastle, a statement that confirmed the woman's initial apprehension.

'You'd better come in. He's in his office. He's not in trouble again, is he?' the woman asked, as an afterthought.

'Remains to be seen,' said Hardcastle, making a mental note to discover if the man had a criminal record.

The woman led the way, and pushed open the door of a small room on the front of the house. A man was sitting at a worn desk, his back to the door, poring over a sheaf of papers. He was wearing a collarless shirt with armbands round the sleeves.

'Percy, there's someone to see you.'

The man carried on studying his papers. 'What do they want, Ethel?' he said, without turning. 'Tell 'em we're booked up till next Wednesday.'

'We're police officers,' said Hardcastle. 'Are you Percy Tranter, a haulier?'

The man swung round in his chair, and then leaped to his feet, a hunted look on his face. He rapidly hooked his braces over his shoulders. 'Yes, what is it? I ain't done nothing wrong, guv'nor, so help me.'

'We'll see about that.' Hardcastle glanced at Tranter's wife. 'Thank you Mrs Tranter,' he said, by way of dismissal, and then turned his attention to the haulier. 'Last Thursday night you removed some furniture from number five Gloucester Street.'

'It was all above board, guv'nor,' said Tranter. 'I wasn't

thieving it. I was doing it for Mr Utting. It weren't nicked, nor nothing like that.'

'At what time did you undertake this removal?' asked Hardcastle, amused at the speed with which the haulier went on the defensive.

'Just before midnight, guv'nor.'

'Funny time to be moving furniture,' said Marriott. 'Very suspicious.'

'Yeah, well, Mr Utting said as how he worked late, and that was the most convenient time. He had to see his stuff out, and he couldn't've done it no earlier. He reckoned he'd got a very important job. Something to do with the war effort, he said.'

Hardcastle laughed. 'War effort be buggered. Did it cross your mind that he might've been doing a moonlight flit, Tranter?' suggested Hardcastle. 'Because the Mutual Life Insurance Company that owns the property is none too pleased about it, and right now they're looking for someone who can pay the rent he owes 'em.'

'His rent ain't nothing to do with me, guv'nor,' pleaded Tranter. 'I was doing him a favour, like. I don't normally work that late.'

'How did he book you for this removal of his?' Marriott stepped a little closer to Tranter, further alarming him.

'I met him down a pub in Vauxhall Bridge Road. We often had a drink together.'

Hardcastle crossed the room to stare out of the dirty window of Tranter's office. 'Have you ever noticed, Marriott, how all the dubious transactions we come across are somehow arranged in a boozer?' he said, apparently addressing the street.

'It's quite remarkable, sir,' said Marriott.

'There was nothing dodgy about it, guv'nor. I swear.' By now, Tranter's voice had assumed a whining tone. But he had had dealings with the police before – a matter of some unaccounted-for lead from a church roof that was found in his van – and the outcome was a stretch in Wandsworth Prison.

'I wouldn't call conspiracy to defraud an insurance company exactly legal,' said Hardcastle, turning from the window to fix the luckless Tranter with an icy gaze. He saw no reason to tell Tranter that Utting's rent arrears were nothing to do with the removal man.

'But I never knew that's what he was up to, so help me.'

'Dear me,' said Hardcastle. 'Well, while I'm considering what to do about you, you can tell me where you took his goods and chattels.'

'Denbigh Street, guv'nor,' said Tranter promptly. 'Number twenty-six.'

'And you actually unloaded his belongings into that house, did you, Tranter?' asked Marriott.

There was a distinct pause before Tranter replied. 'Well, not exactly,' he said eventually.

'Not exactly?' said Hardcastle. 'Either you did or you didn't. What happened . . . *exactly*?'

'Mr Utting said as how it was getting so late, and if I'd like to leave the van outside his new drum overnight, he'd unload it himself. There wasn't a great deal of it, and he said he didn't want to keep me up too late. He said that as I'd done him a favour, he'd do me one in return.'

'So you went back there the following morning, and picked up your van, did you?' asked Marriott.

'Yeah, that's right.'

'And did you see Mr Utting on that Friday morning?'

'No, he wasn't about, but he'd left the key on top of the front wheel, under the mudguard. So I drove it back here.'

'Did Utting pay you?' asked Hardcastle.

'Yeah, course he did. A quid.'

'You were lucky to get it,' said Hardcastle, and turned to his sergeant. 'Isn't that an amazing tale, Marriott? Well, I think we'll pay Mr Tranter's friend Utting a visit. See how he's getting on now he's out of work.' The DDI turned to the haulier. 'And while I'm doing that, I'll think about what to do about you.' He paused. 'As a matter of interest, why aren't you in the army, Tranter?'

'I ain't fit,' said Tranter.

'Really? But you're fit enough to hump furniture about. I might have a word with the War Office about you, just in case they've lowered the standards. Good day to you, Tranter.'

For the past few days the weather had been unbearably hot, and the windows in Hardcastle's office were wide open. The DDI ran a finger around the inside of his starched collar, cursing, yet again, the convention that required him to wear a waistcoat, even in the height of summer.

But on the other side of the channel, the men in the trenches, usually up to their knees – and worse – in mud, were now suffering in the excessive heat. Some of the soldiers had cut the legs from their trousers to turn them into shorts; a form of tailoring that would displease the quartermaster who would undoubtedly make a charge for the damage. On some parts of the Front typhus had struck the enemy, but fortunately the British troops had, so far, escaped its ravages.

Unable to get his usual *Daily Mail*, Hardcastle had reluctantly bought *The Times* that morning, and saw that it carried a letter from a young officer, Captain Siegfried Sassoon, holder of the Military Cross, who had attempted to resign his commission in protest at what he called 'a war of aggression', but he had been transferred to Craiglockhart Hospital in south-west Edinburgh, Scotland, a facility that specialized in neurasthenics or, as the troops called it, shell-shock. It did not, however, stop an outcry from those who suggested he should be court-martialled and shot for cowardice, as so many 'ordinary' soldiers had been.

Hardcastle's first-class sergeant knocked on the DDI's door, and entered.

'Yes, what is it, Marriott?' Hardcastle folded his newspaper, and tossed it to one side.

'A message from the DDI on B, sir,' said Marriott.

'And what does Mr Garwood have to say?'

'He's received another report from a beat-duty constable, sir. Apparently this PC saw a furniture van being unloaded outside a house in Francis Street early in the morning last Friday. The PC did a check on the registration mark, and the van was the same one that the other PC saw taking the furniture from the Gloucester Street house. As it was likely the Uttings' goods and chattels were being shifted, Mr Garwood saw fit to advise us.'

'It strikes me that this murder enquiry has developed into a wild-goose chase, Marriott. We've finished up following a bloody furniture van halfway round the Metropolitan Police District.'

That was Marriott's view, too, but he deemed it impolitic to say as much. In his opinion, the DDI was straying farther and farther away from discovering the actual murderer of

Herbert Somers. And possibly of Ivy Huggins too. Not that the latter was his problem nor, for that matter, Hardcastle's.

'We'd better go and have a look, Marriott.'

The woman who answered the door was holding a baby on her hip. The child looked to be about a year old, which accorded with the statement of Mrs Tolley, the Uttings' previous landlady, that Nancy Utting had been six months pregnant when she was married to Jack Utting in January.

'Good morning, madam.' Hardcastle raised his hat. 'I'm a police officer. Is Jack Utting here?'

A look of alarm spread across the woman's face. 'How did you find us?' she blurted out. Had she had time to think, she would not have said that.

'It's called detective work,' said Hardcastle drily. 'You're Mrs Utting, I take it.' The woman's concern at his arrival had not escaped his notice.

'Yes. What's it about?' Nancy Utting's blonde hair was worn loose, and reached to below her shoulders. She wore a full-length, low-cut, black dress that, fitting tightly to below her hips, displayed her good figure to advantage. It was a form of attire that seemed to confirm Mrs Tolley's view that Nancy Utting was a 'strumpet'.

'We want to talk to him about the murder at Victoria Station a week ago last Wednesday.'

Hardcastle's reason for wanting to speak to her husband seemed to offer no relief to Nancy Utting's concern, and she held the door firmly with her free hand.

'Jack's not here at the moment. He's out looking for work.'

'Has he given up his job at the bank, then, Mrs Utting?' Marriott well knew this to be the case, but he had learned a trick or two from his DDI.

'He reckoned it was too dangerous.'

'Dangerous?' echoed Hardcastle. 'What, being a bank clerk?'

'It was after that poor Mr Somers was killed. I said to Jack that he ought to find something else. What with Archie still being only a baby.'

'How old is the boy?' asked Hardcastle.

'Thirteen months,' replied Nancy Utting promptly.

'He's a nice-looking young fellow. Keep you up much at nights, does he?'

'All too often, I'm afraid. He's teething, you see.'

'Yes, that's always a problem. How long have you been married, then?' Hardcastle knew the answer to his question, and had asked it out of sheer devilment.

Nancy Utting hesitated slightly before answering with a lie. 'About fourteen months.'

Hardcastle nodded. 'Well, when your husband gets in, be so good as to ask him to call round to Cannon Row Police Station. I need to have a word with him about the routine of the teller who runs the money-exchange booth at Victoria. As your husband usually did it, he's the man to help us with our enquiries.'

'All right,' said Nancy. The baby began to cry, and she moved him from her hip into her arms, and gently rocked him to and fro. 'Who should he ask for?'

'Divisional Detective Inspector Hardcastle. I'm investigating Mr Somers' murder.'

Using her elbow, Utting's wife began to nudge the door closed.

'You've only just moved in,' said Hardcastle, placing a staying hand on the door. 'Why did you leave your other place?'

'We had to. Now that Jack's out of work, we couldn't afford the rent. This place is cheaper, you see.'

'One other thing, Mrs Utting,' said Hardcastle, refusing to be forced out of the house until he had had all his questions answered. 'The day your husband got knocked over by a bicycle—'

'Knocked over? He wasn't knocked over.'

'Really? It was the day before Mr Somers was murdered at Victoria Station.'

'Oh, that. Yes, I remember it now,' said Nancy, a flush rising to her cheeks.

'Did he spend all day at home?'

'I don't really remember. I suppose he must've done.' Nancy Utting frowned, clearly at a loss to know what to say. She had no knowledge of her husband being involved in an accident, and she wondered whether this was a story he had told the police. 'But I've had so much on my mind, what with moving house and everything, that I can't really remember.'

'That's all right, Mrs Utting,' said Hardcastle smoothly. 'I was just wondering, that's all.'

'What d'you make of that, Marriott?' asked Hardcastle, as they made their way back to the police station.

'I don't think she's telling the whole truth, sir.'

Hardcastle scoffed. 'The truth? She was lying through her teeth, Marriott. Married fourteen months be buggered. I reckon that Jack Utting's done a runner.'

'But why, sir?'

'He's tied up in this somehow, Marriott, you mark my words.'

'But it's possible that he *is* out looking for work, sir.'

'The reason he gave for chucking in his job at the bank is all my eye and Betty Martin,' said Hardcastle dismissively. 'What are the chances of another bank clerk being murdered in one of them huts at Victoria Station, eh? No, he's up to something.'

'What's our next move, then, sir?'

'I'm thinking about it, Marriott,' said Hardcastle enigmatically.

It was not until Hardcastle had reached his office, and got his pipe going, that he spoke again.

'Who have we got who's not doing anything, Marriott?'

Marriott was aware that Hardcastle wanted to know the availability of Cannon Row's detective officers. He replied promptly. 'Catto and Lipton, sir. They're writing up reports in the office.'

'Good, fetch 'em in.'

Seconds later, the two detective constables appeared in Hardcastle's office.

'Sergeant Marriott tells me you and Lipton haven't got much on at the moment.'

'Er, well, I, that is to say, we . . .' stuttered Catto. Being the senior of the two DCs he felt it incumbent upon him to answer, but, as usual, the DDI had put him in a difficult situation, and he was not quite sure how to reply. If Catto agreed, he would be asked why they were sitting in the office when they could be out on the streets catching criminals. On the other hand, if he told the truth, and said they were writing reports, Hardcastle would want to know what was taking them so long.

'In other words, you've got bugger all to do,' said Hardcastle crushingly.

'Well, sir—' began Catto.

'I thought so. Well, I've got a job for you. I want you to set up an observation on Jack Utting. Sergeant Marriott will give you the address.'

'D'you want him nicked, sir?' asked Catto.

'It strikes me you're all too keen on feeling collars, Catto,' said Hardcastle. 'No, I don't want him arrested. I want to know where he goes when he leaves his house. Once you've done that, and he returns, you can bring him to the nick.'

'But you said you didn't want him arrested, sir.' Catto was now thoroughly confused.

'I don't want him arrested, Catto. I want you to invite him politely to come to the police station in order that I can ask him some questions. And if he refuses, you'll persuade him that it would be very unwise to refuse an invitation from a divisional detective inspector. You got that?'

'Yes, sir,' said Catto, wondering how he was to persuade an unwilling witness to come to the station without arresting him.

'I hope *you've* understood all that, Lipton,' said Hardcastle, turning his gaze on the other detective. 'Even if Catto hasn't.'

'Yes, sir.' Lipton was pleased that he was junior to Catto, sensing that if anything went wrong, it would be Henry Catto who would be in trouble with the DDI.

Once the two detectives had left the office to embark on their unwelcome duty, Hardcastle rubbed his hands together.

'Fetch Wood in here, Marriott.'

When DS Wood entered the office, Hardcastle put his pipe in the ashtray. 'Wood, you got the details of Nancy Utting née Mansfield from Somerset House, didn't you?'

'Yes, sir.'

'Good. Have a word with Vine Street nick and see if they've any record of her being knocked off for soliciting prostitution. I've a feeling in my water that she's the sort of woman who puts herself about. And with Jack Utting being out of work, she might be the family's only breadwinner. Her previous landlady seemed to think so.'

'Right, sir,' said Wood.

'By the way, Wood, did you make those enquiries at the other barracks about Lieutenant Mansfield?'

'Yes, sir. I called at Wellington, Chelsea and Hyde Park Barracks. I even tried Kingston Barracks, but Mr Mansfield hadn't registered with any of them.'

'I thought as much. All right, Wood, carry on. And now, Marriott, I think we'll go and have another chat with Miss Isabella Harcourt,' said Hardcastle, once Wood had left to undertake the DDI's enquiry. 'See if she can shed some light on what's been going on.'

'D'you think she'll be able to help in any way, sir?' Marriott was often puzzled by his DDI's sudden decisions, but could not for the life of him understand what Hardcastle hoped to achieve by interviewing Lieutenant Mansfield's fiancée again. 'After all, we've established that it wasn't her fiancé we spoke to on the day of the murder.'

Hardcastle said nothing, but merely smiled and tapped the side of his nose with his forefinger.

FOURTEEN

It was a pleasant, sunny afternoon, and Detective Sergeant Herbert Wood decided that he would walk from Cannon Row to Vine Street Police Station. It was only about a mile if he went via Cockspur Street and then cut through the back streets to Piccadilly. Being a sergeant, he did not get to do much patrolling, and the opportunity for a stroll in the fresh air was more than welcome.

The constable on duty at the door of the police station, his thumbs tucked under his tunic pocket buttons, looked up in surprise as he saw DS Wood's figure approaching. 'Well, I'm damned, if it ain't Bert Wood.'

'Good grief, "Pincher" Martin,' said Wood, as he shook hands with the PC. Ten years previously, Douglas Martin and Wood had been among the first recruits at the newly opened Peel House, the Metropolitan Police training school in Victoria.

'Where're you doing it, Bert?' asked Martin, using the police shorthand for enquiring where someone was serving.

'On A at Cannon Row.'

Martin laughed. 'Come up to Vine Street to see how proper police work's done?'

'I can see you're not doing much of it, standing on the front door of the nick sunning yourself,' said Wood.

'It's to stop idle callers troubling the high and mighty station officer,' said Martin. 'Anyway, what are you really doing up here?'

'I've come to have a look at your toms' register, Pincher. I'm working on a murder with my DDI.'

'What, the one at Victoria Station? Nasty business that.' Martin half bowed and swept a hand towards the police station entrance. 'Be my guest, Bert. Don't want to hold up detective officers on an important mission for their DDI.'

Once inside the police station, Wood explained to the station officer what he was seeking. 'Anything you've got on a Nancy Utting, or maybe in her maiden name of Mansfield, skip,' he said.

The sergeant quickly produced one of a plethora of bound volumes that were on the shelf behind his desk, and handed it over. 'Help yourself, mate,' he said.

It did not take Wood long to find what he was looking for, or, more to the point, what Hardcastle wanted. He made a few notes, thanked the station officer, and went on his way.

'How about a beer some time, Bert?' suggested Martin as Wood left the station.

'Yeah, why not? You earlies next week?'

'Yes, six-to-two all week.'

'See you Friday at the Coal Hole pub in the Strand, Pincher. That's about halfway between your nick and mine.'

'Look forward to it, Bert,' said Martin, and turned to deal with a young woman approaching the station door.

It was three o'clock that same afternoon when Hardcastle and Marriott arrived at the Westbourne Terrace house where the Harcourts lived.

This time it was a severely countenanced butler who answered the door.

'Yes?' The butler looked down his nose, obviously recognizing the two detectives as not of the class of visitor usually calling at the Harcourt residence.

'I'm a police officer,' said Hardcastle. 'I wish to see Miss Isabella Harcourt.'

'May I enquire what it's about?' asked the butler, still maintaining his haughty attitude.

'No, you may not,' snapped Hardcastle. He had had dealings with supercilious butlers before, and dismissed them as having ideas above their station.

'One moment.' Leaving the two detectives on the doorstep, the butler retreated.

'Toffee-nosed bugger,' muttered Hardcastle. 'He thinks the bell tolls for him,' he added, misquoting John Donne, the sixteenth-century poet.

The butler reappeared at the front door. 'This way,' he said, crooking a beckoning finger.

Hardcastle handed his bowler hat and umbrella to the butler, and signalled to Marriott to do the same. The two detectives followed the Harcourts' flunky into the drawing room at the front of the house where they had previously interviewed Isabella Harcourt.

Geoffrey Mansfield's fiancée appeared almost immediately.

'The two police persons, Miss Isabella,' murmured the butler disdainfully, by way of introduction.

'Thank you, Hoskins,' said Isabella. She waited until the butler had departed, and had closed the door firmly behind him, before speaking again. 'Please take a seat, gentlemen. I presume you have some more questions for me, Inspector.' She sat down on the sofa opposite the two detectives and arranged her skirt.

'No, miss, no questions. But I thought that you'd wish to know that I'm now quite satisfied that your fiancé, Lieutenant Mansfield, was not the officer we spoke to at Victoria Station on the morning of the murder.'

'I can't say I'm surprised, Inspector,' said Billie Harcourt. 'What you said about him waiting at Victoria to meet me off a train was obviously nonsense, but what does it all mean? Who was this man, and why should he have impersonated Geoffrey?'

'That's what's puzzling me at the moment, miss,' said Hardcastle, with an unusual candour. 'The man I spoke to that morning, gave your fiancé's name, knew that he was in the North Staffordshire Regiment – in fact, was dressed in the uniform of such an officer – and also knew that he'd served at Arras. Now, that makes me wonder who would've known Lieutenant Mansfield well enough to have all those facts at his fingertips. And why should he have claimed to have a fiancée, by whom he presumably meant you? Although he didn't mention you by name.'

'I'm afraid I'm unable to help you with that, Inspector.' Billie Harcourt chewed briefly at her bottom lip in vexation. 'It is rather worrying, isn't it?'

'Can you think of anyone who might've known all these things, miss?' asked Marriott.

Billie Harcourt remained silent for a few moments before replying. 'As far as I'm aware, only his parents might know that much about him. His father's in the army, something to do with military bands, I think. And then there's his sister, of course. Her name's Nancy, and I believe she's an actress.'

'I suppose she lives with her parents,' suggested Hardcastle in an offhanded manner. He was playing his usual game of teasing facts from someone when he already knew the answer. But he always liked to have those facts confirmed.

'Oh, no, she's married to someone called Jack Utting, and has a baby.' Billie Harcourt lowered her voice. 'To be perfectly honest, Inspector, I don't much care for Nancy's husband. He's a bank clerk, so Geoffrey told me, but I gather that he's a bit of a disreputable character.'

'Have you met him, then?'

'No, but from what Geoffrey's told me about him, he's a bit of a ne'er-do-well.'

'Surprised he's not in the army,' said Hardcastle, 'but what d'you mean by a disreputable character?'

'It's only what Geoffrey has told me. Jack Utting got mixed up with the stage at one time, before he got a job with a bank, and that's where he met Nancy. I think he was a stage manager at the theatre where she was appearing, but apparently he hops from one job to another, never staying in one for any length of time.'

'Well, Miss Harcourt,' said Hardcastle as he stood up, 'if your fiancé does return in the near future, perhaps you'd be so good as to ask him to contact me at Cannon Row Police Station. He might just be able to shed some light on this whole business.'

The butler reappeared, and proffered the two police officers their hats and umbrellas. But it was out of duty to Billie Harcourt, rather than a courtesy to the detectives.

'Thank you, Hoskins,' said Hardcastle.

'Well, Marriott, we didn't learn much there,' said the DDI, hailing a taxi with his umbrella. 'Apart from discovering that Jack Utting seems to be a bit of a layabout. But we'd guessed that already.'

'No, sir.' Even before their visit to Westbourne Terrace, Marriott had decided that it would be a waste of time, but caution had prevented him from expressing that view to Hardcastle. After all, the DDI moved in mysterious ways, and often brought a murder enquiry to a successful conclusion. And the fact that Billie Harcourt had said that Jack Utting was a ne'er-do-well more or less confirmed the opinion that both he and the DDI had formed. An opinion to which Hardcastle had just given voice.

'Scotland Yard, cabbie,' said Hardcastle to the taxi driver, and in an aside to Marriott, added, 'Tell 'em Cannon Row and half the time you'll finish up at Cannon Street in the City.'

'Yes, sir,' said Marriott wearily.

Detective Constables Catto and Lipton did not relish spending all night keeping observation on the Utting residence in Francis Street. But both were resourceful officers, and it was Gordon Lipton who made the decision to foreshorten their tedious duty.

'It's damned near ten o'clock, Henry,' said Lipton, glancing at his watch. 'I don't reckon the bugger's going anywhere now.'

'If he's there, Gordon,' said an equally dispirited Catto. 'We could be hanging about here until tomorrow morning with nothing to show for it.'

For nine hours now, the two officers had attempted to maintain a discreet surveillance of Jack Utting's house. It was not an easy task, apart from which both officers were certain that they were fairly obvious. It was a self-consciousness shared by all officers attempting a discreet observation. There was little cover, and they had maintained their watch on Utting's house by walking up and down Francis Street. But they had convinced themselves that if Utting had spotted them, he had decided to stay indoors. Either that or he had been out, had spotted them before they saw him, and had no intention of going home until the detectives had gone.

'Well, I'm going to make a duff call,' announced Lipton.

'I don't think the DDI would like us to do that, Gordon,' said Catto nervously. As the senior of the two constables, he bore responsibility for the conduct of their particular duty, and knew that if anything went wrong, Hardcastle would blame him. Henry Catto laboured under the constant fear that the slightest transgression on his part would result in a return to uniformed duty, and the monotony of walking a beat in what Hardcastle termed 'a pointed hat'. What he did not know, and would never be told, was that he had a champion in Detective Sergeant Marriott who regarded him as an efficient detective.

'Well, I'm going to give it a go,' said Lipton, 'and to hell with the DDI.' With that disregard of any sanction that Hardcastle might care to impose, Lipton marched up to the door of number seventeen, and hammered loudly on the brass knocker.

Nancy Utting opened the door a fraction, and peered apprehensively at the man on her doorstep. 'Yes, what is it?'

'Sorry to call so late, ma'am,' said Lipton, at the same time raising his straw boater. He was slightly taken aback by Nancy Utting's somewhat revealing dress, the same dress that she had been wearing when the DDI called. 'I represent the Durham Life Insurance Company. Is the man of the house at home?'

'Are you selling insurance?' asked Nancy.

'I'm offering a very cheap life policy, ma'am. They've proved to be very popular, particularly since the war started.'

'I'm sorry, but my husband deals with all that, and he's away in the army in France.'

'Ah, I see, ma'am,' said Lipton, raising his boater once again. 'I'm sorry to have troubled you.' He turned and paused. 'I hope your man will be safe over there,' he said.

'Thank you,' said Nancy Utting, and closed the door.

Lipton rejoined Catto at the corner of the street. 'Well, that's that, Henry, old son. She reckons her old man's in the army, and I bet the DDI didn't know that. So we'll be wasting our time hanging about here any longer. I suggest we have a pint, and push off home.'

The following morning, a nervous Catto hovered outside Hardcastle's office door.

'Well?' barked the DDI.

'It's about the observation on Jack Utting, sir.'

'What about it?' Hardcastle sat down behind his desk, and filled his pipe.

'Nothing happened, sir.'

'Nothing?' Hardcastle stared at the young DC.

'No, sir. There was no sighting of him at all. Gordon Lipton and me kept discreet observation on the house in Francis Street, but there was no sign of Utting.' Fearing some reproof, Catto spoke apprehensively before uttering his next sentence. 'Lipton knocked on the door, and—'

'He did what?' exclaimed Hardcastle, pausing with a lighted match in his hand. 'Fetch him in here at once.'

Catto fled, and returned almost immediately with Lipton.

'What's this about you knocking on the Uttings' door, Lipton?' demanded Hardcastle.

'I told the woman who came to the door that I was selling insurance, sir, and asked if the man of the house was there.' Lipton spoke hesitantly, expecting an outburst from the DDI.

'And?'

'The woman – Mrs Utting, I suppose she was – said that her husband was away in the army and she didn't know when he'd be coming home.'

'Did she indeed?' Hardcastle waved a hand of dismissal. 'All right, you two, you can break off the observation for the time being. The bugger's up to something,' he said, for the umpteenth time since the murder had occurred. 'Ask Sergeant Marriott to come in.'

'A rum business, sir,' said Marriott, as he entered the DDI's office. Catto had already informed the first-class sergeant of the outcome of his and Lipton's abortive observation. 'D'you think he *has* joined the army, sir?'

'Not bloody likely,' said Hardcastle. 'If Nancy Utting thought that being a bank clerk was too risky, I doubt she'd let her husband join the army. Of course, I suppose it's possible that he got caught up in Lord Derby's conscription scheme.

Not that I think the authorities would've found him, especially as he was at pains to cover his tracks when he left Gloucester Street. Anyway, as far I know, he ain't eligible, what with being married and having a sprog.'

'A search warrant, sir?' suggested Marriott.

'I was just thinking the same thing myself, Marriott. Get up to Bow Street a bit *jildi*, and swear one out.' Hardcastle placed his pipe carefully in the ashtray. 'And I wouldn't mind betting that we'll find the young bugger skulking in a wardrobe when we get there.'

'By the way, sir, DS Wood has some information for you. I'll send him in.'

'Well, Wood, solved it for me, have you?' asked Hardcastle jocularly, when the detective sergeant presented himself.

Wood smiled. 'Not exactly, sir, but you were right about Nancy Utting.'

'I'm usually right about such things, Wood,' said Hardcastle mildly.

'As Nancy Mansfield she had several convictions for prostitution on Vine Street's ground, sir, mainly Piccadilly and Shepherd Market.' Wood paused. 'And she has one in the name of Nancy Utting three weeks ago, sir.'

'Has she, by Jove?' exclaimed Hardcastle. 'So I suppose Jack Utting looks after the nipper while Nancy's out hawking her mutton. Seek and ye shall find, Wood. Seek and ye shall find.'

'Yes, sir,' said Wood, and left the office.

It was half past eleven before Marriott returned from Bow Street Police Court with a search warrant for the Uttings' house. Hardcastle decided that they would execute it after lunch. In Hardcastle's case, and therefore in Marriott's also, lunch consisted of a pint of bitter and a fourpenny cannon in the downstairs bar of the Red Lion in Derby Gate, just outside Scotland Yard.

At around three o'clock, the two detectives arrived once more at the Francis Street house of the errant Jack Utting.

Once again, it was Nancy Utting who answered the door. She looked anxiously at the two police officers, and sighed.

'What is it now?'

'May we come in, Mrs Utting?' asked Hardcastle, doffing his bowler hat.

'I suppose so.' The woman seemed resigned to frequent visits from the police. 'We're still in a muddle after moving, though.'

The parlour was in reasonable order, but there were cardboard packing cases on each of the chairs, and a tea chest in front of the hearth. As a result, the two CID officers were obliged to remain standing.

'Where is your husband, Mrs Utting?' demanded Hardcastle.

'Like I told you the last time, he's out looking for work.'

'Not found anything yet?'

'No. Things are a bit hard these days.'

'Really?' Hardcastle raised his eyebrows in surprise. 'I'd have thought that with so many men at the Front, he'd've found a billet without too much trouble.'

'It's not that easy,' said Nancy Utting, flicking her long, blonde hair over her shoulders.

'I was led to believe he was in the army,' said Hardcastle smoothly, making the entirely fallacious statement without preamble.

'Whatever gave you that idea?' Nancy Utting was plainly surprised by the DDI's comment.

'One of my policemen stopped a man who was calling door-to-door yesterday. We've had reports of confidence tricksters working in the area, and talking people out of precious antiques for a knock down price. However, I was informed that the man was a legitimate insurance salesman, and that he called here yesterday. Apparently, he was told that your husband was in the army.' Hardcastle had no intention of revealing that the 'insurance salesman' was, in fact, Detective Constable Lipton.

Standing beside Hardcastle, Marriott had great difficulty in preventing himself from smiling at the way in which the DDI was weaving his fanciful tale.

'Oh, that.' Nancy Utting smiled, but did not seem at all surprised that Hardcastle's enquiries should have extended to the questioning of callers at her house. 'I only say that to people who come to the door. It stops them pestering me. Anyway, we couldn't've afforded any insurance.'

'I believe you're an actress, Mrs Utting,' said Marriott.

'Yes, but I'm resting at the moment. I have to look after young Archie. I've had parts on the West End stage, though. I was in *Chu Chin Chow* at His Majesty's Theatre last year.'

Yes, and in Shepherd Market last month, thought Hardcastle, who completely ignored the woman's tenuous claim to fame. 'I see you've had time to unpack the family photographs,' he said, having spent the last few seconds studying the framed prints that were lined up, somewhat untidily, on the mantelshelf. 'And there's one of an army officer there. A relative, is he?'

'That's my brother Geoffrey,' said Nancy proudly. 'He won the Military Cross in Arras, you know.'

'Very commendable.' Hardcastle nodded amiably. 'Is that where he is now, in Arras?'

'I don't know. He said that they get moved around quite often, so he could be anywhere.'

'Have you seen him lately?' asked Marriott, posing his question as casually as Hardcastle had posed his.

'Yes. As a matter of fact, he was on leave just over a fortnight ago. He popped in to see us, but he could only stay for an hour.'

'What did he think of your husband not being in the army?'

Nancy Utting paused. 'I think he said something about how Jack should stay out of the army for as long as he could. Otherwise he'd stand a good chance of getting killed, the way things are going.'

Hardcastle made no comment about those he regarded as scrimshankers, and peered yet again at the gallery of photographs. 'Is that you?' he asked, pointing to a wooden-framed print.

'No, that's my sister-in-law Cora, Jack's sister. She's two years younger than me.'

'She looks very much like you,' commented Hardcastle.

'Yes, it's often mentioned, the likeness between us.'

'Does she live here?'

'No, she lives with Jack's father in Clapham.'

Hardcastle turned from his study of the photographs. 'Did you give your husband my message, Mrs Utting?' Having tired of making polite conversation, he almost barked the question.

'Your message?'

'Yes, last time I was here, I asked you to let him know that I'd like a word with him at Cannon Row Police Station.'

'Oh, yes, I told him. Hasn't he been in yet?'

'No, and it is rather urgent.'

'I'll tell him as soon as he gets home.'

'Thank you. I don't think we need to bother you any longer.' Hardcastle turned towards the door. 'You will impress on your husband that it is urgent, won't you?'

'Yes, of course.'

Once again, Hardcastle paused. 'When your brother called here, did he mention anything about a murder at Victoria railway station earlier this month?'

'No,' said Nancy promptly, but the swiftness of the woman's reply gave the DDI further cause for suspicion.

'You didn't execute the warrant, sir,' said Marriott, when the two police officers reached the street. He was still wondering why the DDI persisted in this fiction about Lieutenant Geoffrey Mansfield when it had been proved beyond doubt that he had nothing to do with the case.

'No, we'll keep that for tomorrow, Marriott. If the young bugger hasn't been to see us by then, we'll turn his drum inside out. But I have a shrewd suspicion that we won't see him until we feel his collar.'

'And you didn't tell Mrs Utting that you knew that her husband hadn't been home.'

'You don't tell people everything, Marriott.'

FIFTEEN

The moment he returned to the police station on Thursday afternoon, Hardcastle sent for Catto and Lipton.

'I want the pair of you to resume your observation on Utting's house in Francis Street immediately. I know Utting's there, and when the bugger appears you can nick him this time. Got that, Catto?'

'Yes, sir,' said Catto. 'What for?'

'Anything you can think of. But obstructing police in the execution of their duty might be good for a start. If he doesn't show up, keep the observation going all night, and report back here tomorrow morning at eight thirty sharp.' Hardcastle might have added that Utting could also be arrested for living on immoral earnings, but he kept that surprise to himself for the time being.

'Do you want us to knock again, sir, to see if he's there?' asked Catto.

'If I wanted you to knock on the bloody door, Catto, I'd've said so. And I wouldn't have asked you to keep up the observation all night. Now, have you got that?'

'Yes, sir,' said the two detectives in unison. Catto and Lipton were not at all pleased at being saddled, yet again, with what could well turn out to be an all-night stint of duty, and they hoped fervently that Jack Utting would appear not later than six o'clock that evening. But it was not to be.

Hardcastle arrived at Cannon Row Police Station at eight o'clock on the Friday morning, and waited impatiently until half past the hour.

'Where the hell's Catto, Marriott?' he asked, pulling out his watch and peering at it. 'I told him to report at eight thirty sharp.'

'I'll get him, sir. He's next door.'

'Sir?' Catto hovered nervously in the doorway of the DDI's office.

'Come in, man, for God's sake, and tell me what you've learned.'

The apprehensive Catto moved to the front of the DDI's desk. 'We maintained observation from five o'clock yesterday evening until eight this morning, sir, but Utting didn't show up.'

'What, not at all?'

'No, sir.'

'Right, Marriott, that does it.' Yet again, Hardcastle took out his hunter, stared at it, briefly wound it, and dropped it back into his waistcoat pocket. 'Time we executed that search warrant.'

'D'you want to take anyone with us, sir? One of the DCs for example?'

Hardcastle laughed. 'I think we can manage to turn over Utting's drum quite easily on our own,' he said, and seized his hat and umbrella. 'I'm quite looking forward to this.'

'Where is your husband, Mrs Utting?' demanded Hardcastle, when the two detectives had been shown into the Uttings' parlour once more. The Uttings had made no apparent progress in the process of settling in to their new house, and the same boxes still occupied the armchairs, the sofa, and the floor.

'Out looking for work, Inspector. I told you that yesterday.'

'No he's not,' said Hardcastle bluntly. 'I've had two officers keeping this house under observation since yesterday afternoon, and your husband hasn't been anywhere near here. Now, my girl, where is he?'

Nancy Utting immediately dissolved into tears. 'I don't know where he is, Inspector.' She looked up at Hardcastle with an imploring look on her tear-stained face. 'I'm so worried. I think something might've happened to him.'

'Is that a fact?' Hardcastle did not believe Nancy Utting and, recalling that she was an actress, thought that her display of histrionics was an act put on for his benefit. 'When did you last see him?'

'The day before yesterday, when we moved in here.' Nancy dabbed at her tears with a handkerchief. 'He said he was going out to look for work, but he never came back.'

'Why didn't you report his disappearance to the police, Mrs Utting?' asked Marriott. He shared the DDI's view that the woman was lying. 'You said earlier that you were worried about him being in danger.'

'I thought he'd come home.' Nancy sniffed, and blew her nose noisily.

'I have a warrant to search this house, Mrs Utting,' said Hardcastle, 'and I propose to execute that warrant now.'

This announcement brought about a fresh onset of sobbing. 'But I've only just put Archie down. You'll wake him.'

'Both Sergeant Marriott and I are fathers, and we're accustomed to small children,' said Hardcastle. 'We won't disturb the boy. Come, Marriott.' The DDI turned towards the door. 'We'll start upstairs,' he added.

The two CID officers mounted the stairs, and Hardcastle opened the first door he came to. It proved to be the front bedroom.

A man was in the act of leaving through the window.

'I shouldn't jump out, Utting,' said Hardcastle. 'You'll probably break both your legs.'

Jack Utting turned from the window with a resigned expression on his face. 'I've done nothing wrong,' he said.

'Then why were you trying to escape through that window? Or is that the way you usually go out when you set off to look for work?'

'It's not what you think, Inspector,' said Utting. 'I was just letting some fresh air in.'

Hardcastle emitted a guffaw of sarcastic laughter, and turned to his sergeant. 'Isn't it amazing, Marriott? Every time we find someone in circumstances they can't – or won't – explain, they always say it's not what I think.' He took a step towards Utting. 'And what is it that I'm thinking, lad, eh?'

'You think I had something to do with Mr Somers' murder, don't you?'

'Now why should I think that?'

'Well, you keep calling here, asking for me, and I thought you were out to get me.'

'You're certainly right about that, Utting,' said Hardcastle, a statement that afforded little comfort to the former bank clerk. 'I originally wanted to ask you about the procedure for running that kiosk at Victoria Station, but since you didn't come to see me at my police station, I've come to the conclusion that you might've had something to do with this here murder after all.'

'Well, I never had anything to do with it,' said Utting. It was an anguished denial.

Hardcastle studied Utting for some seconds. 'Well, be that as it may, lad, you're now going to accompany me and Sergeant Marriott here to the police station where we'll have what you might call a heart-to-heart chat.'

They escorted Utting downstairs. Nancy Utting was standing in the doorway of the parlour.

'Jack! What are you doing here?' she asked. 'Where have you been?'

'I've got to go to the police station with these officers,' said Utting.

'Oh, Jack!' exclaimed Nancy, and burst into tears yet again.

'I'm sure you're a very good actress, Mrs Utting,' said Hardcastle, 'but it's no good playing to the gallery, because there ain't one. And I'm not about to sign you up for a play. I'm no angel.'

The interview room at the front of Cannon Row Police Station was a cheerless place. Its only furnishings were a table with a scarred wooden top, and three chairs. The windows were barred, and the view from them obscured with dull brown paint.

'Sit down,' said Hardcastle, and took out his pipe. He spent several minutes scraping out the bowl and refilling it with tobacco. Having got it alight to his satisfaction, he turned his attention to Utting.

'How well d'you know Lieutenant Geoffrey Mansfield, Utting?'

'He's my brother-in-law.'

'I know he's your brother-in-law, but I asked how well you know him.'

'Not very well. I only met him once.'

'Did he come to your wedding?'

'No, he was away in the army. At the Front. It was just Nancy and me, and a couple of witnesses. I don't know who they were. They were just sort of hanging about.'

'And at which church was it that these here witnesses were just sort of hanging about?' asked Hardcastle sarcastically.

'It was the registry office at Caxton Hall.'

'It's a *register* office, not a *registry* office,' murmured Hardcastle, who had an ingrained dislike of people who misused the English language.

'Were Major and Mrs Mansfield there?' asked Marriott.

'Who?'

'The bride's parents.'

'No, they live too far away.'

'I wouldn't have called Twickenham too far away,' commented Hardcastle drily. 'But what I really wanted to ask you was the routine at the exchange office you ran at Victoria Station.'

'Oh, I see.' Utting suddenly sounded much more confident. 'What d'you want to know?'

'What time did you normally get there in the morning?'

'I used to arrive at nine o'clock, in time to meet the van from the bank. That would arrive with a military escort. I'd open up and start business as soon as the first troop train arrived. There'd be quite a few breaks during the day when I could get a cup of tea, or something to eat. Then at six o'clock, I'd shut up shop, supervise the cash being loaded into the truck, and away it'd go with the army. Then I'd go home.'

'You closed down at six o'clock, did you say?' Marriott looked up from his pocketbook. He had been making a pretence of taking notes, but it was all part of putting Utting at ease in the hope that he might say something that would give him away.

'Yeah, that's right.' Utting leaned back in his chair, almost cocky now.

'And when you went for a cup of tea did you lock up?'

'Yes, of course. And I'd get a military policeman to stand guard while I was away. There was always quite a few of them on the station.'

'How many?' asked Marriott, aware that there appeared to be only two on the morning of the murder.

'Six or seven,' replied Utting.

'What regiment is your brother-in-law in?' asked Hardcastle suddenly.

'The North Staffordshire Regiment.' Utting replied quickly, but then realized he might have given himself away. 'Er, I think it's the North Staffordshires.'

'And where do your parents live?'

'My parents?'

'It's a simple enough question. Where do they live?'

'In Clapham, but my mother's dead.'

'Where in Clapham does your father live, then?'

'Acre Lane.'

'And Lieutenant Mansfield is serving in Arras, isn't he?'

'Yes, he—' Utting paused again. The detective's questions were coming too fast, and gave him no time to think. 'Well, I think that's where Nancy said he was.'

'It strikes me you know a lot more about Mr Mansfield than you're letting on, Utting,' suggested Marriott.

But before Utting had time to think about that, the DDI changed the subject, albeit slightly.

'Turning to another matter, Utting,' said Hardcastle, 'you told Mr Richards, the manager of your bank, that the day before Mr Somers was murdered, you were knocked down by a bicycle, and weren't able to go to work.'

'That's right.'

'But when Sergeant Marriott and me saw you after the murder, you told me that you'd had a bilious attack.' Hardcastle turned to his sergeant. 'Ain't that right, Marriott?'

Marriott studied his notes, even though he knew the answer. 'Yes, sir, that's what he said.'

'So which was it?' demanded Hardcastle, facing Utting again. 'Or was it neither, because you knew that Mr Somers was going to get robbed that day.'

'No, I never knew that was going to happen. I can only thank God that I wasn't there, otherwise it might've been me that was killed.'

'Yes, that would've been dreadful,' commented Hardcastle with undisguised sarcasm. 'But you still haven't answered my question. Why did you tell Mr Richards one story, and me another, eh?'

'To tell you the truth—'

'That'll make a change,' observed Hardcastle.

'You see, Inspector, Nancy wasn't very well that day, and young Archie was playing up, what with his teeth coming through and everything. I just didn't feel like leaving them, so I made up that story. But when you asked me, I'd forgotten what I'd told Mr Richards. I didn't think he'd be too pleased if I said I was staying at home to look after my wife.'

'Where did you spend that day?' asked Hardcastle.

'Er, at home, like I just said. Because Nancy wasn't too well, and Archie was playing up.'

Intent upon dividing husband and wife, Hardcastle said, 'Well, your wife didn't seem to think you stayed at home that day.'

'Well, I did.' But uncertain what his wife might have told the police, the question had disturbed Utting.

'Now, let's deal with something else that's been vexing me,' said Hardcastle. 'Your wife.'

'What about her?'

'She's been plying her trade as a common prostitute in the West End.'

'That's a lie.' Utting leaped to his feet in a display of outrage. 'My Nancy's a well brought up, decent girl. She wouldn't do anything like that.'

'Sit down, Utting.' Hardcastle ignored the man's little outburst. 'And I know that to be true because she has several convictions recorded at Vine Street Police Station. She's been up before the Marlborough Street beak several times as Nancy

Mansfield, and at least once as Nancy Utting. Now then, given that you're unemployed, I reckon you're living on her immoral earnings, and that, my lad, is an offence. And if I take you up the steps to the Inner London Sessions you could cop two years in chokey.' The DDI thought there was little chance of securing a conviction without detailed evidence, and he did not intend to bother too much about it; he had more important matters to pursue.

'I never knew nothing about that, so help me!' exclaimed Utting, resuming his seat. 'You wait till I get home. I'll sort her out.'

'I hope you're not contemplating any violence, my lad.' Hardcastle stood up and stared at the young man opposite him. 'All right, Utting, you can go. And I hope you get a job. You could always join the army, of course.'

'I don't think Nancy would let me.'

'I doubt that her opinion would count for much if Lord Derby has anything to do with it,' said Hardcastle.

'I'm surprised you let him go, sir,' said Marriott.

'There was nothing to hold him on,' said Hardcastle. 'Climbing out of a window wasn't an offence the last time I looked. And we'd be pushing it to get him sent down for living on immoral earnings. But don't vex yourself, Marriott, give him enough rope and he'll hang himself.' It was a proposition that he fervently hoped would come true. Literally.

'What about the observation that Catto and Lipton were doing, sir?'

'Take it off. I doubt that we'd learn much. No, Marriott, we've got to cast our net a bit wider.'

The front-office sergeant stood up as Hardcastle and Marriott walked through the station following their lunch at the Red Lion.

'Excuse me, sir. There's a message from Colonel Frobisher at Horse Guards.'

Hardcastle stopped. 'And what does Colonel Frobisher want, skipper?'

'He has some information for you, sir. He said it would be best if you called on him.'

Hardcastle glanced at his watch. 'Now's as good a time as any, Marriott,' he said, and turned on his heel.

'Ah, Mr Hardcastle. Good of you to call in. I thought it better to give you the information that I have personally.'

'I hope it'll help me catch this murderer of mine, Colonel,' said Hardcastle, as he and Marriott sat down opposite the APM's desk.

'I'm not sure about that, Inspector, but it might tidy up a few loose ends. You recall the business of the four officers who appeared to be absent . . .?'

'Bryant, Morrish, Nash and Strawton, if I remember correctly, Colonel.'

'Exactly so.' Frobisher raised his eyebrows, surprised once again at Hardcastle's ability to recall facts. When it suited him. 'We have news of two of them.' The APM referred to a file on his desk. 'Bryant eventually caught up with One Corps Troops Column.' He looked up. 'Apparently they'd moved, several times, but he got there in the end. As for Strawton, his troopship was sunk off the coast of Haifa, and, I'm sorry to say, he was among those drowned.'

Hardcastle said nothing about the loss of the former footman. 'How about Nash and Morrish, Colonel?'

Frobisher looked apologetic. 'Nothing so far, but I'm sure they'll turn up sooner or later.'

'Thank you, Colonel. That reduces my list of suspects. Perhaps you'd let me know if they do surface somewhere.'

'Of course, Inspector.'

Hardcastle nodded, but kept to himself any comments he might have harboured about military efficiency. Or lack of it. But Hardcastle's knowledge of conditions at the Front was extremely limited, as he would be the first to admit. He was not to know that whole divisions could be lost, albeit temporarily, in the heat of war, let alone individual officers.

Hardcastle and Marriott returned to Cannon Row.

'I'm not sure that helps us any, Marriott,' said the DDI. 'We have to consider the possibility that either Nash or Morrish stole the clothing from Buller Barracks. On the other hand, it might've been neither of 'em. We'll just have to wait and see, I suppose.'

But an event occurred later that day that was to change completely the direction of Hardcastle's enquiries.

SIXTEEN

At about eleven o'clock that night, and shortly after the maroons had signalled yet another air raid on the capital, a patrolling A Division PC had knocked at the door of seventeen Francis Street to advise the occupants that they were showing a light. Regulations required houses to be 'blacked out' with heavy curtains. But before the door was answered, an upstairs window had opened, and a man fired a round from a revolver at the policeman.

The constable, fortunately unhurt, had wisely retreated to a safe point, and sent the officer on the adjoining beat to Rochester Row Police Station to inform the station officer of what had occurred.

Within minutes, Superintendent Arthur Hudson, head of A Division, had been advised of the shooting, and he, in turn, had immediately telephoned Sir Edward Henry at home.

The moment Sir Edward Henry, the Commissioner of Police of the Metropolis, had finished talking to Hudson, he tapped the receiver of his telephone. It was immediately answered by the operator at Paddington Green Police Station to which the Commissioner's telephone was directly connected.

'Get me Sir Herbert Samuel at home, as soon as you can, if you please.'

'Yes, sir,' came the response, and within seconds the Commissioner was talking to the Home Secretary.

Henry explained, as succinctly as possible, the situation that had arisen at Francis Street.

'Thank you for telling me, Commissioner,' said Samuel. 'Perhaps you'd be so good as to keep me informed of the outcome.'

'Of course, Home Secretary.' Sir Edward Henry paused. 'Will you be attending the scene?'

'Certainly not, Commissioner. I have the utmost faith in

the Metropolitan Police to resolve the situation. From what you tell me, this is not another Sidney Street, and I am most certainly not another Winston Churchill.'

The so-called 'Siege of Sidney Street' in 1911 had begun when the occupants of number one hundred, believed to be Bolshevik anarchists, began firing at police who were attempting to arrest them for the murder of three City of London policemen at Houndsditch the previous year. A company of Scots Guards had been deployed to contain the situation, and Winston Churchill, then Home Secretary, had arrived at the scene and directed operations, much to the annoyance of the army officers there.

'I appreciate that, Home Secretary, but in the event that I need the services of the military, I shall require your authority.'

'D'you think it will come to that, Commissioner?'

'I hope not, Home Secretary.'

'Well, we'll wait and see. Good night, Commissioner.' The Home Secretary replaced the receiver of his telephone, and went back to sleep.

Hardcastle had not been home for more than an hour – time enough to scan the pages of the *Star* evening newspaper – when there was a furious hammering at the front door.

A policeman stood on the doorstep. 'Mr Hardcastle, sir?'

'Yes. What's all the fuss about, lad?'

The policeman saluted. 'You're required urgently at Francis Street, sir.' He proffered an official message form. 'And the maroons went off at Southwark Fire Station nigh on an hour ago.'

Unconcerned by yet another air raid, Hardcastle put on his glasses, and scanned the brief message. 'Well I'll be buggered! It's bloody Jack Utting,' he exclaimed, and thrust the form into his jacket pocket. 'Find me a cab, lad, as quick as you can.'

While the policeman was searching for a taxi, Hardcastle put on his bowler hat and seized his umbrella. 'I've got to go out, Alice,' he yelled up the stairs, hoping that his wife was still awake. She had lately developed a habit of reading *Woman's Weekly* in bed, much to Hardcastle's irritation. He could not sleep while she still had the light on.

'Take care of yourself, Ernie,' came Alice Hardcastle's reply from upstairs. It was her usual response to the departure of her husband, but secretly she was always worried when he was called out late at night. It was as well that Hardcastle had not told her *why* he had been summoned to Francis Street.

The DDI walked out to the street, and glanced up at the night sky. In the distance, he could see the searchlights mounted on Apsley Gate at Hyde Park Corner criss-crossing as they scoured the sky for the deadly Gotha bombers.

'Your cab's here, sir.' The policeman appeared out of the gloom created by the latest blackout regulations, the result of which was to require that most of London's street lamps were switched off, and that the few that remained were dimmed.

'Francis Street, as quick as you can, cabbie,' said Hardcastle, almost throwing himself into the taxi.

As Hardcastle arrived at Francis Street, the uniformed figure of Superintendent Arthur Hudson appeared out of the gloom, and joined Hardcastle and Harry Marsh, the sub-divisional inspector in charge of the Rochester Row sub-division, who had been called to the scene earlier. Marsh had already ordered the closure of Francis Street a hundred yards in either direction from the Uttings' house, and had had the residents of the street warned to stay away from their windows.

'I've informed the Commissioner, Mr Hardcastle,' said Hudson.

'What exactly has happened, sir?'

'According to Mr Marsh, it all started about thirty-five minutes ago,' said Hudson, and told the DDI what had occurred. 'But why the occupant should have started shooting at the PC remains a mystery.'

'Not to me, sir,' said Hardcastle. 'The man who lives there is Jack Utting, and I fancy him for involvement in the murder of the man Somers at Victoria Station on the eleventh of July.' The DDI quickly brought the superintendent up to date with the outcome of his enquiries.

'It looks as though you were right, Mr Hardcastle,' said Hudson thoughtfully. 'So you think he's a killer.'

'I do, sir,' said Hardcastle, 'but all I need is the evidence. This affair might just provide it.'

At that moment another harmless round was fired from the upstairs window of number seventeen.

'Move down the street,' shouted Hardcastle at the group of policemen who had been summoned to the scene, and were now gathered near the Uttings' house. 'Unless one of you wants to be killed. That blue serge you're wearing ain't bullet-proof.' He steered Superintendent Hudson rapidly out of the line of fire.

'D'you think we're likely to need the military, Mr Hardcastle?' asked Hudson.

'I doubt it, sir. It's not looking like another Sidney Street,' said Hardcastle, unknowingly echoing what the Commissioner had said to the Home Secretary earlier.

'Mr Sankey.' Superintendent Hudson beckoned to the Rochester Row duty officer.

'Sir?' Inspector Jasper Sankey had been the first senior officer at the scene of the shooting. And he and the others were now well away from the Uttings' house.

'I take it you've sent to the station for firearms?'

Each police station held a stock of pistols and revolvers for use in emergencies such as the police were now facing in Francis Street. Some were the more modern point-32 calibre Webley and Scott automatics, but following the outbreak of the war, many of the unreliable Webley revolvers that the automatics had replaced had been reissued.

'Yes, sir. Two PCs should be back here shortly. And I've told them to bring a megaphone, in case you should need it.'

'Good,' said Hudson. 'What chance d'you think they'll have of hitting the chap in the window?'

Sankey, who had served in the First Boer War, shook his head. 'The revolvers don't have as much stopping power as the automatics, sir, but either way the officer would have to get much closer to the target to stand any chance of making a hit. And to do that, he'd risk being shot himself.'

'Yes, I see.' Hudson turned to the DDI. 'Have you any suggestions, Mr Hardcastle?'

'It might be possible to get someone round behind the house, sir, and effect an entry via the garden and the back door. But we don't know whether the man with the gun is the only armed man inside. The last time Marriott and I called there only Utting was living in the house, together with his wife and baby. I suppose it could be Utting who's shooting, but I can't recognize him at this distance. But I have my doubts about that; Jack Utting's a gutless little bastard who's terrified even of being a bank clerk.'

'Have you got someone who could take a look round the back, Mr Hardcastle? Better to send a plain-clothes officer than a uniformed one, don't you think?'

'Yes, sir.' Hardcastle was reluctant to risk one of his own men, but could see the sense of what the superintendent had suggested. He glanced around just as Detective Sergeant Marriott arrived, having been summoned from his quarters in Regency Street at the DDI's behest. DS Wood, and DCs Catto and Lipton, all of whom had also been called out, arrived at the same time. 'Marriott, I've got a job for you.' The DDI quickly explained the situation. 'See if you can get round the back of the Uttings' house, and find out if there's any way in. Best idea is to knock at the house next door and ask if you can go through their garden to have a look.'

'Very good, sir.'

'And keep your head down, Marriott. I can't afford to lose a first-class sergeant. Even you,' he added with a rare grin.

Affecting a stooped posture – which, in the circumstances was pointless, but made him feel safer – Charles Marriott ran quickly along the pavement on the opposite side of the empty road from number seventeen. It was still too near, but was as far away as he could get from the gunman in the upstairs window. Crossing over, he reached number fifteen, the house next door to the one containing the gunman. Lifting the heavy ram's head knocker, he banged repeatedly in his desire to get out of the line of fire.

Eventually, a worried face appeared round the edge of the door.

'What is it?' The man who answered was some fifty years of age.

'I'm a police officer, sir,' said Marriott. 'Detective Sergeant Marriott.'

'How do I know that?' the man asked. Apparently satisfied once Marriott had produced his warrant card, the man opened the door a little wider. 'What's going on at number seventeen?' he demanded.

Marriott pushed his way into the hall. 'There's a man at

the upstairs window shooting at police officers, sir,' he said breathlessly, not telling the man something he did not already know.

'A German spy, is he?' In common with most people, the occupant believed that any untoward incident occurring since the war had started was somehow associated with enemy aliens.

'Not as far as we know, sir.' Marriott closed the front door. 'I wonder if I might go through to your garden. I want to see if there's a back way into the house next door. And tell your family to stay away from the windows,' he added, as an afterthought, even though that advice had already been given earlier by the Rochester Row duty officer.

The house was similar in layout to its neighbour, and the occupant led Marriott through the hallway towards the back door. But as they were passing the sitting room, another man appeared in the doorway. Dressed in army uniform, he wore a colour-sergeant's badges of rank.

Marriott stopped as he recognized the brass shoulder titles denoting that the soldier belonged to the Middlesex Regiment.

'A Diehard, eh?' Marriott knew the regiment's nickname.

'That's right,' said the colour-sergeant.

'My brother-in-law's in your lot,' said Marriott.

'What's his name?'

'Frank Dobson. He's a company sergeant-major.'

'Well, I'm buggered. I know him well. He's not only in my battalion, he's in my company. It's a small world. So you must be Charlie Marriott, the copper. He's talked a lot about you. I'm Cecil Berryman. Pleased to meet you.' The soldier shook hands. 'You've got a bit of a to-do going on next door, then. Someone taking pot shots?'

'Yes,' said Marriott. 'One of our PCs knocked at number seventeen to tell them they were showing a light, and a bloke started shooting at him from an upstairs window. God knows why.'

'Was your man hurt?'

'No. I don't think our gunman's a very good shot.'

Berryman ran a hand round his chin. 'I don't know if I can help,' he said thoughtfully, 'but I've got my rifle upstairs. We always have to bring it home when we come on leave. If you want me to take this bugger out for you, just say the word.'

It was Marriott's turn to appear thoughtful. 'I don't know about that,' he said. 'We're supposed to have the Home Secretary's say-so before we deploy the military, but the truth is that none of our officers can get near enough to pick him off with a pistol, and that's all we've got. Not without our man being put in danger of getting shot. And between you and me, Cecil, I don't think our chaps are very good shots.'

'Well, Charlie, just say the word.' Berryman grinned. 'I'm on leave for a fortnight, but it'd be as well to keep my hand in, so to speak.'

'I'll have a word with my guv'nor, Cecil, and see what he says. In the meantime, I'll have a look at the back of number seventeen to see if we can get in that way, and surprise him.'

'Right. And I'll give your regards to Frank when I get back. He'll like to know I've met you. Even though it wasn't over a pint,' he added with a laugh. 'More's the pity.'

Marriott followed the householder, who proved to be Cecil Berryman's father, into the garden.

'Is the back of number seventeen the same as yours, Mr Berryman?'

'Yes, it is, Mr Marriott. Both houses are of the same design.'

For a moment or two, Marriott studied the rear of the Berrymans' house, and noted the low garden fence. It would be no obstacle for a policeman.

'Thanks, Mr Berryman. It might be possible for some of our men to force an entry through that back door, if you've no objection to them coming through your house.'

'Not at all, Mr Marriott. They're a rum lot in that house. Not long moved in. He doesn't seem to go to work, and his floozy of a wife reckons she's an actress, so she told the missus. But she's not doing much acting lately, because she's got a little one to look after. Mind you, I have seen her going out of an evening. I suppose her husband looks after the bairn.'

'Possibly,' said Marriott, but he thought he knew the real reason for Nancy Utting's late-night excursions.

Marriott explained to Hardcastle and Superintendent Hudson what he had learned, and mentioned that the soldier at number fifteen was willing to take a shot at the gunman now holding the police at bay.

Hardcastle took out his pipe and lit it, while he considered the offer made by Colour-Sergeant Berryman. 'What d'you think about that, sir?' he asked Hudson.

'We really ought to get the Commissioner's authority to use the military, Mr Hardcastle,' said the superintendent doubtfully.

'But that could take hours, sir. The Commissioner would have to get on to the Home Secretary, and he'd have to speak to the Secretary of State for War. Then we'd have to wait while the army got their act together, and managed to turn up here. I've no doubt there are some complicated regulations about use of the military in aid of the civil power, and all sorts of forms to fill up. I reckon we're looking at six or seven hours, at the very least, even though the nearest soldiers are at Wellington Barracks. And it's Friday night, sir. All the people who make those decisions will be away at their places in the country, I shouldn't wonder, war or no war.' Hardcastle came up with a reason that he was certain would convince the superintendent. 'If we delay, sir, innocent people might get killed.'

But still Superintendent Hudson was unsure. After all, Hardcastle was not the officer who would have to bear the responsibility. 'It's taking a chance, Mr Hardcastle, and I do see your point. But just supposing that Berryman killed our gunman, we'd have God knows how much trouble on our hands. The coroner would have to decide whether it was justifiable homicide or even murder.'

'A couple of rounds in our villain's direction, sir, and I reckon he'd throw in the towel.' Hardcastle was never a man to be pessimistic about the outcome of a police operation. 'I reckon it's worth taking the risk.' What the DDI did not say was that if the operation was successful, the superintendent might get promoted, but if it were a failure, he would probably be looking at some sort of disciplinary sanction.

But Hardcastle's conversation with the superintendent was interrupted by the drone of a Gotha bomber right overhead. Seconds later there was an explosion as a bomb fell in a nearby street.

'Bloody hell, that was near,' said Harry Marsh, the sub-divisional inspector. 'I'll bet it was on my patch.'

Suddenly the air was rent with the sound of the anti-aircraft guns in Hyde Park opening up in an attempt to hit the German raiders, while the white fingers of the searchlights swung back and forth as they searched feverishly to find a target for the gunners.

'Pity it didn't hit the Uttings' house,' commented Hardcastle.

'You'd better take a look at where that bomb fell, Mr Marsh,' said Hudson. 'It looks as though all our policemen are here. If you need any, I'm sure we can spare a few.'

'Very good, sir,' said Marsh, and hurried away in the direction of where the bomb had fallen.

'I think we'll take advantage of Colour-Sergeant Berryman's offer, Mr Hardcastle,' said Hudson, at last making a decision.

'Very good, sir.' Hardcastle turned to Marriott. 'Ask the colour-sergeant to join us out here, Marriott, and tell him to bring his rifle.'

'Mr Sankey,' said Hudson, addressing the Rochester Row duty inspector. 'Be so good as to rouse the occupants of the house opposite number seventeen, if they're not awake already, and ask them if we might put a man with a rifle in their upstairs window. If it's all right, signal with your lantern.'

'Yes, sir.' Sankey sped down the road and banged on the door of number fourteen Francis Street, hoping that the gunman would not loose off a round at him.

A man in a dressing gown opened the door an inch or two.

Sankey barged through the door, and promptly shut it behind him. 'I'm sorry to disturb you, sir,' he said. He deemed it unnecessary to explain that he was a police officer; he was in uniform. 'But we have a man with a gun shooting at our officers from the house opposite.'

'So that's what it's all about,' said the man.

'I'd like your permission to put a sniper in your upstairs front window, sir.'

'Well, I suppose it'll be all right, but my wife's in bed,' said the man, as he led the way upstairs to the front bedroom. 'So long as she doesn't get hurt.'

'We'll try not to disturb her, sir,' said Sankey hopefully, but he had time to consider that the appearance of a soldier with a rifle in the lady's bedroom would not exactly be viewed with equanimity by her.

'It's all right, love,' said the man in a vain attempt at pacifying his wife, as he and Sankey entered the room. 'It's only the police.'

The woman, her hair in paper curlers, drew the bedclothes up around her neck. 'What on earth's happening?'

Once again, Sankey explained briefly what the police hoped to do, before moving cautiously to the window. Kneeling down, he held back the corner of one of the curtains and slowly slid up the bottom half of the window a foot or two. As quickly as possible, he leaned out and waved his lantern towards the group of policemen further down the road. That done he raced downstairs, ready to admit Colour-Sergeant Berryman.

By this time, Berryman had joined the little group of police officers, and was conferring with Superintendent Hudson.

'D'you think you'll be able to hit this fellow without killing him, Colour-Sergeant?' asked Hudson.

'Yes, sir.' Berryman spoke confidently. After his experience in the trenches, hitting a stationary target should present no problems. And, in any event, he was acting under police instructions, and any unfortunate outcome would be their responsibility, not his.

'Get down to number fourteen as quickly as you can, then,' said Hudson. 'Mr Sankey will let you in. His signal means that he's arranged for you take a position in the upstairs room of that house. I'll try to reason with the man, but if I'm unsuccessful, I'll signal to you with a lantern. Of course, a couple of rounds near him might persuade him to surrender.' The superintendent was still hoping that the gunman would give up, or at best be wounded rather than killed.

'I'll give it my best shot, sir,' said Berryman, with a grin. He ran down the road to number fourteen, his rifle at the trail, demonstrating clearly that he was more accustomed than the police to moving rapidly while under fire. The door opened, and Berryman went in.

SEVENTEEN

Waiting until he could see Berryman positioned in the bedroom window, his head just above the sill, Hudson took the megaphone from one of the policemen, and raised it to his lips. 'This is the police,' he shouted. 'Give yourself up, or we'll open fire.'

Hudson's message was met with an insolent shout of

defiance from the upstairs window of number seventeen, followed by another shot.

'All right, sir?' asked Hardcastle.

'Yes, go ahead.'

Taking a lantern from one of the PCs, Hardcastle turned and signalled to Berryman.

None of the policemen heard Berryman's shot – the anti-aircraft guns were making it difficult to hear anything – but they saw the man's revolver fall into the front garden of number seventeen as the man himself reeled backwards into the room.

'I reckon Colour-Sergeant Berryman's a good shot, Marriott,' commented Hardcastle drily. Turning to Catto, he said, 'Take possession of that revolver in the front garden, and make sure you don't put your bloody dabs all over it.'

'Yes, sir,' said Catto.

At Hudson's command, two policemen rushed at the front door of the Uttings' house and broke it down. The PCs were followed by Hardcastle, Hudson, Marriott, and some of the other officers.

One of the PCs opened the door of the sitting room to find a man, and a woman holding a baby, cowering on the floor in the corner furthest from the windows.

'What's your name?' asked the PC.

'Jack Utting,' said the white-faced man.

The policeman relayed this information to the DDI.

Having learned that Utting was not the shooter, Hardcastle led the way upstairs, moving extremely fast for so bulky a man. He kicked open the door that he knew, from his previous visit, was the front bedroom. On the floor lay a young man, moaning, and holding his left arm. There was blood seeping between the fingers of his right hand.

Hardcastle bent over the prostrate figure, and quickly checked that he was unarmed. 'And who are you?' he demanded.

'Go to hell!' muttered the man, and continued to moan. 'I was nearly killed.'

'D'you know this man, Mr Hardcastle?' asked Superintendent Hudson. 'From your enquiries, I mean.'

Hardcastle was fairly sure that he had seen the man before, but did not know his true name. However, he had no intention of telling the superintendent until he had made certain. 'Not to my knowledge, sir,' he said enigmatically, 'but I'll sweat it out of the young bugger, you may rest assured of that.'

'Yes, I'm sure you will, Mr Hardcastle,' said Hudson mildly.

'Take Lipton with you, and get this man to hospital, Wood,' said Hardcastle to the sergeant who had followed him up the stairs, 'and make sure that he's kept under guard until he's ready to be interviewed. Arrange with the station officer at Cannon Row for a round-the-clock uniformed presence, on my orders.'

'Yes, sir.' DS Wood dragged the wounded man into an upright position, and he and Lipton hurried him downstairs into the street.

That matter out of the way, Hardcastle turned to DC Catto, who by now had been joined by Carter. 'You and Carter search this room thoroughly, and then the rest of the house. Sergeant Marriott and me will be downstairs talking to Mr and Mrs Utting.'

'What are we looking for, sir?' asked Catto.

'You'll know when you find it, Catto,' said Hardcastle, and turned on his heel.

Having been assured that the danger had passed, Nancy Utting had put young Archie to bed, and went into the kitchen to make tea.

Hardcastle pushed open the door to the sitting room so hard that it crashed back against the wall. Unconvinced, despite police assurances, that the gunman had been captured, Jack Utting leaped to his feet in panic, thinking he was about to be shot.

'Right, Utting, you've got a bit of explaining to do.' Hardcastle sat down in an armchair, now relieved of its packing case, and filled his pipe. 'And you can start by telling me the name of that idiot who my officers are just taking to hospital, on account of him having been shot in the arm.'

'I don't know who he is, Inspector.'

Hardcastle inspected the tobacco in his pipe, and then lit it. 'You'll have to do better than that, my lad,' he said mildly. 'You've had a man in your house attempting to murder my policemen, and you're telling me you don't know who he is. Pull the other one.'

'All I can tell you is that he's Cora's fiancé.'

'Who's Cora?' Hardcastle knew of the existence of Cora Utting. DS Wood's searches at Somerset House had revealed that she was Utting's sister.

'She's my sister.'

'What was he doing here, then, this fiancé of your sister Cora? Just drop in for a cup of tea and a chat, did he, before keeping his hand in with a revolver?'

'No, he came round to give me a message from Cora.'

'Really?' Hardcastle's sarcastic, one-word response indicated that he was not taken in by Utting's statement. 'And he didn't tell you his name? And you claim not to know it.'

'No, I've no idea.'

'And what was this message?'

'I don't know. He never had time to tell me. It was then that there was a knock at the door, and he looked out of the front-room window. Then he said there was a copper at the door, and with that, he ran upstairs.'

'That's what I call guilty knowledge,' commented Hardcastle mildly. 'Where does your sister live?'

'With my parents.'

'And where do your parents live?' Hardcastle's temper was beginning to shorten quite dramatically.

'Clapham, in Acre Lane.'

'How long has your sister been going out with this mysterious stranger?'

'I don't know.'

'But you knew that this man was your sister's fiancé?'

'Yes.'

'I see. Let me get this straight, Utting. Your sister Cora gets herself promised to this mystery man, but she doesn't tell you his name or where he came from, and neither did he. Is that it?'

'Yes,' said Utting unconvincingly.

'Wasn't there an engagement party, then?' asked Marriott, who was standing near the door.

'I mean you'd have been invited, being her brother,' put in Hardcastle. 'Wouldn't you?'

'She never held one, Inspector.' Utting was beginning to sound desperate in the face of the detectives' persistent questioning. 'She said as how they oughtn't to have a party, what with the war and the shortages, and everything.'

'How very patriotic,' said Hardcastle, with icy sarcasm.

There was knock at the door, and a PC looked into the room. 'The All Clear's been signalled, sir. Mr Hudson asked me to tell you that the air raid was over. Oh, and that bomb fell in Vauxhall Bridge Road.'

'All right, lad, thank you,' said Hardcastle.

'How often have you seen this boyfriend of your sister?' asked Marriott.

'I never met him before.'

'So tonight was the first time you'd set eyes on him, was it?' persisted Marriott.

'Yes, that's right.'

'Why isn't he in the army? Looks to be the right age to be serving. Not a conchie, is he?' Marriott knew that many eligible young men had claimed to be conscientious objectors to fighting in the war, but with his brother-in-law at the Front, he had no great sympathy for people he regarded as shirkers of the worst possible kind. Particularly as Ted Kimber, one of Cannon Row's detectives, had been killed at Neuve Chapelle two years ago while serving as a lieutenant with the Suffolk Regiment.

'I don't know,' said Utting. 'I don't know anything about him.'

Hardcastle stood up, and knocked the tobacco out of his pipe on the fire grate. 'Jack Utting, I'm arresting you on suspicion of being involved in the murder of Herbert Somers at Victoria railway station on Wednesday the eleventh of July, and conspiring with a person unknown to attempt to murder police officers.'

Utting's face paled and he swayed to such a degree that Hardcastle thought he was going to faint. But the DDI just stared at him with a cynical expression on his face.

But Utting's surprise was as nothing compared with Marriott's shock at his DDI's sudden decision to arrest the man without any apparent evidence.

Having handed his prisoner over to the custody of DCs Catto and Carter, Hardcastle walked out to the street in time to meet SD Inspector Marsh.

'Where's the guv'nor, Ernie?' he asked.

'I'm here,' said Hudson, appearing out of number seventeen.

'The bomb fell in Vauxhall Bridge Road, sir,' said Marsh.

'Yes, I heard. Casualties?'

'Four dead, three seriously wounded, sir.'

Hudson nodded. 'Been a busy night, Mr Marsh,' he said.

It was three o'clock on the Saturday morning by the time that Utting had been put in a cell, and Hardcastle was able to relax. 'Take the weight off your feet, m'boy,' he said to Marriott. With an uncharacteristic gesture of generosity, the DDI took a bottle of whisky from the bottom drawer of his desk and poured a measure into each of the two glasses he kept with it.

'Have we got any evidence to support a charge against Utting, guv'nor?' asked Marriott, taking a sip of his whisky as he lapsed into a less formal mode of address.

'Utting's tale is all my eye and Betty Martin, m'boy. He claims not to know the name of his sister's intended, and reckons he's never seen him before.' Hardcastle's tone of voice revealed his scepticism. 'Well, if that was the case, how did he know that this stranger who turned up at nearly eleven o'clock at night *was* his sister's fiancé, just because he said so? He hadn't got an answer for that, had he?'

'What will you do next, guv'nor?'

'I'll wait until tomorrow morning and then give Master Utting a bit of a sharp talking to. See if we can't rattle the truth out of the young bugger. And by that time our gunman should be in a fit state to be given a going over. According to Wood, the people at Westminster Hospital said it was only a flesh wound, so he should be up and about by tomorrow. Which reminds me, I must have a word with Colonel Frobisher, see if we can't get that Colour-Sergeant Berryman a pat on the back, and perhaps a letter from the Commissioner.' Hardcastle pulled out his hunter and glanced at it. 'Good gracious, Marriott, it's nearly half past three. You'd better get home, and my apologies to Mrs Marriott.'

'Thank you, sir, and my regards to Mrs H.'

'See you at eight o'clock in the morning, then,' said Hardcastle.

'Yes, sir,' said Marriott, thinking that it was hardly worth going home.

But as Marriott reached the door of Hardcastle's office, the DDI spoke again. 'Didn't you recognize our gunman, Marriott?'

Marriott paused on the threshold. 'I must admit he looked familiar, sir.'

'Of course he did,' said Hardcastle. 'He was the little bastard who passed himself off as Lieutenant Geoffrey Mansfield who we spoke to at Victoria Station on the day of the murder. But he'd shaved off his moustache.'

'Ye Gods!' exclaimed Marriott. 'So he was. But why didn't you challenge him about it when you arrested him?'

'I want him to think I hadn't recognized him, Marriott.' Hardcastle knocked out his pipe in the ashtray, and stood up. 'Now, get off with you, or you'll be in no fit state to start work in the morning.'

True to his word, Hardcastle was in his office at eight o'clock on the Saturday morning. And so was Marriott.

'Has our prisoner been released from hospital yet, sir?'

'Yes, Marriott, he was brought back about half an hour ago. He's tucked up in cell number three.'

'When are you going to interview him, sir?'

'Not yet, Marriott. Get across to the Yard, and ask Mr Collins if he'd be so good as to come over here as soon as he can.' Hardcastle was playing a hunch.

It was fifteen minutes before Marriott returned with Detective Inspector Charles Stockley Collins, head of the Metropolitan Police fingerprint bureau.

'You're up and about early this morning, Ernie,' said Collins cheerfully, as he entered the DDI's office.

'Been up half the bloody night as well,' rejoined Hardcastle. He lit his pipe, and leaned back in his chair, a near-beatific smile on his face. 'I've got a prisoner banged up in number three cell, Charlie, and I'd like you to take his dabs. When you've done that, perhaps you'd do me a favour and make a quick comparison with the prints you found on the revolver that was left at Victoria Station after the murder, and on the knife that killed Ivy Huggins. Oh, and of course the van that was abandoned in Kingston or Malden – I can't remember which – following her murder on Arthur Fitnam's patch. I've got a feeling that we're about to strike lucky.'

'Who is this bloke you've arrested, Ernie?'

'I don't know. At least, not at this stage, but I'll get it out of the bugger, never you mind.'

Collins smiled. 'I'm sure you will, Ernie,' he said, but half suspected that Hardcastle knew already. He knew A Division's DDI of old.

'Marriott here will take you down to the cells.'

'Right, I'll get to it,' said Collins. 'Lead on, skipper.'

Hardcastle and Marriott took their usual lunch of a pint of bitter and a pie in the Red Lion. Unfortunately, Fleet Street journalists knew that Hardcastle frequented this particular public house and, in consequence, so did they in the hope of picking up a valuable snippet of newsworthy information.

Hardcastle had just taken the head off his beer when a reporter sidled up to him.

'Charlie Simpson, *London Daily Chronicle*, Mr Hardcastle,' said the reporter by way of introduction.

'I know who you are, Mr Simpson,' said Hardcastle, as he placed his glass on the bar and turned to face the reporter.

'I hear you're about to make a breakthrough in the Victoria Station murder.'

'I don't know what gave you that idea, Mr Simpson,' Hardcastle said, 'but I should have thought that by now you'd know better than to talk to me about police matters when I'm enjoying a quiet pint. It tends to turn the beer sour.' He turned away dismissively.

When Hardcastle and Marriott returned to the police station at two o'clock that afternoon, DI Collins was waiting for them with the results of his checks.

'You're in luck, Ernie. He's your man.'

'Luck don't enter into it, Charlie,' said Hardcastle. 'It's what's called good detective work.'

'Well, whichever it was, you were right,' said Collins. 'I got a match between your prisoner, and the prints found on the revolver at the scene of the Victoria Station murder, in the van and on the knife from the Kingston job. And they match the prints found on the revolver from Francis Street.'

'I'm pleased about that,' said Hardcastle mildly. 'That'll put a smile on Arthur Fitnam's face down at Wandsworth, too. It'll have cleared up his murder for him. Now, Marriott and me'll go and have a few choice words with our mystery man. See you at the Old Bailey, Charlie.'

*   *   *

At three o'clock that same afternoon, Hardcastle ordered the station officer to have the anonymous prisoner brought to the interview room.

However, Hardcastle's attempts to discover the identity of the young man who had masqueraded as Lieutenant Mansfield, and who had shot at policemen in Francis Street the previous evening, were to no avail. The prisoner sat in the interview room, his left arm in a sling, and a disdainful expression on his face.

'Who are you?' demanded Hardcastle.

'I'm not saying anything, copper,' said the boy, 'and if you're thinking of charging me with anything, you'll have to prove it.'

Hardcastle noticed that the prisoner spoke with an educated voice. Although clearly not the product of a well-known public school, the DDI formed the opinion that he had probably been the beneficiary of a good grammar school education.

'Won't make any difference,' said the frustrated Hardcastle. 'You'll still be taking the eight o'clock walk.'

'They don't hang people for taking a few pot shots out of a window,' said the young man confidently. 'Anyway, I didn't hit anyone.' But his confidence was belied by the change in his demeanour. Hardcastle had worried him, and it showed. 'I'm in a good mind to sue you for shooting me,' he added, with a show of bravado he did not feel.

However, the DDI was determined not to charge the prisoner with two counts of murder until he had made further enquiries.

'Take him back to the cells, Marriott,' said Hardcastle irritably.

EIGHTEEN

'Have you got a reason for not charging the prisoner yet, sir?' asked Marriott, once he and Hardcastle were back in the DDI's office.

'Indeed I have, Marriott. I've got a shrewd suspicion that he didn't carry out that murder on his tod. Where did he get the uniform? From Mansfield? I doubt it. And how did he know enough about the routine of the money-changing place at Victoria Station to carry out the robbery, eh? I'm sure he had someone else helping him, and I think I know who.'

'So what do we do next, sir?'

'We go to the Uttings' house in Clapham and have a word with Cora Utting. But not until you've been to Bow Street Police Court, and sworn out a search warrant.'

'On what grounds, sir?'

'I should've thought that was obvious, Marriott. Cora Utting is Jack Utting's sister. Then, our mystery gunman turns up in Jack Utting's house. According to Jolly Jack, Cora is engaged to the man we've got in custody. In my book that makes a connection.'

The house in Acre Lane, Clapham, in which Jack and Cora Utting's father lived, was a drab dwelling in a road of similarly drab houses.

'I'm Divisional Detective Inspector Hardcastle of the Whitehall Division, and this is Detective Sergeant Marriott,' said the DDI to the man who answered the door. 'Is Cora Utting here?'

'I'm William Utting, Inspector, her father. There's no trouble, I hope.'

'So you'd be the father of Jack Utting as well, would you?'

'That's me, Inspector.' William Utting was a man of about forty-five, and as he led the two detectives into the parlour, he walked with a distinct limp. And his left sleeve was empty.

Seeing that Hardcastle had noticed, Utting volunteered the reason. 'I copped a Blighty one on the Somme last year,' he said. 'Corporal in the Durham Light Infantry, I was. A bloody toc-emma took me left arm off, and buggered up me right leg. Still, can't complain. Most of me mates was killed.'

'What the devil's a toc-emma?' asked Hardcastle.

'It's a trench mortar, but toc-emma is the signallers' code for it, and bloody nasty things they was, too. They was always called toc-emmas by the troops who were on the receiving end of 'em, not that you heard 'em coming,' said Utting, easing himself into an armchair and inviting the policemen to take a seat on the settee. 'Any road, you don't want to hear about my troubles. What was it you wanted?'

'I'd like to have a talk to your daughter Cora about her fiancé.'

'What, young Adrian? He's an officer, you know.'

'Is that a fact? What's this Adrian's surname?' Hardcastle's interest was suddenly aroused.

'Nash,' said Utting. 'Why?'

'In that case, I take it we're talking about Second Lieutenant Adrian Nash of the Army Service Corps.' Hardcastle spoke mildly, at pains to suppress his excitement.

'That's him. But how did you know?'

'Where's he stationed?' asked Hardcastle, answering Utting's question with one of his own.

'Hounslow, I think he said, but I'm not sure. Young Cora will be able to tell you more about him. I think she's upstairs, Inspector. Hang on, and I'll give her a shout.' William Utting, who did not seem at all disturbed that the police had arrived wishing to interview his daughter about her fiancé, stood up and limped to the door. When he reached the bottom of the stairs, he bellowed his daughter's name.

The young woman who entered the room looked to be older than the eighteen years of age that Hardcastle knew she was. She carried herself well, and her hair, worn up in the prevailing fashion, was immaculate. She seated herself sedately in an armchair, folding her hands in her lap, and looking the picture of a demure young lady. It was a pose destined not to last long.

'This is Cora, Inspector,' said Utting, his face radiating pride. 'These gentlemen are police officers, Cora, love.'

'Police?' Cora seemed to be unsettled by that information. 'What's wrong? It's not Adrian, is it?'

'Nothing's happened to him, miss.' Marriott made that monumental understatement with no indication that it was far from the truth. But he had assumed that the girl thought that her fiancé had perhaps fallen in battle.

'I can't wait to walk her down the aisle when she weds young Adrian.' Utting glanced at his daughter with obvious pride.

Hardcastle decided that he would not spoil William Utting's ambitious plans. At least, not yet.

'How long have you known Adrian Nash, Miss Utting?' asked Hardcastle.

A further mention of her fiancé's name disconcerted the young woman even more. 'Er, why d'you want to know?' she asked.

'Perhaps you'd just answer the question.'

'About six months, I suppose.'

'Would that have been just before he went into the army?'

'Yes, it was, as a matter of fact. We met at a tennis club dance. But once he joined up, he'd travel up from Aldershot at the weekends. That's where he was doing his officer training.' Cora Utting almost glowed with pride. 'He's going to wear his officer's uniform when we get married.'

'And he's in the Army Service Corps, is he not?'

'Yes.'

Hardcastle knew that Nash had not 'joined up' but was one of Lord Derby's reluctant recruits. His face took on a grave expression, and he decided it was time to tell the young woman the truth about her fiancé. 'I'm afraid that it's unlikely there'll be a wedding, Miss Utting,' he said. 'I'm sorry to have to tell you that Adrian Nash is in custody at Cannon Row Police Station, and will shortly be charged with two counts of murder, and another of attempted murder.'

With a gasp, Cora Utting's head fell forward, and she swooned from the chair in which she was sitting, and fell to the floor.

'Ye Gods!' exclaimed her father. He stood up and attempted to pick up his daughter, but, having only one arm, was unable to be of any assistance. 'There must be some mistake,' he said, turning to Hardcastle with an anguished expression on his face.

Marriott leaped across the room and scooped the slender young woman into his arms and laid her gently on the settee on which he and Hardcastle had been sitting.

'Perhaps you'd get a glass of water, Mr Utting,' said Hardcastle.

By the time that William Utting returned, Cora had partially recovered.

'I'm sorry to have to break the news to your daughter like that, Mr Utting,' said Hardcastle, 'but there was no other way.'

'It's all this bloody war,' said William Utting, a sad expression on his face. 'The world'll never be the same again, Inspector.'

'I fear you might be right, Mr Utting,' said Hardcastle, who had expressed the same view many times himself.

'Why didn't you tell me straight away, instead of letting me carry on like that?' demanded Cora, dabbing at her tears with a lacy handkerchief.

Hardcastle ignored the question. 'When did Adrian shave off his moustache?' he asked.

'What a funny question,' said Cora. 'He hasn't, as far as I know.'

'When did you last see him, Miss Utting?' asked Marriott.

Cora paused in thought for a few moments. 'It must've been about three weeks ago, I suppose. He told me he'd be away on some special training.' Although the girl gave the impression of being still in a state of shock, she was doing her best to put a brave face on the news she had just received. 'It looks as though I'll be a war widow before I was even wed,' she said sadly. Albeit a contradiction in terms, it was a remarkably mature comment for an eighteen-year-old to have made.

Hardcastle and Marriott glanced at each other. The period of time since Cora had last seen her fiancé was significant. If she was telling the truth, the last occasion they had met was just before the Victoria Station murder.

But the DDI was not wholly convinced. She had made a very quick recovery from her fainting fit, and was once again bright and cogent. All of which made him wonder if she had been putting on an act, and knew all along what Adrian Nash had been doing. She might even have worked out that it had been her fiancé who was involved in what the press had called the 'siege of Francis Street'. The early editions of today's *Star* had carried lurid accounts of the shooting although no mention was made of Nash; even the police had not known who he was until now.

'Mr Utting,' said Hardcastle, 'I have a warrant to search this house in connection with the murder of Herbert Somers at Victoria Station on the eleventh of this month.'

Utting's face expressed astonishment. 'What on earth makes you think that anything in this house is connected with that, Inspector?'

'I have not only arrested Adrian Nash, Mr Utting,' said Hardcastle, 'but I've also arrested your son Jack in connection with the same murder.'

'My God!' exclaimed Utting, sitting down suddenly. 'I don't believe any of this, Inspector.' He was clearly taken aback by Hardcastle's latest announcement, coming so quickly after news of his prospective son-in-law's arrest. 'You'd better do what you have to do, then,' he said, in a voice that had taken on a pitch of despair, as though he was unable to grasp the extent of the crisis that had suddenly beset his family, or the reasons for it. 'I don't know what you expect to find.'

'We'll start upstairs, perhaps with your room,' said Hardcastle to Cora Utting. He noticed that she seemed quite nervous at the prospect.

'Let me go and tidy it up first,' said Cora, swinging her legs off the settee and standing up. 'It's in a bit of a mess.' She seemed fully recovered.

'That won't be necessary, Miss Utting,' said Marriott, as he followed the DDI out of the room. 'But it might be as well if you came with us.'

It was a small bedroom at the back of the house. A crucifix hung over the single bed, and far from being untidy, as Cora Utting had implied, it was clean and orderly. A hairbrush and comb were neatly arranged on the dressing table, and there was a woman's magazine on a small table next to the bed.

Hardcastle looked around, as if trying to decide where to start. He moved towards the small wardrobe and opened the door. Inside was an army uniform. The DDI took it out and laid it on the bed.

'What d'you know about that, Marriott?' When it came to military matters, Hardcastle always deferred to his sergeant.

'The collar badges are the North Staffordshire Regiment, sir. You can't mistake the Staffordshire knot.'

'I thought as much,' said Hardcastle, as he looked closer and examined the two Bath stars on each of the shoulder straps. He turned to Cora Utting. 'And who does this belong to, miss?'

'It's my fiancé's.' But from the hesitant way in which she replied, it was obvious that Cora was lying, or at least uncertain.

'But I thought you agreed that he was in the Army Service Corps, miss.' Hardcastle gave a masterful performance of being completely puzzled by the whole thing. 'Or has he transferred to another regiment of late? And been promoted?'

Cora Utting blushed scarlet, and spread her hand across her neck. 'I don't know anything about the army,' she said. 'All I can tell you is that Adrian said it was his spare uniform, and he wanted to keep it here ready for the wedding.'

'Really?' Hardcastle sounded surprised.

'Your brother Jack is married to a woman called Nancy, isn't he?' asked Marriott.

'Yes, that's right.'

'And Nancy Utting's brother is Lieutenant Geoffrey Mansfield, of the North Staffordshire Regiment. So I would suggest, Miss Utting, that this is his uniform.'

'Well, if that's the case, I don't know what Adrian was doing with it. Perhaps he's looking after it for this . . .' Cora paused. 'What did you say his name was?'

'It won't do, Miss Utting,' said Hardcastle. 'I'm arresting you on suspicion of being an accessory to the murder of Herbert Somers. I shall now take you to Cannon Row Police Station.'

Predictably, Cora Utting burst in to tears. But her father, who had been standing on the landing during this exchange, exploded with fury.

'Now look here, Inspector,' protested William Utting, 'my daughter had nothing to do with this awful business. To suggest that she was somehow involved is outrageous.'

'If she wasn't involved, Mr Utting, she has nothing to worry about,' said Hardcastle. 'But I have to say that there appears to be no reasonable explanation for her possession of a uniform that may have been used in a murder.'

'Aren't you going to search the rest of the house, then?' asked Utting sarcastically.

'Not at this stage,' said Hardcastle. 'I've found what I was looking for.' He glanced at his sergeant. 'We'll take that uniform with us, Marriott. There may be blood stains on it.'

'Bloody marvellous, isn't it? There's me risking life and limb fighting on the Western Front, and damned near getting killed, and all you people can do is make a young woman's life a misery. I don't know why I bothered. I should have joined your lot when I had my health.'

And with that caustic tirade following them, Hardcastle and Marriott escorted Cora Utting out to the street.

*   *   *

Hardcastle's 'unknown' prisoner affected the same surly coun-
tenance when, once again, he was escorted into the interview
room. He flopped into one of the chairs and took out a packet
of Capstan cigarettes.

'Well, Second Lieutenant Adrian Nash of the Army Service
Corps,' said Hardcastle, 'I've just found something else to
charge you with. Desertion. And I understand that you'll likely
get shot at dawn for that.'

Nash jerked upright, almost as if he were a marionette
whose strings had been suddenly tightened. 'Not me,' he
protested.

'Furthermore,' Hardcastle continued, 'I shall charge you
with unlawful possession of an officer's uniform, and wearing
the ribbon of the Military Cross to which you weren't entitled.' Not that the DDI was going to bother with either of
those summary offences, given that Nash was facing two
charges of murder.

'If, as you say, I am an officer,' sneered Nash, 'how can I
be in unlawful possession of an officer's uniform?'

'Because it's a uniform of an officer in the North
Staffordshire Regiment.'

'I don't know anything about it. I've never had such a
uniform. What would I be doing with a North Staffs officer's
uniform?'

'Do you deny ever possessing it, then?' asked Marriott.

'Of course I do.' But Nash was nowhere near as confident
as when he had entered the interview room, and his hands
had started twitching on the table.

'In that case,' said Marriott mildly, 'we'll have to charge
your fiancée with its possession. We found it in her wardrobe
at her father's house in Acre Lane.'

'What fiancée?'

'The young lady we've got locked up here,' said Hardcastle.
'In case you've forgotten, Nash, her name's Cora Utting, and
I'm about to charge her with being an accessory to the murder
of Herbert Somers.'

Nash's face drained of colour. 'You leave her out of this.
She had nothing to with it.'

'Nothing to do with what?' Hardcastle asked the question
gently, rather like a skilled fisherman reeling in a prize salmon.

'She had nothing to do with any murder, and neither did I.'

Hardcastle leaned back in his chair and studied the young renegade officer. 'I am going to charge you with the murder of Herbert Somers at Victoria Station. That was when you cunningly thought to deflect any suspicion from yourself by pretending to be Lieutenant Geoffrey Mansfield, and telling me all about the soldier who didn't salute you, and who ran away. And, on behalf of another police officer, namely Divisional Detective Inspector Arthur Fitnam of the Wandsworth Division, I shall likely be charging you with the murder of a prostitute, Ivy Huggins, at Kingston upon Thames. Mr Fitnam will probably charge you with stealing a motor van as well.' Hardcastle did not think that Arthur Fitnam would bother with that, but, as with the question of the uniform and the medal ribbon, he never avoided putting such psychological pressure on a prisoner.

'I had nothing to do with any of that,' said Nash lamely, but his protestation carried no conviction.

'You see, Nash, your fingerprints were on the revolver which you used to club Somers to death.' Hardcastle spoke as though Nash had not denied any involvement. 'And they were also on the knife with which you stabbed Ivy Huggins, and they were all over the van you stole from the lock-up at the baker's shop in Cowleaze Road, Kingston upon Thames.'

'I want a lawyer,' said Nash.

'Yes, I think you do,' commented Hardcastle. 'And when you see him perhaps you'll tell him I shall also charge you with the attempted murder of a police officer in Francis Street on Friday the twenty-seventh of this month. Incidentally, where did you get the revolver you used to shoot at my officers?'

'I was issued with it, of course.' The reply was surly.

'And the one you used to club Herbert Somers to death?'

'Find out.'

It was nearing nine o'clock that evening by the time that Hardcastle turned his attention to Cora Utting.

Languishing in a cell for nigh on two and a half hours had terrified Adrian Nash's eighteen-year-old fiancée, and she had spent most of the time sobbing. It was a combination of fear, and the certain knowledge that her fiancé was to be hanged.

'Well, young lady,' Hardcastle began, as he and Marriott

entered the interview room, 'I think it's time you told us all you know.'

'I don't know anything,' said the tearful Cora, staring imploringly at the DDI with red-rimmed eyes.

'Let me explain the situation to you, then,' said Hardcastle. 'Your fiancé has been arrested for murder. That much I told you before.'

'I don't believe he had anything to do with a murder.'

'Just listen.' Hardcastle spoke softly, and tried to bear in mind that the young woman opposite him was only a year younger than his daughter Maud, and he was aware of how immature, on occasion, she could be, despite nursing wounded soldiers. 'There is no doubt in my mind that Adrian Nash was responsible for two murders, and one of the victims was a prostitute who he'd picked up in Kingston after stealing a van from a lock-up garage.'

'A prostitute?' Cora could not disguise her shock at this revelation. 'I don't believe it.' But it was obvious that she did, and was starting to realize that Adrian Nash was not the man, resplendent in an officer's uniform, whom she thought would make a dashing and gallant husband.

'He will be charged with those murders, and doubtless your brother Jack will also be charged as an accessory.' Hardcastle was by no means sure that Jack Utting *was* involved in any way with the killings, but saw no reason to share those doubts with Utting's sister. 'Now, unless you want to join your fiancé and your brother in the dock at the Old Bailey, it would be best if you told me all you know.'

Cora Utting plucked a handkerchief from her sleeve, and began to cry again. 'I don't know anything about it, honestly,' she blurted out between sobs.

'You know nothing about the uniform we found at your house, then?' asked Marriott.

'No, honestly, I thought it belonged to Adrian.'

'But it had different badges on it, and two stars on the shoulder straps,' said Marriott. 'Your fiancé is a second-lieutenant, and that merits only one star.'

'I told you, I know nothing about the army. All I can tell you is they made Adrian an officer, and I was very proud of him.'

Marriott glanced at Hardcastle and sighed. 'What d'you think, sir?'

Hardcastle leaned back in his chair, and lit his pipe. Then he spent a little while studying the young woman on the other side of the table. 'Release her, Marriott,' he said eventually. He looked closely at Cora Utting. 'But if I find out you've been lying to me, miss, I'll come after you. D'you understand?'

'Oh, yes, I do. But I never knew anything about that uniform, honestly. Adrian said it was his, and I believed him.'

'Make sure she gets a taxi, Marriott. I don't want a young girl like Miss Utting roaming about the streets of London this late at night.'

'Her father's here, sir,' said Marriott. 'He arrived just before we started to talk to Miss Utting.'

'Is he? Well, in that case, I'll have a word with him.'

'Do you think she knew about the murder, sir?' asked Marriott.

'Maybe,' said Hardcastle, 'but I see no profit in taking her to court. Her brief would only have to say that she knew nothing about the uniform or the murder, and we'd be hard pressed to prove that she did.'

'But she must've known about Nash masquerading as Mansfield, sir.'

'Why d'you say that, Marriott?'

'Well, sir, when we arrested Nash at Francis Street, he was in civilian clothing. But we found the North Staffs uniform in Cora's wardrobe. Now, she said that she hadn't seen Adrian for three weeks, which takes us back to *before* the murder. But he must've called at Acre Lane after the murder to leave the uniform there.'

'Yes, well, I spotted that, Marriott,' said Hardcastle.

NINETEEN

Cora Utting had been handed over to the care of the police station matron – who promptly made the girl a cup of tea – while Hardcastle and Marriott escorted the girl's father to the DDI's office for a brief conversation.

'I want to know the meaning of this, Inspector,' Utting began. He was clearly very annoyed at the DDI's arrest of his daughter. 'I don't know how you can possibly think that a young girl like my Cora could've had anything to do with a murder.'

Hardcastle told Utting the details of the murder at Victoria Station, and about Nash pretending to be a North Staffordshire officer. 'And so you see, Mr Utting, when we found the uniform of an officer of that regiment in your daughter's wardrobe there had to be some explanation of how it got there. To my mind there is only one explanation.'

'Well, I've no idea where it came from,' said Utting, his fury slowly abating in the face of Hardcastle's irrefutable account of the facts surrounding Somers' murder.

'Did Adrian Nash visit your house often, Mr Utting?' asked Marriott.

'Yes, as often as his duties would allow. As my daughter told you, he was in training at Aldershot, but he seemed to get home almost every weekend.' There was an element of resentment in Utting's voice; it was clear that he thought there was a set of privileges for officers that were not extended to other ranks, of which he had been one.

'But you said that he was stationed at Hounslow, Mr Utting,' said Hardcastle.

'That's where I thought he was. At least that's what he told me. But now Cora's telling you something different.' Utting sighed; he was having difficulty in understanding it all. But he was slowly beginning to realize that Adrian Nash was not the upstanding, unblemished young man he thought he was. And he had rapidly changed his mind about his suitability as a match for Cora, not that that was any longer a consideration.

'Were you aware of him bringing any luggage with him when he came for the weekend?' Hardcastle asked.

'He usually had a small suitcase; a valise he called it,' Utting added with a contemptuous sniff. 'We'd put him up in the spare bedroom. He seemed to be such a nice young lad that I can't believe that he's a murderer. It just goes to show that you can never tell.'

'Did perhaps your wife notice whether—?'

But Utting broke into Marriott's question. 'My wife died some six months ago of the consumption, Sergeant,' said Utting.

'Oh, I'm sorry,' said Marriott.

'I won't detain you any longer, Mr Utting,' said Hardcastle, as he and Marriott stood up. 'You'll be wanting to get Cora home.'

'Well, what d'you think?' asked Hardcastle, after Marriott had returned from escorting William Utting, and his daughter, to the door of the police station.

'I think Cora's probably right when she said she didn't know anything about the uniform or the murders, sir,' said Marriott, repeating what the DDI had said earlier. 'She didn't strike me as being particularly bright.'

'Maybe,' said Hardcastle doubtfully. 'But I suppose it's possible that Nash put it in her bedroom wardrobe without her knowledge, or, as she said, she did know but believed it to be his uniform.'

'There was another thing, sir. Although the collar badges were of the North Staffordshire Regiment, the buttons on the uniform we found were Army Service Corps.'

'So the young bugger used his own uniform, Marriott.'

'Looks that way, sir.'

'I'm surprised you didn't notice that at the time, Marriott,' said Hardcastle. 'Being as how you're so knowledgeable about all things to do with the army. Anyway, first thing tomorrow morning, we'll go and see Adrian Nash's parents again.'

'Tomorrow's Sunday, sir,' said Marriott, suffering Hardcastle's rebuke without comment.

'So it is, Marriott.'

'Don't you think we ought to tell Colonel Frobisher first that we've arrested Nash, sir? He is a deserter, after all.'

'What on a Sunday?' said Hardcastle, conjuring up an expression of surprise. 'Don't be silly, Marriott. Whatever gave you the idea that Colonel Frobisher would work on a Sunday? Anyway, we haven't finished here yet. Time we had a go at Jack Utting.'

'I'll get him brought up, sir,' said Marriott, and departed to arrange for Utting to be put in the interview room.

When Hardcastle joined the two of them, Utting was lounging in his chair smoking a cigarette.

'Well, Utting, Adrian Nash has cooked your goose for you good and proper.' The DDI took a seat opposite Utting and lit his pipe while he allowed that falsehood to sink in.

'I don't know what you mean,' said Utting, but the expression on his face showed that he had clearly been worried by Hardcastle's opening statement.

'It's no good you beating about the bush, my lad.' Hardcastle dropped his spent match into the tin lid that served as an ashtray. 'You see, Nash has admitted it all, and told me about your part in it.'

Marriott, who of course, had been present when Hardcastle had questioned Nash, was amazed, yet again, at his chief's interrogation technique. Nash had said nothing about Jack Utting, much less had he involved him in the murder of Herbert Somers. But Hardcastle had made his allegation with a confidence that brooked no argument.

'I only told him about the exchange bureau at Victoria, and how it operated,' said Utting. 'I didn't know he was going to do a murder.'

Hardcastle scoffed. 'He didn't know, Marriott,' he said, in an aside to his sergeant. 'What did you think he was going to do, then, Utting? Admire the view, perhaps? Or was he going to write a book about the experiences of soldiers trying to change their francs for pounds. You'll have to do better than that.'

'He said he was going to rob the clerk.'

'Oh, so that's all right, is it? That lets you off the hook. Don't talk daft, lad. You're in this over your head, and you'd best tell me what took place. If you want to save your neck from being stretched by His Majesty's hangman early one morning at Wormwood Scrubs, that is.'

Jack Utting's face paled dramatically, and he gripped the edge of the table so hard that his fingers were white. 'I never knew he was going to kill poor old Bert Somers, Inspector, honest.' The prospect of finishing up on the gallows had terrified the former bank clerk. 'I wouldn't have told him anything otherwise.'

'I'm waiting.' Hardcastle leaned back in his chair, and linked his hands across his waistcoat.

'It was being made an officer that did it,' began Utting. 'He ran up an awful lot of debts. He told me that being an officer he had to spend money on drinks in the officers' mess, and buy extra uniform, and all that sort of thing. And him and all the other officers would go up to London on a Friday to see a show, or go to some nightclub. And he said that he took a showgirl to supper a couple of times. It all costs money, you see.'

'Quite the toff, your brother-in-law to be, ain't he?' observed Hardcastle.

'So how much was this debt?' asked Marriott.

Utting switched his gaze to Hardcastle's assistant. 'He reckoned he was in Queer Street to the tune of two hundred quid.'

'*Two hundred!*' exclaimed Hardcastle in amazement. 'That's half what I earn in a year.'

'Well, that's how much he said it was,' admitted Utting.

'I see. So he decided to carry out a robbery, did he?'

'Yes, but he never meant to hurt anyone.'

'Is that why he had a revolver with him, Utting?' scoffed Hardcastle. 'What was he going to do, wave it at Somers and say, "Give me the money"? You must be even more simple than I thought in the first place. And so must Nash.'

'And that's why you took the day off, was it?' asked Marriott. 'Because you knew that Nash was going to rob the booth on that day.'

'Yes.' Utting mumbled the word, and looked down at the table.

'Well, that's conspiracy to rob, if not to murder,' said Marriott. 'Don't you agree, sir?' he asked, turning to the DDI.

'Without a doubt, Marriott,' said Hardcastle. 'And how much was it that he nicked?'

Marriott referred briefly to his pocket book. 'According to Mr Richards, the bank manager, some three hundred pounds was taken.'

'I see. So he took an extra hundred against future outgoings, I suppose,' said Hardcastle sarcastically. 'But he didn't, did he, Utting, because he gave you that extra money?'

'I, er . . . well—'

'It's no good shilly-shallying, Utting,' put in Hardcastle. 'Nash told me all about it. But I want to hear it from you.' Once again, the DDI made a statement that sounded positive, but was without any foundation.

'Yes, he gave me fifty quid.'

'Make a note of that, Marriott,' said Hardcastle, and returned his attention to the prisoner. 'Where did the uniform come from?'

'Uniform? What uniform?'

Hardcastle smote the tabletop with the flat of his hand, and Utting jerked back in alarm. 'Don't bugger me about, lad. You know perfectly well what I'm talking about. How did Nash know to get himself all dressed up as Lieutenant Geoffrey Mansfield, eh?'

'My Nancy is Geoffrey's sister,' said Utting miserably.

'Yes, I know that. And your sister Cora is Nash's fiancée. So which one of you provided Nash with the information, eh?'

'It was Nancy. Adrian asked her what regiment Geoffrey was in, and she told him he was in the North Staffordshires. But she didn't know why he wanted to know. She just thought he was interested in Geoff.'

'And she told him what the badges looked like, I suppose,' suggested Marriott.

'She didn't have to. Adrian knew already, and he went to some uniform shop in Aldershot, and bought the badges. Oh, and the medal ribbons. He's got an MC, has Geoff. Then he decked up one of his own uniforms to look like Geoff's. He said that if he got caught running away, he'd say he was chasing after the man that did it. But apparently, a copper came on the scene almost as soon as Adrian had knocked over poor old Bert. So he couldn't leg it. It would've looked suspicious, so he said.'

'So the cheeky bugger waited, and then told me some fanny about a soldier who hadn't saluted him, and had done a runner.' Ever since he had discovered the true identity of the officer he had spoken to, Hardcastle had been furious that he had allowed himself to be deceived by a nineteen-year-old newly commissioned army officer. Furthermore, after murdering Herbert Somers, Nash then had the audacity to go on to murder a prostitute at Kingston. 'What about the cap, and the other bits of uniform he stole from soldiers at Aldershot?' The DDI was now in no doubt that Nash had been the thief.

'He said that he'd leave the cap in the booth to throw the police off the scent. I s'pose he must've forgotten in all the panic of having killed old Bert. He never meant to do that. And I think he pinched the other stuff because his first idea was to pretend to be an ordinary soldier. But then he changed his mind, and said that he wouldn't be stopped by the military rozzers if he was in officer's uniform.'

'I strikes me that your friend Adrian is not the brightest of men,' said Hardcastle. 'I've never heard such a daft tale in all my life.'

'If he hadn't gone to all that trouble,' said Utting, 'I s'pose he'd've got away with it.'

Hardcastle fixed Utting with a withering gaze. 'You think so, do you, Utting? Well, I'll tell you this: from the very moment he struck Mr Somers on the head, he'd assured himself of a trip to the scaffold. Because with me dealing with it, he'd've stood no chance. And you'll likely be joining him.'

Utting gulped at the prospect of being hanged, but before he could respond, another question was fired at him.

'What d'you know about the prostitute he murdered?' asked Marriott.

'Prostitute?' Utting sounded genuinely surprised by that. 'I read about that in the paper. Was that really him?' he said. 'What did he do?'

'He stole a van, picked up a prostitute in Kingston, and murdered her,' said Marriott. 'And he stole the keys to the lock-up from a poor private soldier who was supposed to be in his care at Aldershot.'

'Whatever did he do that for? He must've gone mad if he picked up a pro, and then topped her.'

'Maybe,' said Hardcastle, 'but if he's thinking of pleading guilty but insane, he's got another thing coming. By the way, where did he stay all the time he was on the run?'

There was a long pause before Utting replied, but Hardcastle had guessed the answer anyway.

'At my place.'

'I hope he helped you to move house,' said Hardcastle sarcastically. The DDI stood up, but he had not finished yet. 'Put him down, Marriott, and get Nash up to the interview room. We'll see what he's got to say about the murder of Ivy Huggins.'

'Yes, sir,' said Marriott, glancing briefly at his wristwatch. It was now almost midnight, but once Hardcastle got going, he paid no attention to the time. 'But that's Mr Fitnam's job. Shouldn't we let him interview Nash about that?'

'I'm sure Mr Fitnam won't mind me clearing up his murder

for him, Marriott,' said Hardcastle, rubbing his hands together.
'After all, the two are connected.'

'It seems that you were two hundred pounds in debt, Nash.'
Adrian Nash managed a sneer. 'Who told you that?'

'Your mate Jack Utting. He's told us the whole story, and
he dropped you right in it. Apparently you've been living the
high life ever since you were commissioned.'

'Some mate he turned out to be,' said Nash.

'Now, what about Ivy Huggins?'

'Who's Ivy Huggins?'

'She's the prostitute you murdered in Kingston, the same
day that you did for Bert Somers.'

'I don't know what you're talking about,' said Nash loftily.

Hardcastle leaned closer to the prisoner. 'The army might've
been stupid enough to make you an officer, Nash, but underneath that uniform you're just a water board clerk. The only
reason that I can think of is that the average life of a subaltern on the Western Front is about six months, so they've got
to keep filling up the vacancies. But you needn't worry about
that because you're going to hang.'

Nash was petrified at Hardcastle's mention of a hanging;
he had spent the time since his arrest hoping that he might
still come up with a way of avoiding the consequence of his
crimes. 'I don't know anything about this Ivy woman you're
talking about.'

'Just because the army was daft enough to give a nineteen-
year-old kid like you an officer's uniform, Nash, won't stop
a judge sentencing you to take the drop at eight o'clock one
fine morning. Let me put it to you in simple terms. After
murdering Mr Somers, you went down to Kingston and used
Private Stacey's keys – which you'd stolen from his barrack
room – to gain admittance to the garage where the baker's
van was kept. Presumably to celebrate your theft of three
hundred quid you then picked up a prostitute, and you
murdered her. And it's no good denying it because your fingerprints were found in the van, and on the knife that you used
to kill the woman. But what interests me is *why* you should've
killed her.'

Nash slumped in his chair as the realization dawned upon
him that he had nowhere to run. 'She knew about the money.'

'How did she know?'

'After I'd picked her up, she wanted the money in advance. I took out this roll of notes to pay her, and she suddenly said, "It was you, wasn't it?" I asked her what she meant, and she said I'd killed the bank clerk at Victoria Station. She said she'd read about it in the evening paper. I told her that I was a witness, but she didn't believe it. She said she'd been with army officers before, and they never had that much money.'

'And I suppose you were still stupid enough to be wearing your uniform, were you?' asked Hardcastle.

'Yes, I'd gone straight to Kingston. I couldn't go home because my folks would wonder what I was doing there when I should've been in Boulogne.'

'As a matter of interest, Nash, where did you stay while you were on the run?' But Hardcastle knew; Utting had told him.

Nash came rapidly to the conclusion that as Jack Utting had apparently ratted on him, he would do the same for Utting. 'I stayed at Jack Utting's place.'

'So the night you started shooting at my policemen in Francis Street, you'd been there all the time, had you? And Utting's story that you'd just called at the house when a policeman came to the door was all my eye and Betty Martin.' To his annoyance Hardcastle realized that when he and Marriott had visited Jack Utting's house, and detained him, they had not bothered to search the rest of the house. And Nash was probably in another room.

'Of course it was, but Jack didn't want to get involved.'

Hardcastle laughed. 'Well, he's left it a bit late for that. Right, Nash, you'll be charged with the murder of Herbert Somers and Ivy Huggins.' He turned to his sergeant. 'Put him down, Marriott.'

'I hope they're not churchgoers,' said Hardcastle, as he rang the bell of the Nashes' house in Stanstead Road, Forest Hill on the Sunday morning.

The man who answered the door was probably in his mid-forties. For a moment or two, he gazed at the two detectives. 'Yes, what is it? I hope you're not some of those people who call at houses preaching religion.'

'We're police officers, sir. I'm Divisional Detective Inspector Hardcastle of the Whitehall Division, and this is Detective Sergeant Marriott. Mr Reginald Nash, is it?'

'Yes. What's wrong? Is it young Adrian? He's not dead, is he?' Nash took hold of the door jamb for support.

Not yet, thought Hardcastle. 'No, sir, he isn't. However, there are some matters I wish to discuss with you.'

'You'd better come in.' Nash opened the door wide, and escorted the two detectives into the parlour.

Mrs Nash appeared in the doorway. 'Oh, *you're* here again,' she said, recognizing the two officers, and followed them into the room. 'It's not about Adrian, is it?'

'In a manner of speaking,' said Hardcastle, 'but he's quite safe, if that's what's worrying you.'

'Well, what *is* it about?' asked Reginald Nash, as he invited the detectives to sit down.

'I've come to inform you that your son Adrian Nash is presently in custody at Cannon Row Police Station, and will shortly be charged with two counts of murder.'

'*Murder?*' Rose Nash paled significantly and leaned back against the cushions of her armchair, almost in a faint. 'There must be some mistake,' she mumbled.

'This is nonsense,' said Reginald Nash. 'Adrian's an officer in the army, and he's serving on the Western Front.'

'I'm afraid there's no doubt about it, Mr Nash. He's made a full confession. Your son never arrived at his unit in Boulogne, and has been posted as a deserter.'

'But we saw him off at Waterloo Station at the beginning of this month. The fifth it was, a Thursday evening. Isn't that right, Rose?' he asked, turning to his prostrate wife, but received only an incomprehensible mumble in reply.

'You may have seen him off, Mr Nash,' said Marriott, 'but I doubt that he boarded the train. Or if he did, then he got off at some station before Southampton. Either that, or he reached his destination, turned round and came straight back again.'

'Good God Almighty!' exclaimed Nash. 'But what are these murders he's supposed to have committed?'

'I shall be charging him with the murder of a bank clerk at Victoria Station on the eleventh of July,' said Hardcastle. He paused. 'And a prostitute at Kingston upon Thames later the same day, or early the next.'

'A prostitute?' exclaimed Rose Nash, as she recovered herself. 'I don't believe it. In fact, I don't believe any of it. He's an officer in the army.'

'I can quite understand your disbelief, Mrs Nash,' said Hardcastle patiently, 'but it happens to be the truth.' It was not the first time that the DDI had come across a mother who, when faced with overwhelming evidence, maintained an inflexible faith in the probity of her children.

'Would it be possible to see our son, Inspector?' asked Nash quietly. Adrian's father seemed to have accepted the state of affairs more readily than his wife.

'Not until he's appeared before the magistrate, Mr Nash. Now then, I have a warrant to search these premises.' Hardcastle took a sheet of paper from his pocket, examined it, and then returned it. Only he knew it was a gas bill that had been delivered to his house yesterday morning. 'However, rather than formally execute this document,' he said, tapping his pocket, 'I'd prefer to have your co-operation. We don't wish to appear heavy-handed about this matter, do we?'

Marriott gasped inwardly at his DDI's sheer effrontery. He knew that Hardcastle did not have a warrant, and that neither he nor the DDI would have been able to obtain one in the short time available to them. Not without disturbing a magistrate at home, and in the middle of the night. And that was never a wise thing to do.

'Of course, Inspector,' said Nash wearily, 'although I don't know what you expect to find.'

'As I think I made clear, sir,' said Hardcastle, rising from his seat, 'we don't want to seem tactless. Just a look at your son's room will suffice. As a matter of interest, when was your son last here?'

'A few days before we saw him off. We haven't seen him since, obviously. But then we believed him to be in France.'

Leaving his distressed wife on the sofa, Nash led the way upstairs. 'This is Adrian's room,' he said, opening a door. 'I don't really know what's happened to the lad. He had a promising career ahead of him at the Metropolitan Water Board. I've worked there all my life, and I'd hoped that Adrian would do the same. It's this wretched war, Inspector. It's upset everyone.'

'Very true, sir,' said Hardcastle, not that he could see how the war could be used as an excuse for young Nash to commit two murders.

Adrian Nash's room was neat and tidy, the bed made, and the furniture polished.

'It's exactly as he left it, Inspector,' said Nash.

Hardcastle remained just inside the door, and signalled to Marriott to see what he could find. He knew what they were looking for, and it did not take long.

Marriott opened the chest of drawers, and ferreted around. 'I think this is what we're after, sir,' he said, holding up a pair of army trousers and a tunic.

'You've got the numbers that those lads at Aldershot gave you, Marriott, haven't you?' said Hardcastle. 'See if they match. Unless I'm very much mistaken, that'll be Private Ash's tunic, and Private Joliffe's trousers.'

Even after years working with the DDI, Marriott could still be surprised at his chief's oft-disguised prodigious memory for detail.

Reginald Nash stood in the doorway, clearly bewildered by this cryptic conversation. 'Is there something wrong, Inspector?' he asked.

Hardcastle waited until Marriott had confirmed that the clothing was indeed marked with the regimental numbers of the soldiers he had named.

'Yes, Mr Nash. Those items of military clothing that Sergeant Marriott found were stolen from soldiers under training at Buller Barracks when your son was there. And it looks very much as though your lad nicked 'em. Although quite why he did is a bit of a mystery.' Hardcastle did not bother to explain that Nash had stolen them with the original intention of masquerading as a private soldier.

Marriott completed his search of the room, but found nothing more that would further their investigation. Not that he thought they needed any more, but he knew that Hardcastle was a stickler for putting together what he would describe as a 'gold-plated' case for the prosecution.

'Thank you for your co-operation, Mr Nash. We'll not need to trouble you further. Your son will be appearing before the Bow Street magistrate at ten o'clock tomorrow morning. If you care to attend there, it will probably be possible for you to have a few words with him before he's taken to Brixton Prison.'

'Brixton Prison? But surely, being an officer—'

'He'll be remanded in custody, Mr Nash, officer or not. Prisoners facing a murder charge don't get bail,' said Hardcastle unsympathetically.

TWENTY

'**A**ll rise!' At ten o'clock precisely on the following Monday morning, the usher in Court Number One at Bow Street Police Court had his moment of glory.

The Chief Metropolitan Magistrate took his seat on the bench and spent a few moments searching for his pen. He took out his pince-nez and polished them with a red pocket handkerchief. Satisfied, he replaced the handkerchief in his top pocket and clipped his glasses carefully on to his nose before perusing the register.

Aware that a man accused of murder was to appear, the public section of the courtroom was crowded. There were a few men – mainly Covent Garden layabouts with nothing better to do – but the majority were women who, judging by their fine apparel and their elegant hats, were ladies of substance possessed of a macabre curiosity. After all, it was this very courtroom that had witnessed the initial arraignments of Hawley Harvey Crippen and Ethel Le Neve, George Joseph Smith, and countless other notorious murderers and murderesses.

'Yes?' Once again, the magistrate adjusted his pince-nez, and glanced first at the clerk, and then down at the register.

'Adrian Nash, Your Worship,' intoned the clerk. 'Two counts of murder, and one of attempted murder.'

'Very well.' The magistrate peered over his spectacles at the young man in the dock.

'Adrian Nash,' began the clerk in a reedy voice, 'you are charged with the murder of Herbert Somers on Wednesday the eleventh of July this year, and with the murder of Ivy Huggins on Wednesday the eleventh, or Thursday the twelfth, of July this year. You are further charged with the attempted murder of Police Constable Donald Wallis on Friday the twenty-seventh of July this year. Against the Peace. How do you plead?'

'Not guilty,' said Nash in a halting and tremulous voice.

'Officer in the case,' said the clerk, and gazed searchingly around the courtroom.

The DDI stepped into the witness box. 'Divisional Detective Inspector Ernest Hardcastle, attached to A Division, Metropolitan Police, Your Worship.'

'Do you have an application, Mr Hardcastle?' queried the magistrate.

'I respectfully ask for a remand in custody, Your Worship.'

The magistrate glanced at his register once more, and made an entry. 'Very well, Mr Hardcastle. Remanded in custody to Tuesday the seventh of August,' he said. 'Next.'

As Nash was taken down, and Hardcastle left the courtroom, a cheeky young prostitute – her breasts almost popping out of the top of her provocative dress – entered the dock, and blew an insolent kiss to the magistrate.

Hardcastle walked out to the echoing entrance hall of the court. There was a low hubbub of conversation among the people there, but Reginald Nash was sitting silent and alone on one of the benches, his head bowed, and his hands linked loosely between his knees.

'If you care to come with me, Mr Nash, you can have a word with your son.'

'Thank you, Inspector.' Nash followed the DDI into the dank cell passage that ran alongside Number One Court.

The miserable figure of Adrian Nash was seated in the holding cell at the end of the passageway near the gaoler's office. Dressed in an ill-fitting suit, he no longer appeared the suave, dashing officer who had wined and dined ungrateful showgirls during his forays into London with his brother officers.

'Adrian, what the hell have you done?' Reginald Nash's face clearly showed his torment. 'Is this true?'

'No, Pa, I never did these things, not like they're saying I did,' said the younger Nash, but the expression on his face belied his reply. And it was clear that he was close to tears.

'D'you mean the police are making it all up?' Reginald Nash shot a sideways glance of censure at Hardcastle.

'It was all an accident,' blurted out Adrian. 'I never meant to kill either of them. It just sort of happened.'

But it was obvious, in the face of the evidence that had been expounded by Hardcastle on his previous meeting with Reginald Nash, that Adrian's father had come to the reluctant conclusion that his son had indeed committed the terrible murders with which he had been charged, with – to use the legal term – malice aforethought.

'You had everything, son. You'd even got a commission in the army. Why?' Adrian's father shook his head in disbelief and despair, as if asking himself where he had gone wrong in bringing up his only son. 'Why did you do these terrible things?'

'I'd got into debt, Pa. Two hundred pounds. I needed the money.'

'*Two hundred pounds?*' Reginald Nash was shocked, as indeed Hardcastle had been earlier, at the enormity of his son's indebtedness. 'You could've come to me, son. I'd've worked something out. You didn't have to kill people for it.' But even as he said it, he realized that there would have been no chance of him amassing so large a sum of money. Not on his pay as a water board engineer.

'Anyway, I couldn't go to the Front, Pa,' muttered Adrian, adding another untenable excuse for his conduct.

'But you weren't going to the Front, my boy. You were going to Boulogne. That's what you said the day we saw you off at Waterloo. You'd've been safe there, surely? I don't know much about the war, but I do know that Boulogne's quite a way behind the lines.'

'Yes, but that wouldn't have lasted long, would it? I'd have had to take supplies right up to the front line. That's what officers are for. A lot of our people have been killed doing that. I just couldn't face it.'

'Well, it's no excuse for committing murder,' said Reginald Nash sharply, his tone of voice indicating that he had finally abandoned his son. 'All you've done is to bring disgrace on your family. Your mother's quite distraught. We're going to have to move house because of the shame of it all. Probably change our names, too.' Following that announcement, which had more to do with his own reputation than with Adrian's plight, he turned to Hardcastle. 'I'm ready to leave, Inspector.'

The DDI escorted Reginald Nash to the front door of the court.

'What will happen to him, Inspector?'

'He'll hang,' said Hardcastle bluntly. 'And if he don't, the army will shoot him at dawn for cowardice.'

Reginald Nash said nothing, just shook his head. With that he stepped out into the July sunshine, and with head bowed, walked slowly down Bow Street towards the Strand, a broken man.

Hardcastle and Marriott were back at Cannon Row by eleven o'clock.

The DDI always pretended that he was unfamiliar with the telephone, and frequently described it as an invention of the devil that would not last. However, on this occasion, using his own instrument he quickly had the operator connect him to the DDI of V Division at Wandsworth.

'Arthur, it's Ernest Hardcastle on A.'

'What can I do for you, Ernie?' asked Fitnam, somewhat wearily.

'It's rather a case of what I've done for you, Arthur. I had a young army officer called Adrian Nash up at Bow Street this morning charged with murder.'

'Congratulations, Ernie,' said Fitnam, 'but what's that got to do with me?'

'Because I charged him with the murder of Herbert Somers at Victoria Station, and I also charged him with the murder of Ivy Huggins on your toby, Arthur. So I suggest you start putting your case together. And get the mothballs out of your Old Bailey suit, ready for an appearance at the Central Criminal Court. You do know where the Old Bailey is, don't you, Arthur?' Hardcastle added impishly. 'If not I'll send you a map.'

'How the hell did you manage that, Ernie?' Fitnam's voice suddenly took on a brighter note.

'Good old-fashioned police work, Arthur. I talked to him like a Dutch uncle, and he confessed. We do a lot of that up here in the centre of the great Metropolis.'

'Well, I'm very grateful,' said Fitnam.

'I'm pleased to hear it, Arthur. And I reckon your gratitude would be best shown by a bottle of Scotch. I'm rather partial to Johnny Walker's Black Label. It'll only set you back about five shillings.'

'It's as good as done, Ernie,' said Fitnam who, after replacing the receiver, let out a loud whoop of delight, much to the astonishment of the detectives in the next office.

Hardcastle next decided to pay a visit to Colonel Frobisher, the assistant provost marshal.

'Good morning to you, Inspector,' said Frobisher. 'I'm glad you've dropped in. I've got some more news for you. Second Lieutenant Bertram Morrish has finally turned up at 233 Supply Company ASC in Fort William. It seems he was mistakenly sent to 232 Supply in Taunton, Somerset. They tried to hold on to him, but eventually the records office made sure he went to the right place. But these things happen. However, I've no news yet of Adrian Nash who should've gone to 143 Mechanical Transport Company in Boulogne.'

'Ah, but I have, Colonel,' said Hardcastle. 'Which is why I'm here. I thought I'd let you know that I've captured him for you.'

Frobisher looked up with an amused smile on his face. 'So you've found him, have you? And how did that come about?'

'He made the mistake of loosing off a few rounds at some of my policemen in Francis Street last Friday night. He was promptly arrested, and I've got him locked up in Brixton police station charged with two counts of murder.'

'Have you, by Jove? Did he kill some of your policemen, then?' Frobisher had read an account of the Francis Street incident in *The Times*, but no mention had been made of fatalities.

'No, he was arrested without anyone being hurt. And while I'm at it, I'd like to mention the part played in the siege by Colour-Sergeant Cecil Berryman of the Middlesex Regiment who volunteered to resolve the matter for us.'

'What did he do?'

'He was instrumental in wounding our man with a carefully aimed rifle shot, thereby enabling police to make an arrest. I thought he deserved some sort of commendation.'

'I think the less said about that the better, Inspector. I gather from what you say, that he acted without authority from a superior officer. An army officer, I mean.'

'Police can call on anyone to assist them in arresting a felon, Colonel,' said Hardcastle.

'Yes, that's as maybe, but I still think it's best forgotten. You see there'll be all sorts of questions asked, like where did he get the ammunition from, and how he is to account for it. Once the military machine gets going on that sort of thing, Mr Hardcastle, it's very difficult to stop it.' Frobisher shook his head apologetically. 'Your people aren't going to do anything silly, like submitting official reports, are they?'

'I'll make sure they don't, Colonel. Wouldn't want to get Berryman into any trouble.' Hardcastle was somewhat surprised at the colonel's reaction. The colour-sergeant had done a first-class job in assisting the police, but now the army did not want to know because of some pettifogging regulation. In that respect the army was not unlike the police force, and if his part in the incident became known, it was possible that Berryman could finish up being court-martialled for his actions.

'Now, to return to Second Lieutenant Nash. Who exactly is he charged with murdering?' asked the APM.

'I've charged him with murdering Herbert Somers, the cashier at the Victoria Station exchange booth that you know about, and, on behalf of the DDI on V Division, with the murder of a prostitute called Ivy Huggins at Kingston upon Thames.'

'Good grief!' exclaimed Frobisher. 'This war has produced some unlikely murderers, Inspector. I suppose you've no idea when he'll be appearing in court.' The APM pulled a writing pad across his desk ready to make a few notes.

'I took him before the Bow Street magistrate this morning and got an eight-day lay down.'

'A what?' Frobisher looked up. Despite being a senior army policeman, he still had trouble with some of Hardcastle's jargon.

'A remand in custody for eight days, Colonel,' volunteered Marriott.

'I see.' Frobisher made a further note, and leaned back in his chair. 'D'you think there's any doubt about his guilt, Inspector?'

'Certainly not,' said Hardcastle firmly. 'He's as guilty as hell.'

'I thought you'd say that.' Frobisher knew Hardcastle well, and knew that he rarely made mistakes. 'Once he's convicted, I'll arrange to have him cashiered.'

'What's the point of that?' asked Hardcastle, once again bemused by the army's slavish adherence to *King's Regulations*. 'He's going down.'

'Keeps it all neat and tidy, Mr Hardcastle,' said Frobisher.

As the two detectives were returning to Cannon Row Police Station, Hardcastle saw a barrel organ being played near the Red Lion pub on the corner of Derby Gate.

'Good God, Marriott!' exclaimed Hardcastle loudly. 'A barrel organ in Whitehall. I've never seen such a thing. Whatever next?' But as he drew closer, he saw that the organ was in the charge of a one-legged man with a row of medals who was leaning on a crutch. He was operating the organ with his free hand. A small monkey wearing a red waistcoat sat atop the organ.

Hardcastle paused, and tossed a sixpence into the man's cap that was on the pavement.

'Bless you, guv'nor.' The organ grinder touched his forehead with a calloused finger. The monkey bared its teeth at Hardcastle.

Having informed the army of what had happened to Nash, in itself a cause of great self-satisfaction, Hardcastle decided that it was time to interview Jack Utting again.

Once again in the gloomy interview room at the police station, the DDI settled himself in a chair opposite the unfortunate Utting. DS Marriott sat beside him, ready to take notes. But, in the event, there were not many notes to be taken.

'When I last spoke to you, Utting, you told me that you were instrumental in giving Adrian Nash information about Lieutenant Mansfield's uniform, information you'd obtained from your wife. You also told Nash about the routine at the money-changing kiosk at Victoria Station that he intended to rob. For your assistance in this matter you received the princely sum of fifty pounds from the proceeds of the robbery and murder.'

'But I didn't know he was going to kill Bert Somers,' responded Utting in anguished tones.

'You knew he intended to rob Somers, and you aided and

abetted him. In fact, I'd go so far as to say that you conspired with him.' Hardcastle stood up. 'Consequently, I shall charge you with conspiracy to commit murder, Utting.'

'But I didn't know he was going to kill Bert Somers,' implored Utting, now terrified that, like Nash, he too could soon have an appointment with the hangman.

'Bit late to think about that now, my lad,' said Hardcastle brutally. 'Somers was murdered, and that's it and all about it. You'll hang alongside your sister's fiancé.'

The trial of Adrian Nash and Jack Utting took place at the Central Criminal Court at Old Bailey some months later amid the full panoply of the law.

'The Director of Public Prosecutions got cold feet over Utting, Marriott,' whispered Hardcastle, as he, his sergeant, and DDI Fitnam sat down in the entrance hall outside the four courts that the building contained. As witnesses they were not allowed in court until their turn came to give evidence.

'How so, sir?'

'He was happy to charge him with conspiracy to rob, but didn't think we'd got enough to put him on the sheet for conspiracy to murder. He said that Utting only agreed to rob, not to murder. Personally I'd've given it a run, but there we are.'

'But couldn't we have put him up for conspiracy to murder anyway, sir?'

Hardcastle sighed. 'You should know by now, Marriott, that the DPP has to approve murder cases, and without that approval there ain't a case. And he's not indicting Nash with robbery, or with attempting to murder PC Wallis. He said there was no point, and I agree with him.'

Inside the courtroom, there was a sudden rustle of activity as the red-robed judge – who enjoyed the splendid title of the Common Serjeant of London – entered, and took his place on the bench. The usher intoned the time-honoured catechism for the commencement of the proceedings, including such obscure words as 'oyer and terminer and general gaol delivery', the meaning of which, and the reason for, were lost on the accused, the public high in the gallery, and even on some of the junior barristers in the well of the court.

The clerk rose and read the counts of the indictments against

Nash and Utting. 'Adrian Nash, you are charged with the murders of Herbert Somers on Wednesday the eleventh of July at Victoria in the County of Middlesex, of Ivy Huggins on Wednesday the eleventh, or Thursday the twelfth, of July at Kingston upon Thames in the County of Surrey, each in the year of Our Lord one thousand, nine hundred and seventeen. Against the Peace. How say you? Guilty or not guilty?'

'Not guilty, sir,' said Nash, straining to make his voice heard.

And so it went on. Utting pleaded not guilty to conspiracy to rob, and the prisoners were told to sit down.

Once the jury had been empanelled, Sir Robert Winter – a distinguished King's Counsel – rose from the front bench, and took a sip of water. 'My Lord, I appear for the prosecution in this case, and my learned friend Sir Richard Strong appears for the defence.' Winter spoke in a strong and confident voice.

Those formal introductions made, Winter began to outline the case against both the accused. He made great play of the fact that Nash held the King's Commission, but had got himself into debt, a situation, he suggested, entirely of his own making, and had sought to resolve those debts by the murder of an innocent bank clerk.

Winter took another sip of water. And then, he continued, not satisfied with that, Nash decided to spend some of his illgotten gains on the services of a prostitute, but, for reasons that will be made clear later in the trial, he murdered her.

As for Utting, he said, almost contemptuously, he was merely an opportunist who saw what he thought was a safe way to obtain money without any risk to himself. But in that he was mistaken.

One by one, a string of prosecution witnesses entered the box: Dr Bernard Spilsbury, DDI Hardcastle, DDI Fitnam, DS Marriott and DI Charles Collins among them. Over the next days, each was examined in chief, cross-examined and, in one or two cases, re-examined.

At the beginning of the third week, Sir Richard Strong – a KC of equal eminence as his opponent – opened the case for the defence, such as it was; his vast experience, and an examination of the evidence, had already told him that he had little chance of success. After taking a pinch of snuff, something he was to do at intervals throughout the trial, he suggested to the jury of twelve stern-looking gentlemen landowners that Adrian Nash was a weak-willed young man who had been misled by other, more mature, men to spend more than he was worth. The outcome of this was that he saw fit to devise a way in which to settle his debts.

Failure to do so, continued counsel, was to risk the dishonour of being cashiered from the army. However, what began as a robbery, resulted in the death of the cashier Herbert Somers who, not unnaturally, had resisted, and paid for that resistance with his life.

Sir Richard Strong then drew the attention of the jury to the fact that it was within their power to bring in a verdict of manslaughter should they believe that there was no intention to murder. But Strong knew that it was a legal nicety, and would be made meaningless by the death of Ivy Huggins, which did not warrant a verdict of manslaughter.

After this untenable plea, Sir Richard began to call the first of a precious few witnesses, none of whom was of any real help to his case. But he wisely decided not to call either Nash or Utting to testify in his own defence.

It was to no avail. At the end of the fourth week, the jury returned a guilty verdict in respect of all the counts on each of the indictments against both the accused.

The Common Serjeant donned the black cap, and peered closely at Nash. 'Adrian Nash, you have been found guilty of the crimes of murder, most heinous crimes. Without regard to anything but your own self-interest, you wilfully murdered Herbert Somers, a man going about his lawful occasions and, as if that were not sufficient, you then went on to murder a defenceless prostitute. The sentence of this court is that you shall be taken from this place to the place from whence you came, and thence to a place of lawful execution. After three Sundays have elapsed you will be hanged by the neck until you are dead.'

The judge's chaplain intoned a few pointless words beseeching the Almighty to have mercy on the prisoner's soul, and it was over.

The judge looked at Nash again. 'Take him down,' he said.

The near-collapsing and sobbing figure of Adrian Nash was half-carried down the steps from the dock by two stalwart prison warders. Within the hour he was in the condemned cell at Wormwood Scrubs prison.

That done, the judge turned his attention to Jack Utting, but wasted few words on him. 'You are a man of previous good character,' he said, 'and for that reason I am inclined to treat you more leniently than otherwise I would have done. You are sentenced to ten years penal servitude for conspiracy to rob. Take him down.'

Immediately after Nash had been removed to the cells beneath the courtroom, and unbeknown to Hardcastle, a small drama was played out there. Lieutenant Colonel Ralph Frobisher appeared in Nash's cell.

'Adrian Nash,' he said, 'I am serving you with a notice stating that you are hereby cashiered from the army.' Somewhat pointlessly, but as a military requirement, he added, 'You may appeal if you wish.'

'Serve the buggers right,' said Hardcastle, as he led the way across the road to the Magpie and Stump public house where, with uncharacteristic generosity, he bought beer for Arthur Fitnam, Charlie Collins and Charles Marriott.

It was a cold, dank morning in December when the hangman entered the condemned cell. With a speed born of years of experience, he quickly pinioned Nash's arms. In less than a minute, the condemned man was hustled through a door, and on to the trap. His legs were secured, and a hood placed over his head. Seconds later Adrian Nash was consigned to oblivion.

At five minutes to eight that same morning, in a small villa in Eddystone Road, Brockley, Reginald and Rose Simmons – they had changed their name from Nash, and moved house – had been sitting at the kitchen table drinking tea. As the long-case clock in the hall struck eight o'clock, Rose burst into tears.

The thick fog had lasted all night, and refused to lift even in the face of a watery sun. But the miserable weather had not prevented the usual crowd of ghoulish sightseers, their coat collars turned up, from gathering at the gates of Wormwood Scrubs prison.

At ten minutes past eight, a warder appeared and placed a black-framed notice on the wicket gate. It announced that penalty of death by hanging had been carried out on one Adrian Nash. According to the law.

It was fast approaching Christmas. Holding a newspaper, Marriott tapped on the DDI's door and entered.

'What is it, Marriott?' asked Hardcastle.

'I wondered if you'd seen this report in the paper about the bomb that fell in Acre Lane yesterday morning, sir.'

'Acre Lane in Clapham?' Hardcastle took off his spectacles and paid attention. 'What about it? Sit down and read it.'

Marriott took a seat, and turned to the page containing the report. 'It's only a short piece, sir. "At a quarter past ten yesterday morning,"' he read, '"German raiders launched an attack on South London. A house in Acre Lane, Clapham received a direct hit resulting in the death of the two occupants, a Mr William Utting and his daughter Cora." Then there's a piece about Jack Utting's part in the Victoria Station murder, sir.'

'He was the chap who lost an arm at the Somme, wasn't he?' asked Hardcastle, as he stood up.

'That's him, sir, and his leg was badly damaged at the same time.'

'Looks as though Fritz was determined to get him, doesn't it, Marriott?' Hardcastle took out his watch, glanced at it, and dropped it back into his waistcoat pocket. 'I think I fancy a pint,' he said. 'If you're buying, Marriott.'

GLOSSARY

ACK EMMA: signallers' code for a.m. (*cf* PIP EMMA.)

ALL MY EYE AND BETTY MARTIN: nonsense.

APM: assistant provost marshal (a lieutenant colonel of the military police).

BAILEY, the: Central Criminal Court, Old Bailey, London.

BEAK: a magistrate.

BEF: British Expeditionary Force in France and Flanders.

BLIGHTY ONE: a battle wound that necessitated repatriation to the UK.

BOCHE: derogatory term for Germans, particularly soldiers.

BOOZER: a public house.

BRIEF, a: a warrant *or* a police warrant card *or* a lawyer.

CHOKEY: a prison (*ex* Hindi).

CID: Criminal Investigation Department.

CIGS: Chief of the Imperial General Staff.

COPPER: a policeman.

CRIMED: military slang for receiving punishment.

DABS: fingerprints.

DDI: Divisional Detective Inspector.

DRUM: a dwelling house.

DUTCH UNCLE, to talk to like a: to talk to in a kindly fashion.

EARWIGGING: listening.

EIGHT O'CLOCK WALK, to take the: to be hanged.

FEEL THE COLLAR, to: to make an arrest.

FIVE-AND-NINE ON THE BRIGHTON LINE: the fare from London to Brighton was five shillings and ninepence, so 'Brighton Line' was a popular call for '59' in housey-housey (qv).

FLEET STREET: former centre of the newspaper industry

FOURPENNY CANNON, a: a steak and kidney pie.

GAMP: an umbrella (from Sarah Gamp in Dickens's *Martin Chuzzlewit*).

GUNNERS, The: the Royal Horse Artillery, the Royal Garrison Artillery and the Royal Field Artillery.

HAND AMBULANCE: a two-wheeled barrow used for conveying drunkards to the police station, and occasionally for removing dead bodies.

HAWKING THE MUTTON: leading a life of prostitution.

HOUSEY-HOUSEY: army term for lotto, bingo or tombola.

JILDI: quickly (*ex* Hindi).

KC: King's Counsel: a senior barrister.

KNOCK OFF to: to arrest.

LAY-DOWN, a: a remand in custody.

LINEN DRAPERS: newspapers (rhyming slang).

MC: Military Cross.

NCO: non-commissioned officer.

NICK: a police station *or* prison *or* to arrest *or* to steal.

PIP EMMA: signallers' code for p.m. (*cf* ACK EMMA.)

POT AND PAN, OLD: father (rhyming slang: old man).

PROVOST, the: military police.

QUEER STREET, in: in serious difficulty; short of money.

REDCAPS: The Corps of Military Police.

ROZZER: a policeman.

RP: regimental police, not to be confused with the Corps of Military Police.

RSM: regimental sergeant major (a senior warrant officer).

SAM BROWNE: a military officer's belt with shoulder strap.

SAUSAGE AND MASH: cash (rhyming slang).

SCRIMSHANKER: one who evades duty or work.

SILK, a: a King's Counsel, from the silk gowns they wear.

SKIP *or* SKIPPER: an informal police alternative to sergeant.

SMOKE, The: London.

SPROG: a child.

STONEY: broke.

STRETCH, a: one year's imprisonment.

SWADDY: a soldier.

TEA LEAF: a thief (rhyming slang).

THREE SHEETS TO THE WIND: drunk.

TITFER: a hat (rhyming slang: tit for tat).

TOBY: a police area.

TOD (SLOAN), on one's: on one's own (rhyming slang).

TOM: a prostitute.

TOPPED: murdered or hanged.

TWO-AND-EIGHT, in a: in a state (rhyming slang).

WALLAH: someone employed in a specific office (*ex* Hindi).

WAR OFFICE: Department of State overseeing the army.

WIPERS: Army slang for Ypres in Belgium.